Cheryl—
I hope you
enjoy the suspense!

Dena Netherton
D

Haven's Flight

by
Dena Netherton

W

Dena Netherton

Write Integrity Press
Haven's Flight
© 2017 Dena Netherton

ISBN-10: 1-944120-30-0
ISBN-13: 978-1-944120-30-6
E-book ISBN: 1-978-944120-36-8

Scripture quotations are from The New International Version ®NIV ®. Copyright © 1973, 1978, 1984, 2011 by Biblica, Inc. ™ Used by permission of Zondervan. All rights reserved worldwide. www.zondervan.com.

Published by Write Integrity Press, 4475 Trinity Mills Road, PO Box 702852, Dallas, TX 75370
Find out more about the author, **Dena Netherton,** at her website,
www.denanetherton.com
www.WriteIntegrity.com
Printed in the United States of America.

Acknowledgements:

The Lord has graciously placed people in my writing path who have offered me encouragement, instruction, and advice. Thank you, Jeannie Campbell, for believing in my story concept and giving me a great start in writing the rest of the novel. Thank you to all my friends at Front Range Christian Fiction Writers, especially the late Pamela Trawick. Your critiques helped me immensely. Thank you, Kim Stewart, for faithfully meeting with me each week to discuss the craft of writing. Thank you, American Christian Fiction Writers and the judges on the Genesis Contest for offering me invaluable writing advice.

Thank you, Kiri, my precious and insightful daughter for being a beta reader. God bless you, Marji Clubine, for taking a chance on a new author. You and Write Integrity Press are simply the best. Finally, a special thank you to my editor, Fran Williams, and to Marji Clubine for helping me polish the manuscript.

Dena Netherton

Dedication

I dedicate this book to my husband,

Bruce,

who possesses

the gift of encouragement

in abundance.

Dena Netherton

Prologue

Thomas Dade Boone held his breath and eased the back door shut. Then he listened hard, fearing the creak of his father's pursuing foot on the upstairs landing. Hearing nothing, he turned noiselessly, hefted his duffle bag, and stepped onto the dark, dew-filled grass.

He patted his back pocket one more time to reassure himself that his wallet hadn't somehow fallen out. He'd failed to escape his drunken father before. This time, he had money. This time, he would not fail.

A June fog eerily shrouded the half-acre that separated the old Tennessee country house from the barn and chicken coop. Beyond those buildings, in the midnight gloom of trees, his girl waited for him. Beautiful, dainty, and blue-eyed.

If the moon had been out, he would have glimpsed the shimmer of her long, pale hair reflected by the rays of the moon. Ruth. He crept around the barn and strained to see her. Once reunited in the trees, she'd reach her arms around his neck the way she'd done that other day in the barn, and pull his face down to hers for a kiss.

In the morning, his father would see that his bed hadn't been slept in. Then he'd phone Ruth's mama and find that her things were missing, too. They'd know. They should've known from the day Mrs. Gatling—soon to be Mrs. Bartholomew Boone, Thomas's step-mama—brought Ruth over and introduced her as his future step-sister. That was nigh on four months ago. Ruth could never be his sister. Not when he'd fallen in love with her on first gander.

He cleared the open space in front of the barnyard, felt with his foot for the drainage ditch that formed the boundary of his father's property, and leaped the six feet to the soft dirt on the other side. Beyond the ditch, a row of maple trees hid his father's property from neighbors.

"Here, Tommy." A feminine hand grasped his and tugged him under the branches of the nearest maple. "Did you get your daddy's money?" Her fingers wormed around his back pocket.

"Hold your horses," he whispered and nudged her hand away. "I got it. C'mon. Let's git a ways down the road before we do any more talkin'."

He gripped his duffle and they took off diagonally across the woods. In another quarter mile, they met the gravel lane to his father's farm where it rounded the last acre of baby corn before intersecting with the county road. Though he couldn't see it through the fog, just a tad farther down the road lay the bridge, then the town and the bus station.

He used his flashlight just long enough to help Ruth scramble across the dry ditch and up onto the road. Distant lights from the closest neighboring farm glowed like fading embers. A dog's bark echoed from somewhere far off. His nostrils twitched at the familiar earthy scent of cow manure rising from the nearby fields.

"Can't we use the flashlight? It's too dark, Tommy. I'm gonna trip."

"No, girl." He pulled her closer. "Too risky jes yet. Someone might see the light and git suspicious."

The warmth of her body and the brush of her bare arm filled his gut with fire. If they hadn't been in such a hurry to get to town he would have held her and shown her just how she made him feel. "After we git over the bridge we can use the flashlight. There're so many trees on the other side, nobody'll see us."

Minutes passed. No sign of pursuit. It had to be safe enough to talk now. "Once we're in town we'll have 'bout an hour till the bus comes through."

Ruth gasped when she stumbled into an unseen rut in the road. She gripped his hand. "How long will it take to get to Cincinnati?"

"'Bout six hours, I think." He shifted the duffle bag and rolled his shoulder to work out the stiffness. "But once we git there, we can buy a ticket to anywhere."

"We got that much money?"

"Uh-huh. Tons." A soft breeze cleared the haze for a moment, and the sickle moon dimly revealed Ruth's pretty face. She gazed up at him with such adoration that he dropped the duffle, scooped her up and swung her around, making him dizzy.

"I love you, Ruth." He lowered his lips to hers, and she clung to his neck.

They'd get so far away that his father would never be able to knock him around anymore. Some safe place. In a few months, he'd be old enough to marry Ruth, and then they could get started on having all those babies she was always talking about. His father wouldn't win this time.

He set her down and they started to walk again.

"How come you didn't bring your rifle? How you gonna hunt

without it?"

Thomas gave a little snort. "Now can you just see us gittin' onto the bus and me totin' that thing? Looks suspicious enough, us being teenagers."

Their boots crunched on the gravel road. A cricket chirped, then silenced as they passed nearby. "Besides, I'll get a job, and then I can buy a really good gun. I'll bag a deer, and you can make us venison steaks every night."

Ruth sighed with a voice as sweet as molasses on a cornmeal biscuit. He ran his hand down her soft hair. Yes, they'd find a place where his father wouldn't be able to track them. As far as his money would take them.

The foggy night air laid a sheen over his face. Gurgling sounds, the echo of currents slapping the banks, the silken slipping of leaves as they washed over soggy branches—the song of the river—made him quicken his pace. They rounded a bend and their feet met concrete. The bridge loomed up ahead. Thomas hadn't set foot on the bridge since …. A pain, hardly dulled by the passage of nine years, squeezed his heart … since his Mama had died.

She'd been running from Father, too.

He held his breath for the last seconds it took to reach the structure. At the edge, he peered over the bridge's guardrail. The water flowed swift and deep. Deadly, after a season of rain, with a jagged log or two hiding in the murky underwater, like mean old snapping turtles. Crazy currents. He'd taken the canoe out last year when it was like this. Wanted—out of some perverse need—to see the spot where his mama had died. He'd accidentally rammed the canoe into a submerged log. When his father saw the hole in the boat and found out where he'd been, he beat him with two belts tied up together.

Thomas started at the approaching crunch of tires on the gravel road behind him. His heart pounded at the sound of the motor. Had to be Father's truck. The lights of a big vehicle crashed through the murk, and its diesel engine snorted like a raging feral hog. Fear and hatred seized Thomas's gut and twisted it till his breath came out in short gasps. Ruth stood paralyzed and her big eyes searched his with a pleading look.

"I'm scared, Tommy."

"Quick, Ruth, run 'n hide down the bank."

But Ruth seemed glued to her spot on the paved bridge. "Run, girl, before he sees you." The roar of the truck drowned out his voice. Thomas shoved her behind his body and braced his legs as if fixing to stand up to the blast of a hurricane. He blinked into the glare of Father's headlights.

The truck screeched to a halt and Judge Bartholomew Boone opened the door and launched himself onto the pavement. He stuffed the truck keys into his pocket. Thomas trembled when the silhouette of his father's form passed in front of the headlights. Strong, purposeful steps approached. Though not as tall as Thomas, he had a head and shoulders of massive proportion and a voice to match. Even big men trembled when Father's voice thundered from the judge's bench.

"Thomas, step aside." His father's eyes dismissed him as if he were no more than another small-time criminal in his court, facing sentence.

Thomas turned slightly and shook his head. "N-no, Sir."

Only a twitch in his father's graying mustache betrayed surprise. "Boy, do you dare to disobey your father?" The man raised his arm to backhand Thomas's face.

No, no, no, no. You won't win this time. Before the slap

connected, Thomas lunged and sent his own fist into the man's gut.

Judge Boone hunched over and clutched his stomach, unable to speak.

"You're never going to hit me again." Thomas's jaw clenched so tight he almost couldn't get the words out.

Ruth started to cry.

"You-you made Mama go away. You take away everything I care about. Well, you can't take Ruth."

Thomas turned, pushed Ruth ahead of him, and hurried away. They'd made it halfway across the bridge when a hand grasped his shoulder and spun him around. His father's fist met bone and flesh. Thomas crashed to the pavement, clutching his jaw. The world seemed to tilt and twirl. It took Ruth's scream to bring him back to full consciousness. His eyes focused on his father, dragging Ruth toward the truck.

Thomas scrambled to his feet and ran after them. He threw himself onto his father's shoulders. Ruth scurried out of the way of his flying fists. But this time the judge was ready. He guarded his head and blocked his son's punches.

"You come at me again, boy, and I'll have you thrown in jail for a year."

Breathing hard, Thomas stared at his father, at the sagging jowls and the discolored cheeks that came from hard drinking, the cruelty that had etched deep lines around the man's eyes.

"I'll tell them about you—how you beat me like an old mule."

"You think they'd believe you?"

When his father snickered, Thomas's breath emptied like a punch to the gut.

"I'm a judge and you, well, you're just a troubled boy who never got over his ma dying."

From somewhere deep, a roar thundered up Thomas's torso and erupted. He lurched for the man's throat. But strong as he was, he could not overpower his father. Another blow made him stagger backward.

Ruth ran to him and tried to stop him. "Please, Tommy, take me away from here. Let's go."

Thomas's father laughed. "You think you're going to get far? The police will pick you up before you even get over the county line." He straightened and swaggered back to the truck. In the glare of the headlights he called out, "By tomorrow morning, you'll be in jail and Ruth will be back where she belongs."

All true. The police would be looking on every road, every bus station, every train station. At the age of seventeen, the law would say Thomas had no safer place than his parent's home. And Ruth was only sixteen. After Mrs. Gatling married his father, Ruth would surely have to endure the same kind of beatings Thomas had lived with all his life.

"You can't beat me, Thomas. I always win." As if to rub it in, he lifted the corner of his lip like a dog at a fire hydrant.

Thomas's face drained of expression. His father would win again. There was no way to keep Ruth safe. Except.

The whoosh of Tommy's pulse surged in his brain, rivaling the roar of the river fifty feet below them. He shut his eyes and saw again the image of his mama's car as it sailed off the bridge, sailed far away from his father. The river had rescued Mama. It would do the same again.

He looked down at Ruth.

"Please, Tommy, let's get away."

Yes, get away. For good.

He scooped her up into his arms and carried her toward the

guardrail. Ruth screamed and struggled as he lifted her high. Thomas released her body to the protective arms of the river. One more scream echoed and then silenced as her body slammed into the water. Ruth's head sank under the surge of the deep, welcoming current.

Chapter One

"Never will I leave you; never will I forsake you."
Hebrews 13:5b

Cascade Mountains, near Lily, Washington. June 7th

The river's current nearly swept Haven's legs out from under her. This would be a good time to pray, except she wasn't so sure she still trusted God.

The river was not deep, only thirty or so inches, but the frigid temperature numbed the skin on her bare thighs. As the smallest, lightest adult in the group of seven therapy students and one counselor, she'd been positioned at the end for the river crossing.

Turn around. Give up. The self-defeating message pounded her brain with power greater than the icy surge of water. As if to mock her, an image of her recently vacated college apartment leaped into her mind. What wouldn't she give to be back there right now?

It had been a mistake to come here. These wilderness exercises would not help her learn to control the panic attacks that sometimes ambushed and overwhelmed her on the music stage. Each icy step confirmed that. She gripped the long pole the Life

Ventures students used to steady themselves against the strength of the current, and stepped in tandem with them. They groped for secure footing. With each step, Haven's breath jerked out in shallow puffs. A step ... and ... another. How many more to the shore? Twenty? Thirty? A cold and dangerous dunking threatened with each forward movement. The blue-green water frothed around a moss-covered rock. She side-stepped the slick, hard mound.

The roar of the river drowned out Counselor Jennie's instructions. To Haven's left, her new friend, Latrice, shouted, "Hey, Ellingsen, we're almost there." In the split second it took to hear and register the tall black woman's words, Haven lost her footing. She yelled a warning, then went down.

The shocking cold slammed at her skull, grabbed her eyeballs, wrapped around her jaw and neck. Bubbles churned about her submerged head. Her legs flailed uselessly on the crest of the surging current, while the weight of her backpack trapped her underwater. *God help me!* The river sucked at her and held her down with icy fingers. *Let go, let go.* Panic knifed her heart. Rocks scraped and tore at her exposed flesh like ragged fingernails.

The students had halted in mid-stream. Through the green, bubbly chaos she glimpsed their legs, braced against the current. The need to breathe screamed like a fire siren in her brain.

A hand seized her hair and tugged hard. Haven surfaced and drew her first desperate gasp. Latrice released Haven's hair and wrapped her long skinny arms around her. "Just hold onto me until you catch your breath." She pressed Haven against her own goose-fleshed body.

"Th-thanks." Haven's chest heaved as she clung to Latrice. She dug her heels into the slippery gravel to regain her footing.

The roar of the river seemed deafening after having been submerged in its muffling and deadly grip.

Jennie shouted, "You okay?"

Panting hard, she could only nod in response. Jennie stared at her for a moment as if to make sure, then signaled for everyone to continue moving forward. Haven grasped the pole again and the group of eight resumed their 45-degree angle across the river.

When they reached the shore's safety, she released her backpack. Her knees gave way and she sank onto the warm pebbly surface next to the pack, still gasping. If she'd had the strength, she would have pounded her fist against the ground and shouted, "Dad, I told you this was going to be a mistake." But then, they'd all think she was a big baby. None of the other students knew how much courage she had needed to register for Life Ventures. And she wasn't about to explain, either.

She raked her dripping hair back, turned, and waited for the thudding of her pulse to return to normal.

Footsteps crunched nearby. Jennie's slender form stood silhouetted in the glaring sun, her head tilted in a question.

Haven waved in a feeble gesture to reassure the counselor. "I'll be fine." *Soon as I high-tail it back to Oregon.* "Just need to rest for a minute."

When she was able to sit up, still numbed by adrenaline, she grimaced at her gouged and scraped skin. It reminded her of the day in junior high she'd tried to play tackle football with the neighborhood boys. Not a pretty sight.

Above the banks, wind hissed through the boughs of the ponderosa trees. On sweltering days that hiss had always beckoned her into their fragrant shade. But after her cold dunking, the voice of the trees seemed to communicate a warning. She opened her pack, and hurried to don dry clothing. Pulling off her light-weight tennis shoes, she rubbed her feet vigorously.

Latrice lay on her back next to Haven. Apparently, the river crossing had exhausted her as well. She'd hardly stirred since they reached the shore.

"Some introduction to Life Ventures, huh?" Latrice pushed herself up wearily. Her teeth chattered as she slipped a sweatshirt over her head.

"Thanks for your help out there. That was risky to let go of the pole to help me up."

"No problem, Blondie." Latrice chuckled. "I'll bet you thought Life Ventures would start out with a nice lecture on first aid and maybe some CPR practice."

Haven had almost stopped shivering. "Something like that."

Or not. The brochure for Life Ventures Wilderness Survival Therapy Camp showed a photo of fit and grinning twenty-something adults zooming across zip-lines, fifty feet above the forest floor. In another, a young woman with a serene expression paddled a blue-green lake in a kayak. The brochure stated, "Our wilderness challenges are designed to equip you with the physical and emotional skills to face life with renewed focus and confidence."

Fording a river was bad enough. What other challenges would the counselors dream up in the days and weeks ahead?

"This won't be an easy experience," Grant, the head counselor had said by way of introduction to the two dozen adults who'd registered for the therapy program. "The Cascade Mountains are not some romp in the park."

And on this first day, with twenty-eight yet to face, she had already discovered that.

Later that same afternoon, Haven and the others set up their tents on a wide, flat area, carpeted by pine needles and surrounded on three sides by steep, pine-covered hills.

Besides Latrice, a red-haired woman named Kara joined them in the tent.

"Gonna be a long four weeks," Kara said as she spread out her sleeping bag next to Latrice's. "My allergies are kickin' in big time."

Latrice crouched to unroll her own sleeping bag. "Did you have to cross that river, too?"

"Who didn't?" Kara flopped down onto her bag. "Ah … ah … achoo." She reached into her pocket and drew out a tissue. "I heard a couple of other women complaining about it."

"Good grief," Haven said, "why don't they just throw a couple of logs across the river for us to walk over?" She couldn't have been the only Life Ventures student to have taken a dunking in the river.

Latrice nudged her bag over to make room for Haven's things. "I get the feeling the counselors do the river crossing to sorta initiate us."

Kara blew her nose discreetly and stuffed the tissue back into her pocket. "Well, I guess those counselors know what they're doing. Since we left Lily this morning, I haven't had time to even think about cutting myself." She lay back and rested her head on her skinny arms.

Angry red gouges on the woman's wrists had scabbed over. At least Life Ventures seemed to be doing some good for the woman. She hoped Kara would continue to heal. She doubted her own problem would respond so quickly.

"You've got to face your fear," her father had told her. "I know it was traumatic when you witnessed your mother's murder. But that was over a year ago. You've got to get back to playing in public."

But could this wilderness therapy help her face and conquer her crushing panic attacks? Post-Traumatic Stress Disorder, the doctor back home had called it. Dad agreed with him that Life Ventures might help. He'd said, "Life Ventures might prove to be a good start for your journey toward healing." But she wasn't so sure. At twenty-one, she certainly could've said no to his persistent urging to register for the program. But listening to her father—even now, when she wasn't on the best of terms with him—was a hard habit to break.

Latrice raised her head and sniffed the air. "Hey, smell that?" The aroma of simmering beans and bacon had wafted into the tent. "Hurry up 'n finish or you'll miss supper."

"You guys go on ahead of me," Haven said. "I'll be out in a couple of minutes."

"Okay, I'll save a spot for you." Latrice slipped on her jacket.

"Hurry up!" Kara followed the other woman out of the tent.

The departing women disappeared behind Haven's wet sleeping bag, strung over a rope line to dry.

The bag was a beautiful blue green color, like the river they'd just crossed. The memory of her terror while submerged under the cold water bushwhacked her mind. The same kind of crushing fear she often experienced out of the blue at the most appalling times. More than once, the panic attacks had broadsided her in the middle of playing her piano in front of an audience. A monstrous, unconquerable foe, wielding a rifle. Nausea gripped her gut, numbness dulled her nimble fingers, and death loomed over her like Goliath menacing little David.

Until that one terrible night with her mother and that gunman, she'd confidently played her piano and sung to share her faith. Now her faith faltered under the weight of tragedy and doubt. Just the thought of performing made her stomach churn. Fear controlled her. She hated to agree with her father—and her Aunt Joy—but if she didn't get a handle on her terror her musical talent and her plans for a life as a professional pianist wouldn't go any farther than the grand piano sitting in the oversized living room of the Ellingsen family estate.

She threw on her jacket and hurried out toward base camp supper.

Journal Entry #1

Evening campfire time. First of twenty-eight. Grant asked us to introduce ourselves and tell one interesting piece of info. I couldn't think of anything because this annoying guy was sitting across from me, staring. He's the same guy who tried to talk to me at the Lily Hotel this morning while we were packing our backpacks. I think his name is TD. He's really handsome, but with a creep factor about an 8 on the Richter scale. Then he made a kiss face at me, right in front of all the other campers. Disgusting.

He got me so flustered that when it was my turn, the only thing I could think of to say was, "I once played the piano for the Governor of Oregon." Afterward, this tall male counselor wanted to know all about my playing. But while I was answering his questions, TD stood a few feet away with a friend, leering. My hands started shaking. But Latrice seemed to realize what was going on. She came over and pulled me away with some sort of excuse and we took a walk uphill to get away from everybody.

She hiked with her friend. Up the path. To the rocky outcropping. He followed them and found a good private spot to watch them. The girl had such wonderful, pale blonde hair and fair, creamy skin. She'd hardly changed since … well, since *that* day. And before the daylight had gone, he'd seen that her eyes were still as blue as ever.

She'd barely noticed him during campfire time. Just kept her eyes down most of the time and looked nervous. He'd tried to talk to her, but she must be shy. If only she'd looked up. Called him, "Tommy." But mostly, she talked to the black woman.

The little beauty turned at the top of the hill and said something to her friend. She reached up with both hands and pushed her long, silky hair away from her face.

Instinct screamed in his brain. Reason held him still and silent.

Dainty. Pretty and sweet.

Ruth.

Chapter Two

My soul thirsts for God, for the living God.
Psalm 42:2a

Journal Entry #2
Thank the Lord it's raining heavily.

For most of the morning Haven had hung out with Josh—the only male student in their group—and Kara and Latrice. They'd sat under tarps while Jennie instructed them on first aid.

Haven shivered. Oh, how she hated being cold and wet. But at least it spared them from having to cross any more icy rivers, or scramble up mountains, or catch and eat river sushi.

Jennie announced, "Okay, Haven has tumbled down a steep hill and she can't get up. She can't put any weight on her left leg."

Haven slumped down onto the tarp. Now this was an exercise she could handle. She grabbed her leg and moaned like a cow in labor.

Jennie grinned as she scanned her students. "Let's see, who can show me what you should do?" When no one volunteered, she tapped Josh on the shoulder.

"How about you show us?"

Josh shot Jennie a panicked look. "Me? M-maybe someone else could examine her leg?"

"Don't worry," Jennie said. "She won't bite. Just pretend she's a big, gnarly dude with hairy legs."

Haven resumed her overacting.

"Oh, brother," Latrice muttered. "Give the girl an Oscar."

Josh stared at Haven's leg. "A big, gnarly dude?"

"Yep." Kara came up and patted him on the back. "Just keep picturing how hairy her legs are going to be in a couple of weeks."

Haven frowned. "My legs are never hairy." *Well, hardly.* She stuck her leg straight up in the air. "Here, Josh, come and fix my broken leg."

He wiped a bead of perspiration from his upper lip and crouched to examine her leg. "Well ... I, uh, guess I check to make sure there's no bone sticking out of her skin."

"Eww." Kara made a face.

Poor Josh, he'd probably never been this close to a girl. His fingers trembled as he pulled up her pant leg to examine her shin. "But if she can't stand, it might still be broken. I check for signs of shock, and if her leg's not broken, I elevate her feet and keep her head low."

"Good," Jennie said. "And if it's broken?"

"Then I guess we splint her leg with whatever we can find that'll hold her leg really straight and still."

Latrice and the others left to search for sticks the right size for splints. What a great exercise. If the whole month could just rain and rain, maybe the therapy program wouldn't turn out to be such a big, scary deal after all. She could deal with CPR, Heimlich, and bandages and splints. First-aid class was pure theory. It wasn't like sitting at a piano on a stage in front of two thousand people. Each time, she felt their collective minds, souls, and energies as a force bigger and more terrifying than a demon warrior.

Just as Josh finished splinting her leg, the rain ended and sunlight poured through the wet ponderosa needles.

"Hey," Jennie said with a smile, "it looks like we can get on our hiking boots again. You're gonna love this next exercise."

Oh, goody. Haven untied the splint around her leg. Another confidence-building exercise in the wet, slippery, Cascade jungle. *What am I doing here?*

Later that evening, after a simple dinner in the camp common area, mosquitoes and the cold night air arrived. Haven ran toward the tent, swatting at the insects, followed by Latrice and Kara. Once inside the bug-proof safety of their tent, they slipped into the warmth of their sleeping bags. Sleep was going to feel wonderful after a long day of hiking and zip-lining.

"Goodnight," Grant called as he roamed the area outside the tents. "Lights out, everyone. We get up with the sun."

Haven switched off her flashlight.

Latrice and Kara settled into an exhausted sleep. But tired as she was, Haven could not fall asleep. She turned over onto her back and stared into the blackness, listening to the night sounds. Little drops of rain smacked the tent. Off to the east, someone zipped up his tent. A man chuckled. The distant roar of the river echoed against the river's steep banks. Breath-like sounds from the forest penetrated the thin walls of her tent. They seemed to whisper messages she wished she could comprehend.

She stared up at the blackness. *God, are you there?*

But God didn't answer. He never answered anymore.

A sob muscled its way up her throat. She forced it down and kept her eyes wide open. Maybe that would prevent the horrible memory from replaying inside her head. But it didn't work. It came like it always did, without her permission.

"Don't scream or I'll shoot." The tall stranger leveled the rifle from his shoulder. He stepped out from the darkness of the street alley. "Hand over your purse and your car keys, lady, or you'll get hurt."

The robber didn't see Haven standing in the deeper shadow behind Mom, who stood as tall as her petite frame could muster. Mom's coat was unbuttoned, and she opened it wider as if trying to make herself look bigger.

"Lady," the criminal growled in warning, "what are you doing?" He raised the rifle higher.

"Just showing you I'm not armed."

The man crept nearer, aiming at her heart.

Mom kept her voice steady. "Here, take my purse. My key fob is in it." She held her bag straight out. "Take the car. Just leave us alone."

The criminal took one more step so he could grab Mom's purse. But he was tall, and that one step brought him close enough to see over Mom's shoulders. A harsh gasp exploded from his lips. He swore under his breath. Then his tone changed. "What do we have here?" Haven hated the way he said it. "Not one pretty lady, but two pretty ladies. Move aside, lady. I wanna better look at the girl," he muttered.

"You leave my daughter alone." Mom lurched forward and

thrust out her arm.

The man jerked back and fired.

"Mom!"

Haven bolted upright and clamped her hand over her mouth. She heaved several deep breaths, trying to tamp down the mental image of her mother, lying crumpled on the bloodied sidewalk.

Why did God let that man kill her mother? How could she ever trust Him again? No one as wonderful as her mom should have had to die that way.

With their lantern on, he could clearly make out which one of the girls was Ruth. Her sleeping bag was closest to the west wall. He ducked down when Grant walked by and announced, "Lights out, everyone. Goodnight." Then the director headed for his own tent. The women switched off their light. Their sleeping bags rustled for a minute, then grew quiet. Too bad Ruth didn't have her own tent. It would have made things so much easier.

Morning dawned cold and damp. *Twenty-seven more days.* Haven shivered as she slid her journal out of her backpack and pulled on her hooded sweatshirt. This morning she'd again claim that perfect flat rock down by the river before any of the students with their own journals could snag it. As she climbed noiselessly out of the tent she almost stepped on the flower. Another one. The note attached to it said, "You're really beautiful." She crumpled the note, threw it into the trash, and scanned the tent area. No one was up yet. *Too bad. I'd sure like to give whoever is writing these notes a piece of my mind.* She turned and hurried down the hill, eager to pour out her heart on a fresh page of her journal.

Journal Entry #3

June 9th. God and my father: they both promised they'd be around when things got rough. I don't believe them. I don't know what I believe anymore. I don't know if I trust God anymore. I feel like I'm still standing with my mom on that dark sidewalk and I'm crying for help, but God has turned His back.

From his hiding place across the river he watched her settle onto a rock by the water. Second morning this week that she'd sat there to write. Did she mention him? Maybe she wrote about the flowers. She didn't seem to realize it was for her. Who else would it be for? This morning he'd wrapped a piece of paper around the stem with her name and a little note. Of course, he didn't sign his name or anything. She picked up the flower, read the note, and looked up quickly to see if anyone was watching her. She looked nervous, marched over to the trash bag and dropped it in. Maybe flowers and little notes weren't her thing. Maybe she'd appreciate a moonlight visit from him the next time she headed for her private washing spot in the woods.

He threw a pinecone across the water and into the bushes just a few feet above her. She looked up, but went right back to her writing. It didn't seem to frighten her.

But she should be frightened. She needed him. There were a lot of dangerous things out in the hills. Soon he'd make her see that.

Guy set his coffee mug on the kitchen table and leaned over to grab his cell phone.

His sister's cheery voice greeted him.

"Did Haven get off okay?"

"Oh, hi, Joy. Yep, I drove her to the airport day before yesterday. But I think she's still not convinced this wilderness therapy thing is going to help." He sat down in front of his coffee mug and inhaled a swirl of steam rising from the hot liquid.

"Don't worry. These Life Ventures people are professionals. They'll get her to talk about her thoughts. And she'll be surrounded by other women who are also struggling. Sometimes the best thing is to see that you're not the only one dealing with traumatic memories."

"You think so, Doc?"

"Sure do. And you know how Haven is. Once she starts listening to her new friends, she'll want to help them. That'll help heal her faster than just about anything I can think of."

He didn't know what else to say, so he said nothing.

"Guy?"

"Huh."

"She'll get her performing spunk back, you'll see."

"I hope so. Thanks, Joy."

"This is Mr. Colton," Jennie announced to the group of students assembled in the camp arena in a circle around her. She stood next to a tall, bearded man in a red-flannel jacket, "Just in case you didn't catch his name that first day of camp."

Haven only vaguely remembered Mr. Colton from their get-acquainted session the other night around the campfire. She'd been much too distracted by fighting off the beginnings of a panic attack, being annoyed by TD, and trying to act normal in front of all the other campers. She furtively examined him. Thick brown hair, short beard, shoulders wide as the Grand Canyon. He looked about thirty-five. Very tall. Not a giant. But close. With a powerful build and a face that looked like it had been chiseled from granite. His long nose was slightly crooked, as if he'd seen one too many fistfights.

"I'll bet no bully ever messed with him when he was a kid," Latrice said under her breath.

"He looks scary," Kara whispered.

Haven nudged her. "Shh, he'll hear you."

Jennie frowned at them before addressing the other students. "Mr. Colton is well-known in this area of Washington for his hunting and tracking skills. Even though he's a carpenter, he hikes down here from time to time—when he's not fixing someone's roof or building a house—to teach us a bit about tracking."

Jennie's group had combined with another group, led by a male counselor named Lance. Good grief, it was TD's group. As soon as he noticed Haven, he sidled closer. She inched back and tried to make herself inconspicuous behind Latrice.

Mr. Colton opened a backpack, rummaged around and pulled out a section of animal pelt.

His powerful, bass voice startled the crowd. Even TD jerked his head up slightly when the man spoke. "Can anyone tell me what kind of animal wore this?"

Several students answered simultaneously, "Bear."

"Okay," Mr. Colton laid the pelt on the ground. "But that was an easy one. How about this?" He spread out another pelt next to the first one.

Latrice leaned over and eyed the fur. "That's a coyote. We see 'em all the time in Colorado."

"I'm glad you didn't say wolf," Mr. Colton said.

TD sneered. "Only an idiot wouldn't be able to tell the difference between a coyote and a wolf."

"Oh?" Colton stepped up to TD and his cold green eyes pierced the young man's stare. TD stiffened but held his ground.

Latrice gasped when the big man reached out suddenly and grasped TD's name tag.

"TD," Colton said, letting the tag fall back onto his chest. "What's that stand for? Tall Dude?"

A couple of the students laughed, but stopped when TD narrowed his eyes at them.

Mr. Colton's lips spread into a toothy grin. "Okay, TD, explain how you tell the difference."

"It's ... it's easy. A wolf is bigger and its fur is a different color ... kind of gray-like. And they'd be runnin' in bigger packs, so you'd see tons of tracks all together."

Mr. Colton reached into the backpack again and took out a box. He opened it, then held up a cast of a dog-like track. "Coyote or wolf? What do you think, TD?"

A flicker of uncertainty crossed TD's face, but he answered without hesitating, "It's way too big for a coyote, so it has to be a wolf."

"You sure?" Colton brought the cast closer to TD.

"I'm sure. I don't need to look at it closer. I've been huntin' coyotes since I was a kid." A hint of annoyance tightened TD's attractive mouth.

Haven had planned to keep her mouth shut during the session, but before she knew what she was doing, she'd stepped out from behind Latrice and blurted, "I don't think it is ... Sir."

Mr. Colton turned and stared at her. Heat spread over her face and neck. "I ... I mean, it's like when you're barefoot in the mud ... and you take a step and your feet press the mud out. It makes your tracks look bigger. So, it could maybe be a coyote or dog if the cast was made from a muddy print."

She held her breath, her cheeks throbbing, while the man continued to stare. Had she just made a complete fool of herself?

Finally, Colton nodded. "Very good, little lady. I can tell that you're going to be a good student."

TD said something rude under his breath and rolled his eyes.

Mr. Colton ignored him and smiled at her. This time the smile looked sincere.

Relief flooded her chest. Why she'd chosen that moment to speak up and risk looking stupid, especially in front of such an intimidating man, she couldn't figure. Maybe it was TD's arrogance. Whatever the reason, it felt good.

Mr. Colton addressed the crowd. "Actually, TD is right. The cast is a wolf print. But that comment about the mud making the print look bigger is still a good one. The point is that when you're tracking an animal you may not have a perfect print. Other times the condition of the dirt makes the track look different. Like TD said, sometimes there's a whole group of animals and their tracks cover up what you're looking for. So, you look at more than just the track. You think about what the weather's been like recently. You look for scat. At how the grass is bent, or a broken twig on a tree. Maybe you find fur stuck on a tree trunk."

Colton stuffed the pelts back into his pack. "Okay, let's go down to the river and find some tracks."

Just before he turned to head for the river, he caught Haven's eye, grinned, and winked good-naturedly. The smile completely defrosted his austere features. Why, for all of his imposing size and scary green eyes, Mr. Colton was actually a teddy bear. A little feather-stroke of pleasure caressed her insides as the man turned to trudge downhill. TD sneered when he passed her, but she thrust out her chin at him.

Jennie came over and put her arm around her. "That was pretty spunky for a young woman who says she can't perform in front of a crowd. You're full of surprises."

Haven met her counselor's eyes. "Good surprises, I hope."

Jennie grinned. "Absolutely."

Journal Entry #4

June 12th. Today we met Mr. Colton: I think I'm going to like him. He put TD in his place. Evidently, he dislikes bullies as much as I do.

I heard footsteps outside our tent late last night. They were so soft it was more like the steps of a cat. I wanted to look, but chickened out. I'm such a wimp.

I feel okay today, except when I have time to remember.

Her tent was on the northwest side, the one closest to the trail that they climbed every day for talk sessions. Ruth usually got up first. She'd come out of the tent with her bucket of girl things. Her long pretty hair would be a little messed up. She had her own private spot for washing. It was a good spot. Really well hidden.

Some women looked better from a distance. But Ruth had always been a real beauty queen. Face all dainty and sweet.

Wasn't she afraid to wander away from camp all by herself? Any guy would get ideas just watching her. Not safe.

He had ideas, too.

All the men—even the counselors—sneaked looks at her, too. They were supposed to be all decent and Christian. It made him crazy.

Those guys in the Middle East had the right idea when it came to their women; make them wear those burkas so no one but their husbands and close male relatives could see them. If she were his, well, there'd be some changes. In the meantime, it was a good thing he was around to watch over her.

Chapter Three

Before the mountains were born
or You brought forth the earth and the world,
from everlasting to everlasting, You are God.
Psalm 90:2

Journal Entry #5

June 13th. I don't get these counselors out here. Today, when we were hiking, a doe came out of nowhere and reared up and attacked Josh with her hooves. I've seen YouTube videos of deer attacks. Awful. The deer must have hidden her fawn nearby.

Kara and Latrice and I surrounded Josh afterward and tried to make sure he was okay. But Jennie acted like being bludgeoned by a deer was something that happened every day. Not to worry. I don't understand her or the rest of the counselors. It's like they try to take every random thing that happens and turn it into some kind of metaphor for life. So, to them, a deer attack is just like fending off all those panic attacks that come out of the blue and clobber me.

It's bad enough that they keep throwing us into these scary exercises. But now I've got another worry: I think someone's watching me. At first I thought it was an animal, or something falling from a tree branch and making a noise. Yesterday, while I was cutting tree branches for cordage, I saw a shadow. It looked like a man's shape. I yelled and it moved away quickly. I know that's not my imagination. Also, I've gotten some flowers and "love" notes. Latrice thinks it's TD or one of the guys playing a little joke. I sure hope that's all it is.

Twenty-two more days to go. Haven's group fell into their usual places as they followed Jennie down the trail, two miles from base camp. After half an hour, the path narrowed and they hiked down along the banks of a small river. At a cairn, Jennie turned westward, away from the water. They headed for a jumble of boulders piled at the south end of a sheer rock face.

Whatever Jennie was planning, it couldn't be good. Haven examined the cliff, following it from bottom to top, which loomed sixty or more feet above the forest floor. Bolt anchors had been driven into the wall at successively higher points. One long crack in the rock, beginning at the base, finished halfway up. Knowing Jennie, this utterly perpendicular, completely impossible wall of granite was going to be the day's challenge. Something that tasted like burning, black poison burned her throat. Rivers were bad enough. But heights were worse.

She turned and glanced at Kara whose face had grown pale. She'd had the same look in her eyes the first time they met at base camp.

"Are we going to climb that?" Kara's voice quavered.

"Nope," Jennie said. "Just rappel down from the top."

"What?" Kara stopped and planted her hands on her slender hips. Her thin lips twisted into a snarl. Josh muttered something under his breath.

Haven rubbed her finger against her bottom lip while she stared at the wall. The Life Ventures brochure hadn't said anything about spider-webbing down cliffs. Suddenly, the thought of playing a piano sonata for an audience didn't seem so daunting.

"C'mon." Jennie started climbing one of the boulders piled up against the cliff.

Latrice chuckled at Haven's frown. She wrapped an arm around her. "Aw, it's really not bad at all. I did this back in Colorado. C'mon." She headed toward the boulders. As Haven took tentative steps to follow her, Latrice said, "Here, just follow me and put your feet exactly where I put mine. It's easy."

Some of the boulders were nearly twice her height and there were scarce footholds from which to launch to the next resting place. Placing her fingers on the spots just vacated by Latrice's feet, she tried not to think about the waiting cliff. She had to squeeze between narrow crevices in the jumble of boulders. Her shoes dislodged small rocks and pebbles, which clattered, bounced and ricocheted between the hard surfaces on their way down to the forest floor. She cringed each time a startled spider dove from its web into the shadows to avoid her hands and feet.

After they had climbed halfway above the base, they met a narrow ledge that led toward the summit. There was just enough room for a sure-footed climber to skirt the rock wall.

"It's about as wide as a balance beam," she said out loud. Except a gymnast would only fall about four feet if she lost her balance. A fall from this narrow dirt path could be deadly. Jennie had said the climb was only sixty or so feet, but looking down, the boulders at the bottom of the cliff looked like pebbles.

"What did you say?" Kara snuffled. She was following so

closely that Haven could feel the woman's ragged breath on the backs of her ankles.

"I just remembered why I quit gymnastics."

"Oh," Kara wheezed.

Poor Kara. Usually, her allergies made her sneeze all the time. But she'd stopped sneezing the second Jennie made her announcement about rappelling down the side of Mount-wannabe-Everest. Fear did that. Even the need to sneeze took a back seat when a person had to concentrate on not dying. "How are you doing back there?"

"Fantastic," Kara said. "But I think I'd rather be back in Tacoma, listening to my ex explain why he got fired again."

"Haven," Jennie called from further up the trail, "it's just a couple more steps and then the path gets nice and wide."

Minutes later the entire group made it safely to the flat top of the rock wall. As they came around the wall Lance greeted them. Jennie hadn't mentioned that she'd have an assistant. Lance must have been up at the top waiting for some time because all the climbing equipment had been carefully unrolled and prepared. Haven stared at the ropes, helmets, climbing shoes, and harnesses. Her knees grew weak.

Lance motioned for everyone to approach and surround him. "Remember that big rock we practiced rappelling down two days ago? Well, this is the same thing. You just gotta walk a little farther to get to the ground."

Jennie picked up the harnesses. "Okay, guys, grab your shoes and helmets, and practice putting these on. Then show me how you attach the carabiner and the belay device." When she seemed satisfied that they remembered each part, how it functioned, and could demonstrate the technique of belaying, she stepped out toward the edge of the precipice. "Okay, c'mon and watch while I go over. You'll see how simple it is."

Haven crept closer and took deep, slow breaths. Just getting within ten feet of the edge made her head swim. Her heart drummed against her chest. What would the counselors do if she just stomped out of base camp and hopped the next bus for Portland?

Jennie bent over and attached the draws. "Once you're over the edge, you just walk down, letting a little rope go through, like we practiced the other day." She went over the edge and began to lower herself.

"Just remember to keep your right hand down. That's how you control how fast you go."

When the demonstration ended, Haven eyed her friends. A tight rope of cold coiled around her ribs. Who would be next? She fought an impulse to yell at Lance and refuse to do the rappelling exercise. But Latrice had already placed herself directly in front of Lance, hopping up and down, begging to be first. Haven shook her head. Didn't anything frighten that woman?

"Okay, Haven," Lance's booming voice startled her. He raised his eyebrows and looked at her expectantly. "You look the most nervous, so you should go first."

"Me?"

She must have looked pitiful because he burst out laughing. "You can't fool me, Haven. Your registration form said you're a former gymnast. If you can handle tumbling and vaulting, then you can certainly do this."

"But I ... I can't."

"Sure, you can." Lance checked her attachments once more, then guided her toward the edge. "No sweat. I'll be right here, helping you. And Jennie will be doing fireman's belay. She won't let you fall."

Standing far below, Jennie held the rope and smiled encouragement. She gave Haven a thumbs-up.

Think, Haven, think. Don't let your emotions rule you. She fought the urge to be sick. In his Life Ventures welcome speech, Grant had said, "Fear can be managed." But some fear couldn't be managed. Some fear was too big.

Why was this different? Vaulting, tumbling, uneven parallels. Before her mother's murder she'd done it all without fear.

It wasn't different. She grasped the rope and shot Lance a look of determination. If her mom were still alive, she'd be cheering Haven along right now, just as she'd cheered at all of her gymnastics tournaments. The rope went taut as she took her final step before the earth bent downward. "Belay on." Gritting her teeth, she went over. She caught one last glimpse of Josh's pale face, watching from the edge. The voices of her friends dimmed. Sky and rock blurred. Her feet seemed to have a mind of their own as they pushed against the rock face. Her vision tunneled on the one spot in front of her. Bit by bit, the rope metered through her hands. *Keep your hand down.* She descended another ten feet. *That's it, watch that crack.* She placed her feet on either side of the crevice. *You're halfway down.* Just like climbing the ropes in the gym, only it took longer.

"Keep leaning back," Lance called from somewhere above.

A sensation of connection to the rock spread through Haven's feet and into her limbs and torso. Rock and sky and wind and trees seemed to embrace her. Through the thin climbing gloves her pianist's grip controlled her descent. Her muscles, toned from hours of tumbling practice held her body in position. If she could climb down a sixty-foot cliff, what else could she do?

Jennie's voice thrust into her consciousness. "Great job, Haven. Two more steps and you're down."

When her feet touched the ground, she hurried to disengage from the harness. Whooping with glee, she grabbed Jennie and swung her around in a little dance.

Jennie hugged her. "Told you, you could do it, Haven. Congrats!"

Kara was next. As Jennie gave her attention to the next rappeler, Haven shaded her eyes and looked upward. "Keep your arm down at your side," she called. "That's it, just go slow. Great job. You're almost there."

After Josh safely rappelled down the wall, Lance patted Latrice on the shoulder. "Okay, Miss Eager-Beaver. Finally, it's your turn."

The two stood near the precipice. Lance gave Latrice one quick check before allowing her to step onto the edge. He helped her attach the draws.

Latrice shouted down to Jennie. "I don't need you to do the belaying. I've done this before."

Haven stiffened. Surely, they wouldn't let her do this by herself. They just couldn't. They'd have to know Latrice only *thinks* she can do everything. She clenched her fists against her chest. She'd felt empowered while rappelling, but the sense of euphoria faded at Latrice's over-confidence.

Jennie called up, "Latrice, how many times have you rappelled?"

"Oh, lots of times. Please, I'm not afraid. I can do this without any help."

"Okay, but I'm still going to hold the rope loosely, just in case."

Latrice made a dramatic shrug of her shoulders. "I really don't need any help."

Haven glanced up at her friend. "You be careful, girl."

Latrice made it down to the halfway mark, and seemed to be doing everything right as she fed the rope slowly. She laughed and talked to the group waiting, thirty feet below. She paused in her descent to look down and make some joke about how she was ready to join the Life Ventures Staff. Her right foot tapped the top of the crack that Haven had avoided during her rappel. As she turned her head back to the rock face, a bat flew out of the crack and skimmed her hair. Latrice screamed and threw up her right hand in a panic to ward off the creature. She plummeted earthward.

Jennie reacted in a fraction of a second and pulled the rope taut again. But Latrice had plunged fifteen feet and the snap of the rope wrenched her back. Jennie hurried to lower her the rest of the way. Haven and Kara ran up to support her body. They lowered her gently onto the soft dirt.

Latrice moaned loudly and drew her knees up. She turned onto her side. "I'm okay," she hissed through clenched teeth. "Just let me lie still for a while."

Jennie knelt over her. "Tell me if it hurts where I'm touching." She probed Latrice's spine from top to bottom.

"I'm sorry, Jennie."

"It's okay."

"No, I was real stupid about the belaying. I thought I could handle anything."

Haven, crouched next to Jennie, took Latrice's hand to try to press comfort into her. Tears filled her eyes. Latrice had made another foolish move. When would she learn to look at life realistically?

Latrice was quiet for a moment. Then she shook her head and laughed as she slowly sat up. "Bats. Ugh. I should have stuck with my nice, safe climbing wall at the gym."

Haven flipped over in her sleeping bag. Every time she closed her eyes, she saw Latrice's flailing body hurtle toward the ground. What if Jennie hadn't been right there to catch her?

This was no game out here. She pounded her fist into the mat beneath her. Life Ventures was supposed to be a transforming experience. Making you face your fears and do risky things. But Latrice had almost died today. How was that supposed to make her a better person?

It could've happened to her, falling off that cliff. Didn't her dad know that? She'd been lucky today not to have had the same mishap as Latrice. Tomorrow she'd tell Jennie she wasn't going to do any more dangerous activities. She buried her face in her arms.

She woke with a start and tried to breathe. Giant, icy hands wrapped around her throat and squeezed.

She sprang to her feet.

Clawed at her throat.

Clawed at the zipper of the tent flap.

Gasped, but no air came.

She threw herself out of the tent opening. Landed hard on her side. The impact knocked air into her.

The giant rose up from the blackness beyond the tent door. Towered over her. He thrust a sword into her chest.

She grabbed at her heart, jumped up again, and scrambled into the light of the moon.

Danced around like a boxer in the ring. Flailed her fists against her Goliath.

The immense, inky form swallowed her. Pressed suffocating sludge into her nose and mouth.

Jesus, help me!

The giant released her and backed away.

She bent over. Opened her mouth wide to gulp air.

He's just in your head. You're not dying.

Her heart pounded like a kettledrum.

The sirens and alarms in her head faded.

He comes and it feels awful.

Her breathing slowed.

He's not real. He can't be.

Minutes passed. *Oh, God.* Her heart slowly returned to its normal rhythm. She breathed. Almost normal breathing now. Just a little shuddering.

The giant retreated into the pines, but his icy green eyes gleamed through the branches like tiny, malevolent points of light before finally winking out.

He's gone. She just had to let her mind clear a little bit more. Get away from the tents. In case she needed to cry. Yes, she definitely needed to cry.

The bright moon guided her uphill to the little plateau where she'd first talked with Latrice. Talking, just talking. No river fording, no dangerous animals, no climbing of boulders or rappelling off a mountain. Talk was safe. Talk was hypothetical. It was something she did well.

As she approached the plateau, the tightness around her throat eased. But waves of nausea roiled. She sank down onto a flat rock and dropped her head in her hands. "Oh, God, are you here?"

Wind in the trees sounded like God's breath.

Oh, to hear His voice. Oh, to hear an explanation for the evil He allowed.

The campsite slept on. No one had heard her struggle to live. The giant never said anything. No taunts, no threats, no unholy howls to magnify its malevolence. If only it would speak. Then, maybe, she'd comprehend the monster. Her counselor back in Portland said she had created the dark figure as a personification of her terror. But if that were true, why did it attack in the middle of sleep?

Had God witnessed this attack? If she prayed, would He communicate His comfort? The wind through the pines said, "Shh." And the only words she heard weren't God's, but part of a song in her head. It had come many times before, just as she was drifting off to sleep in her nice little apartment in Eugene. A man's deep and mellow voice, singing a love song. Imprinted from some TV show or movie she'd heard years ago. "My cup runneth over with love." She hugged herself and swayed to the rhythm of the beautiful song.

The snap of a twig jerked her out of the music.

"Do you want to talk, or would you rather I leave you alone?"

Jennie stood a few feet away, head cocked to one side. She hated to think her counselor had seen her boxing match with Goliath.

Haven straightened and pushed her tangled hair away from her face. How much should she explain? "I … I'm just trying to work out how I feel about this whole therapy program. And my dad. I can't seem to figure him out."

She looked down at the ring of tents in the valley. Loss squeezed her soul. How would she make it through the next three weeks? "What's the purpose of learning how to take care of myself in the wilderness? It's back there, in Oregon, that I can't face." She steepled her fingers in front of her mouth just in case she started to cry. "I'd thought all this therapy stuff might help, but now I can see it isn't going to help me be a performer again."

Jennie moved nearer. Oh, how she wished the counselor would put her arms around her and hold her, like her mother used to do when she was a child.

"What do you think would help you get over these panic attacks?"

Haven shook her head. "I don't know. I had many sessions with a counselor. But I'm not sure if it helped." Maybe it was too soon after her mother was murdered.

"That was a horrible thing you went through, watching your mother die violently. These experiences forever change a person."

Haven searched Jennie's face. "You know, I used to think some people were weak when they said that they couldn't worship God anymore. Sometimes it was because their business went under, or they got sick, or they went through a divorce. Of course, those are really hard things. But where was their faith?"

She looked down at her hands. "Then it happened to me. Now I get it. I'll never understand why God let a monster take my mother's life. Up until that happened, my whole life was wrapped up in Him. But He let me down. He abandoned me."

Jennie settled a warm hand on Haven's shoulder. "I can't even imagine how that must hurt."

"That night, I felt so helpless. I just stood there ... behind my mother. I let her shield me." She raised her fists and pounded them onto her thighs. "I should have done something."

"Shh." Jennie sat down next to her and pulled her close. "It's not your fault. A man comes out of nowhere and levels a rifle at you and your mom. What could you have done?"

Haven hunched over and pressed her fingers hard into her temples. Jennie's embrace released some of the tension in Haven's belly. If only she could rub out the terror and agony of that night. "I don't know. I've been beating myself up for months thinking about it, seeing it happen in my head, over and over. I promised myself I'd never be helpless again. That's why I came to Life Ventures."

She tried to swallow the lump in her throat. It had been many months since she'd expressed her hurt to anyone. "And then there's my feelings about my dad. You know, even when I went off to college, got my own apartment, and started making my own life, I stayed close to my parents. I'd drive home lots of weekends because I missed them. After Mom's death, when I needed to feel close to my dad, I'd drive back from college to be near him. I needed to talk about Mom and how I missed her. I wanted to talk about that night. But he shut me out, emotionally. And so, I shut him out, too. I said horrible things to him and—"

A spasm in her throat stole her voice. She swallowed again to relax her throat. "We'd both just lost the most important person in our lives."

"We all handle grief in different ways," Jennie said. "Some people look like they're doing fine after a loved one dies. But they're usually hiding their feelings, trying to cope with it all by retreating into their emotional cave."

"But he went on like nothing had happened."

"What does your dad do?"

"He's an executive in a big bank. And he's also an elder at our church."

"Well, there you go, Haven. Sometimes a man with that amount of responsibility or authority feels that people expect him to keep 'steering the ship.' Even in a storm."

Jennie bent over and picked up a small rock. She turned it over in her hand several times. "Maybe your father thought he needed to be strong for you."

"I didn't need him to be strong. I just needed him to listen and listen and listen."

"Have you ever told him this?"

"I-I ... couldn't."

"Maybe when you go back to Portland, you could try." She closed both her hands around the rock, as if it were a small bird needing protection. "I think your flashbacks and panic attacks are your mind's way of telling you that you still feel like a victim. But facing these wilderness challenges might help you feel more like a conqueror. If you can make yourself rappel off a cliff, then I'll bet you can go back to Oregon and play your piano for people again."

"Maybe your dad knows you better than you think. It must have taken some tough kind of love to coax you into coming to Life Ventures. But I'll bet the next time you see your father, he'll say, 'I knew you could do this. Not even a man with a rifle can take away your courage.'"

She let the rock drop from her hand. "C'mon, it's late. Tomorrow's going to be a tough one."

Chapter Four

Wisdom will save you from the ways of wicked men ...
Proverbs 2:12a

Journal Entry #12

June 19*th*. More creepy things happened this week. I was coming back at sundown from my washing spot and TD stepped onto the path. We just stared at each other for a minute. Then I said, "Are you going to let me get by?"

He said, "Doesn't it scare you to be out in these woods all by yourself?"

I said, "No. Help is only a scream away."

"Oh yeah?" Then he got this spooky sound in his voice. "I've heard stories about people getting lost out here just going for firewood. One wrong turn. No one ever sees them again."

"Well, I'm not about to take a wrong turn." I started to walk around him, but he moved over and blocked my path again.

He said, "That big guy said I shouldn't be staring at you all the time."

"What big guy?"

"You know, that tall dude, the one who teaches tracking."

I thought, good for Mr. Colton. Maybe I'll just keep close to him whenever he's around and TD won't have the nerve to scare me.

Then TD came closer. He made me nervous. He's tall and he loomed over me like a wolf that's about to tear into a fresh kill. He said, "Do you think I stare at you?"

I put my hands on my hips just so he could see I wasn't intimidated. "Do hens lay eggs?"

He ignored that and said, "It's just 'cause I like you." He started to bend over me like he was going to kiss me. I ducked and pushed past him and started running. He laughed and ran after me. Then he caught up and—

"Blondie," Latrice called as she stepped through the tent door and plopped down onto her sleeping bag, "lose the journal. Jennie says we gotta meet down by the river."

Journal Entry #15

June 21st. That first day, back in Lily when we were packing the Life Ventures backpacks, I decided that I wasn't going to bring this journal along. Even though Aunt Joy gave it to me. But it's hard to say 'no' when your aunt is a licensed family therapist and knows what she's talking about. Besides, when I get back to Oregon, she'll probably ask me if I wrote in the journal. Now I'm glad I brought it.

Over the past couple of weeks, we've been learning a lot about how to make survival decisions. Most of them are about choosing the safest route, how and when to make a shelter and hole up, or who to leave behind when someone's sick, and who should go get help. These decisions could make the difference between someone living or dying. Scary.

I've been getting to know Latrice much better. At first I thought she was kind of thoughtless. She jumps into things and never seems to think anything bad could happen. I'm just the opposite. I've always been the cautious type, even though I'm athletic. But she's been through some tough times and she's always sweet and positive. Her faith is real. She made me memorize Psalm 91, the whole thing. Part of it says,

'He who dwells in the shelter of the Most High will rest in the shadow of the Almighty.... He will cover you with His feathers and under His wings you will find refuge. His faithfulness will be your shield and rampart.... He will command His angels concerning you and will guard you in all your ways.'[1]

Latrice says that bad things happen, but God will never leave you. He'll keep your heart in a safe place if you'll just let Him. Why can't I believe that? I feel like God is very far away and that I can't trust Him. Why does my giant keep attacking?

"You put this shelter together like a pro," Jennie said as she examined the interior of the teepee shelter Haven had just finished constructing. She sat on the layer of thick grassy padding Haven had added for insulation and picked up her notebook. "You even chose the warmest, driest spot to build it. Did you ever think you'd be a survival expert in wilderness?"

No, in fact, she had done a lot of things she never imagined she'd be able to do. But still, when would she ever need to be a 'survival expert' once she got back to Oregon and her piano?

Another week had passed and as the students explored plants, terrain, and weather, the wilderness yielded its secrets. Jennie had shown them where to find plants to make vitamin-rich teas. Not exactly Earl Grey tea, Haven sniffed, but it would do in a pinch. The counselor taught them about roots that could be boiled and eaten, which plants to avoid eating, which ones that could be utilized for rope-making or basket-weaving. Haven had learned to assess the weather by the types of clouds, or the movement and strength of the wind. She'd become almost an expert at building various kinds of fires, using flint and steel and whatever plant materials she could find for tinder and fuel. Even making a fish trap hadn't been too difficult.

Haven settled herself on the soft floor next to Jennie.

"So," Jennie folded her legs and set her notebook on her knees, "I read your writing assignment and I really liked what you wrote." She opened the folder and flipped through several pages before coming to Haven's writing.

Haven shifted uncomfortably, fiddling with the seams that ran down her pants legs. "I felt like I was writing a pack of lies. It's hard to write about what I'm going to be like in the future. Sometimes when I remember playing in front of a big audience, I can hardly believe I had the courage to do that."

Jennie looked down at Haven's handwritten entry. "You wrote, 'In five years I will play with a symphony; I will play for hurting people and my music will comfort them; I will teach children; I will be a hero to someone; I will meet a wonderful man and get married; I will raise great kids; I will be a much better person than I am now. I will do something that will make the world—or maybe just my small corner of the world—a better place. My faith will be stronger and I will face all of my challenges—my Goliaths—as if

I were David with his slingshot and smooth stones. And someday I will restore a good relationship with my dad.'"

The counselor reached over and touched Haven's knee. "None of those things sound like lies. Just getting to know you for a couple of weeks, I can see that you want so much to be the person you described in this paper."

Tears welled and Haven fought to control her voice. "But that's just it. Every time I close my eyes I see that tall man with the rifle and my mother lying on the sidewalk. Those horrible memories are keeping me from becoming that person."

"I don't think so." Jennie ran her finger over the last sentence. "I think your faith—"

"My faith?" Haven jerked her head away and her mouth twisted.

"Yes, your faith, Haven. It's still there, buried under all that hurt and unforgiveness. It will give you an awesome power to heal and become that person you wrote about. The last thing you wrote is probably the first thing you're going to take care of."

"My father?"

"Yep."

"I can't forgive him." She heaved a spasmodic breath. "At least not yet. He hurt me. I'm afraid. I don't feel safe with him. I don't feel like I can ever trust him again."

"Forgiveness isn't a feeling. It's a decision." Jennie slipped the brief essay back into her notebook. "And when you're ready, you'll make that decision."

He watched the girl and her counselor climb out of the teepee and head back toward base camp. Her father hurt her. Just like his father hurt him. Weren't all fathers evil? How could anyone hurt such a beautiful creature? And in a few weeks, she'd be going back to him. Back to more hurt. He couldn't let that happen.

He closed his eyes for a second. Ruth's beautiful, anguished face filled his mind. "Please, Tommy, take me away from here." She was so little, so helpless.

Yes, Ruth, I'll take you away.

After the women disappeared behind a ridge, he crawled out of the tangle of vines a dozen feet from the teepee and approached. He crouched and peered inside. She'd done a good job constructing the shelter. Bit too big for warmth, but sturdy. He could still sniff the scent of the soap she used to wash with and see the imprint of her body on the grassy floor.

He caressed the spot where she'd sat and imagined how it would feel to run his hands over her beautiful hair.

Back at camp she'd looked at him. He was sure of it. She'd glanced at him while he sat by himself, reading his Bible. Then she caught his eye for just a second. "Please, Tommy," she seemed to plead with her big, innocent eyes. She couldn't just come out and say it, though, not with all the counselors and students around.

He wanted to tell her how he felt, but she wouldn't give him the chance. She stayed away from men. She wasn't cheap or trashy like his father's women.

So, he'd have to make the first move. And make it fast. Camp would end in a week.

And if she wouldn't do what he wanted, there was always that nice, deep river.

Journal Entry #18

June 27th. I've had a couple of really nice talks with Mr. Colton. I sketched him in my journal. He's a thinker, like me. A quiet type you just feel safe around.

Less than a week to go. Each day has gotten easier. I probably wouldn't have made it if it hadn't been for Latrice and Kara. Of course, they have their own problems. Together we've listened and cried and prayed. And I've told them things I'd locked up in my mind and heart for months.

Jennie's been wonderful, too. But I'm not ready to admit that my (almost) month in the wilderness has given me the courage to perform again. Still, it's been—

What was that? Haven lifted her pen and listened.

Probably just an animal that made the rustling in the undergrowth. She turned around and scanned the woods above the river where she sat. Still. Like the forest was holding its breath.

"Hello?" Her voice echoed against the rocks across the river. She put her journal down. "TD, is that you?" An edge sharpened her tone. Would the guy ever give up hounding her? She listened and strained her ears for the slightest movement. It wasn't funny. Never had been. The woods were creepy enough without someone constantly trying to frighten her.

Snap.

She jumped up. Adrenaline surged through her limbs. "Who's out there?"

A mist had been gathering at the top of the ridge for the past half hour, and at that moment it tumbled and swirled down the hill, obscuring details of trees, vines and ferns.

"Answer me!"

Straining to hear, she gathered up her boots—no time to put them on—and writing things and stuffed them into her satchel. She made herself walk slowly and calmly in the other direction along the beach. She'd gotten to know this stretch of river well. Around a bend, in thirty or so paces, the sandy part would end and she'd be forced uphill onto the wet, slippery bank. Besides the path behind her, where a danger possibly lurked, the steep hill was the only other way back up to the river trail.

She scanned the shore across the river. Fog and drizzle made it impossible to see the steep topography above it. But the river was too wide and swift to ford. Even if she could, what would prevent whoever was following her to cross, as well?

Crunch.

From behind, what sounded like boots jumping down onto the pebbly shore forced a gasp from her lips. More footsteps, slow and stealthy. Someone was definitely following her. What if she stopped and faced him? It could be someone from camp playing with her. Probably that awful TD. The base camp was at least a mile away, though. *Think, Haven. Don't panic.* If this was just play, whoever was following her had gone way past playfulness.

The pebbly shore ended and with nowhere else to go she jumped up onto the steep bank. Her un-shod feet slipped on the moss-covered rocks. Loose pebbles clattered down to the bank.

What if the stranger caught up to her and grabbed her from behind? She dug her fingers into the moss and scrabbled on all fours. In seconds, she'd propelled her body up, over the last slippery rocks and into the deep foliage of ferns. Scooting back as far as possible, she lay prone and peered through the feathery leaves. She covered her mouth to muffle the sound of her breathing. By now, whoever was following her would be coming into view. She'd find out who her practical joker was, and give him a piece of her mind.

Or maybe it was better to keep quiet. She waited, hardly daring to breathe.

Slow seconds passed. Around the bend a figure stepped, covered from head to ankles in a rain poncho. The hood completely shadowed his face. Was it a man? Probably. The figure seemed tall. But it was impossible to tell at this distance and from above the shore. The man approached, turned and scanned the undergrowth. He took another step closer and looked up as if he could see right through the thick leaves.

This was silly. In another minute, she'd get the courage to stand up and reveal herself, and the man would laugh at her for hiding in the bushes. He'd think she was crazy. Paranoid. He'd throw back his hood and it'd be Grant or the always-joking Lance or big, but kind Mr. Colton.

But what if it wasn't a joke? *Go away. Please go away, whoever you are.*

The figure in the poncho put a mud-encrusted hiking boot on the bank and bent to study the scratch marks her fingers had etched into the moss. He moved to take another step.

A woman's voice echoed somewhere up in the hills, and sudden rain unleashed a deluge which pelted the man's nylon covering. He stepped back, turned and hurried back up the beach from where he'd come.

As soon as the man was out of sight again, Haven sprang up and hurried to pull her boots on. Already soaked, she slipped her satchel under her sweater and started back to camp.

The rain and fog made it difficult to see her way, and by the time she'd made it back to camp, lanterns had been lit and hung outside each tent. A man in a poncho crouched underneath the tarp where the collection of camp stoves sat, tending pots of soup. Fury rose in her throat even as she shivered in her wet clothes. How dare her prankster go about camp business so nonchalantly after scaring her and forcing her to hide in the cold and wet? He'd get an earful right here, right now.

She marched up behind him and tapped him insistently on the shoulder. "Hey, I don't appreciate—"

The figure whirled around. "Girl, 'bout time you got here." A flick of the fingers revealed Latrice's dark curly hair from under her hood. She laughed at Haven's shocked expression. Standing up, she shook water off her yellow galoshes. "Blondie, where you been? You better get out of those wet clothes and come and help me. It's our night to cook dinner, remember?"

Journal Entry #19

June 26th. I finally told Latrice about my mystery prankster. I held off telling her because she'd probably say it was TD. She thinks every weird thing that happens around camp is TD's fault.

But I'm not convinced. I said, "He's not smart enough to do all the things you accuse him of."

But Latrice says the guy is evil. She really doesn't like him. "Just look at how he's always talking about his church back east and how he was the pastor's right hand man."

"So?" I said

"So, sometimes it's those people who talk the most about how religious they are that are the really evil ones. Remember that serial killer they executed a few years back? Wasn't he some deacon or elder in his church?"

"Are you trying to scare me out of my wits?"

"No," she said, "but we only got a few more days, and I'm telling you, Blondie, don't go off by yourself anymore."

Definitely not the kind of talk I was expecting from Latrice. I was hoping she'd say something about the guys just trying to get me to admit that I'm scared so they could hang around and try to 'protect' me."

So, what am I supposed to do for the next couple of days?

Chapter Five

... Forgive as the Lord forgave you.
Colossians 3:13b

Journal Entry #20

I've lost count, but I'm pretty sure it's July 2nd or 3rd. In the last few days of the course each of us was assigned the duty of leading their group from one camp spot to another specified by their counselor. It was a final challenge, one last lesson for us grimy and weary students before 'graduation.' My confidence has grown a lot in the past week or so and I felt almost ready for my leadership assignment. My thinking has become more and more focused and I'm working well with my team. Even though I miss my music, I've discovered a subtle kind of pleasure in treating my survival assignments as if they were challenging musical performances. The wilderness still feels like a foreign environment. It's an eerie, dense, silent place, except when the cry of a hawk or a chattering squirrel shatters that silence. But it's not nearly so frightening as it was when we started.

My assignment was to lead our team from base camp to Rock Vista, using my compass and topographical map. Of course, we had to cross over a stream, but this one wasn't deep. I had to wade across and attach a tensionless anchor knot on a sturdy tree. (We've had to study lots of types of knots.) The other members attached their side of the rope to another tree. Then Jennie came over to inspect my knot. She said it was perfect.

Then we crossed, using the rappel seat method. We each attached our harnesses to the rope and, one by one, we slid across, hand over hand. I felt like some sort of army commando. At the end of the exercise Jennie said to leave the ropes in place for the next group to use.

I've surprised myself this month.

Still, I don't know yet if I'm ready to perform again.

He didn't enjoy the graduation ceremony last night. It wasn't the kind at a high school where the graduating seniors come up to get their diplomas. They just sat around in a big circle. Everybody said what they liked about each other. He hadn't said anything. He didn't like anyone. Except the girl. But the things he'd like to say to her would have to wait for a better time. A private time with just the two of them. Then he'd tell her, and she could make a decision: to be with him, or to be dead.

On the last day of Life Ventures Haven stuffed a letter into her jacket and stepped out of her tent. She had one last thing to do before the students hiked back to their rendezvous spot with the Life Ventures truck. Everyone was so busy with their last-minute packing that no one noticed when she left camp and struck out onto the river trail. Last night's rain had soaked the earth and her boots made no sound on the carpet of pine needles. Drops of rain, glistening on the leaves of maple vines, soaked her thighs when she brushed past on the narrow trail. She had an important assignment to complete, and hopefully no one would be at her favorite outlook above the river. Half a mile farther down the trail the river roared a morning greeting. She pulled the letter out of her jacket pocket and opened it for one final reading.

July 5th

Dear Dad, When I was a kid, you used to be my closest buddy. You came to all my gymnastics meets; you took me to my piano lessons. You taught me how to ride a horse, how to shoot hoops, how to roast the perfect marshmallow. I thought you were the greatest guy that ever tied his running shoes. Even when I grew up and moved out to my own place, you were still my hero.

I know it's not your fault that you were away on business the night Mom was killed. The police investigated, we had a funeral for Mom, and you cried for a while. But then, you went back to work each morning like nothing was different. You left me alone because you probably thought that I needed some space. It wasn't your fault that you didn't know what I was feeling or thinking. I should have told you. I felt abandoned by both you and God. And so, I pushed you away because I was afraid to love you anymore. What if I lost you, too? I was terribly mean to you. But I wanted you to bust through that meanness and tell me that even though Mom was gone, you'd still be here. I wanted to scream and yell and get all my grief out. And I wanted you to do the same thing.

Jennie says forgiveness isn't a feeling; it's a decision. So, I'm deciding to let all that hurt and misunderstanding go. I'm going to stop living in the past and get on with healing.

Love, Haven

PS: You won't see this letter because I'm going to rip it up and throw it in the river. I'd rather tell you in person.

She stood at the edge of the bank and gazed down into the surging water. The force of the blue-green water churned a fine mist that settled on her face. She tore the letter into bits, then opened her hand and let the shreds fall like snowflakes. They struck the surface of the water and flowed swiftly away.

With her eyes closed, she drew a deep breath and exhaled as if she could release an entire year's grief and anger. "I forgive you, Dad."

"Well, that's a touching scene."

She whirled around at the sound of the voice and lost her balance. The slippery bank gave way, and her cry pierced the air.

A man seized Haven's arm and halted her tumble into the pounding river. "Whoa. Are you trying to commit suicide? That river would kill you for sure."

Haven's head swam with vertigo, and she pitched forward to get away from the precipice.

He put his arm around her shoulder and walked her a couple more steps away from the pounding water.

When she recovered from her fright, she looked up for the first time. TD. Ick. She grimaced and pulled away. "I was just doing something my counselor suggested."

TD looked unconvinced. "You sure hiked far out just to do an assignment."

Like you're really all that concerned for me. "So, what were you doing sneaking up on me like that? I really don't appreciate having my private moment ruined."

TD backed up and held his hands up, palms out. "Look, I saw you standing by the river like you were going to jump. What was I supposed to do?"

"I don't know. I came way out here so I could be alone. Did you follow me here?"

TD swept off his cap and bowed. "I cannot tell a lie, fair lady." He grinned when she rolled her eyes.

"So now that you can see I'm all right, you can go." She folded her arms, cocked her head to one side, and glared up into his face.

"Aw, c'mon, I've been waiting all month for some alone time with you. This is my last chance." He stepped closer, held her gaze, and reached out for her hand. "You know, it's hard to catch you away from camp and all your protective girlfriends. Now we can talk and ... well, you know."

"No, I don't know." She put her hands behind her and backed away. "I think I should be getting back to camp. I've got some packing to do." Escape looked impossible. *Think, Haven, think. Don't let him intimidate you.* The river was behind her and her path was blocked by the wolfman.

TD chuckled. "You're all bluff, Haven. As soon as I get close, you get nervous."

White-hot anger shot through her torso. *You bully. Oh, if only I could be a man for just five minutes. I'd make your nose look like Mr. Colton's.*

TD's face turned serious. "Remember when I asked if you thought I was staring at you?"

"I remember." If he took one more step toward her she might be able to swing around him and run up the path again.

"Well?"

"Well, what?" She pursed her lips. This was maddening. Why couldn't the guy just get the message that she wasn't interested?

"Well, I have been staring. I can't help it." His fingers came to rest on her shoulders. "You're driving me crazy … the way you pretend not to notice me."

"What?" She tried to back up again but the river made it impossible. "Is this another joke, like all the other things you've been pulling in camp?"

"I don't like practical jokes."

"Me neither." She braced herself to run. A couple more inches and she'd have room to dash past him.

TD pulled her forward and his breath warmed the top of her head. She tried to push him away.

"I can tell you're scared of me."

Bravo. The man's powers of observation were truly remarkable. Her hand closed into a fist.

He bent over her and whispered close to her ear. "I like that. Makes it more exciting." He cupped her face in his hands.

Haven pulled her elbow back, then slammed her fist into the man's gut with all her strength. "Get off me, you creep!" Taking advantage of his pain and surprise, she shoved him while he still clutched his stomach, and dashed up the path. She kept her fists clenched for a fight just in case he ran after her and caught up the way he'd done two weeks earlier. Still running and breathing hard she looked back. TD was gone. But when she faced forward again, a wall of red plaid blocked her way. No time to apply the brakes. With a gasp, she ploughed headlong into the man's unyielding body.

"Hey. Hold on there."

Strong hands steadied her. When she raised her head, Mr. Colton's green eyes stared past her down the path she'd just come up. His mouth tightened into a deep frown.

"Not a good idea to run in this kind of terrain, girl. Too many things to snag you and throw you down."

She followed his gaze. TD was slinking away into the cover of dense forest. Relief washed over her. "I-I apologize for running ..." She had to pause to catch her breath ... "into you like that, Mr. Colton ... but there's this guy ... He's been bothering me."

"TD. Yes, that ... boy." A contemptuous drawl elongated the last word.

"I've told him to leave me alone."

"He's not right for you." Mr. Colton continued to stare down the trail.

She tried to read Mr. Colton's rock-hard face. The man's mysterious manner and the fog shrouded sky reminded her of an old black and white mystery movie. "I-I came out here by myself. At least, I thought I was alone. But then—"

"You do realize that boy only wants one thing from you," he cut her off again, going on as if he hadn't heard her.

"Well, yes, of course. That's why I don't like—"

"Guys like TD, they don't care about you." Mr. Colton looked down at her for the first time, and something close to tenderness softened his chiseled features.

"Haven," a high-pitched voice shouted from somewhere up the hill.

Mr. Colton and Haven both started. She craned her neck in the direction of the voice. Latrice appeared at the top of the path above the river. "Finally. I've been looking all over for you."

Mr. Colton straightened and released his hold.

Latrice rushed down the hill and hugged her. "Jennie was worried about you." She pulled her hood up over her hair and glanced up at the threatening sky. "I think she's out looking for you, too."

Haven threw her hands up. "Good grief. Is the whole camp looking for me? I've been gone less than half an hour."

She turned back to Mr. Colton. "Did Jennie send you out here to find me?"

Mr. Colton blinked. "Why, yes. I'm just glad we found you so quickly." He patted her awkwardly on the back. "Well, young lady, as long as you've got your friend with you I'll head on out … there." He pointed toward the river and without any more explanation started to hike down the path.

Latrice waited for the man to get out of earshot. She tilted her head. "Man, Mr. Colton really *is* a great tracker. I can't believe how quickly he found you."

Warmth spread across Haven's chest. Mr. Colton was concerned for her, looking for her. Maybe this was an indication that God still cared, too.

"Hey, earth to Blondie. Anybody home?"

"Oh, sorry. I heard you, but I was just thinking." She slid her arm around Latrice's waist. They started up the path toward base camp.

"And?"

"It's been a very strange morning." *Bizarre was more like it.* "Want to hear about it?"

"Duh."

"Well, to begin with, I think they should add lessons in self-defense as part of this wilderness therapy course."

Chapter Six

The Lord is good, a refuge in times of trouble.
He cares for those who trust in Him ...
Nahum 1:7

The survival course completed, Haven and her friends rode the same trucks back to the Lily Hotel that had carried them into the wilderness only four weeks earlier. And just in time. A powerful storm tumbled over the Cascades, dumping hail and rain.

Wind tore around the old hotel, screaming like a mad cat. Haven dumped her backpack next to the reception desk and waited for her room assignment. What a relief that by tomorrow evening she'd be back at her piano, working on the Brahms Rhapsody she'd left behind a month earlier.

Latrice leaned close and whispered, "I'm so glad TD went back home earlier in the day. I'd hate to have to see him again."

Haven nodded. "What a relief. No more creepy stuff happening."

"Hoo-wee," Latrice said as she peeked out the front window. "Listen to that wind. Hey, can we have tornadoes up here?" Her big eyes widened.

Josh joined her at the window. "My mother grew up in this state and she never heard about one in the mountains. I just hope we don't have any power outages. I'm ready for some electricity."

A flash of lightning, followed almost immediately by an earth shaking "boom," made Latrice jump. The lights in the lobby flickered. Liz, the receptionist at the front desk called for everyone to line up for room assignments.

Haven was assigned a room with Kara, and they lugged their dusty gear up to their door. Kara unlocked the door and pushed it open. They both sighed at the sight of the twin beds, a television, and most of all, a bathroom with a big tub.

"You go first, Kara. I just want to sit here and look around at all this luxury. Did you ever think four walls could be so beautiful?"

Kara giggled in response, and hurried into the bathroom with her bath supplies.

Haven set her backpack down next to the closet door. She rummaged inside, drew out her leather journal, and traced the graceful patterns on its cover. She opened it and thumbed through her many dated entries.

Later, she wandered the spacious room and listened to the wind and rain. Framed lithographs of nineteenth century farm life decorated the walls. High ceilings and crown molding lent the room a certain rustic elegance. An antique needlepoint chair at the desk caught her eye. The mirrored dresser by the door was topped with real marble. She'd toured many old mansions with her mother in the Portland area, but it seemed strange that the tiny town of Lily would boast a hotel with such lovely furnishings.

The lights flickered inside, accompanied by startled squeals coming from the bathroom. Kara plainly did not like bathing in darkness. Haven drew back the lace curtains and pressed her face to the window. It had grown dark outside, and she could see nothing except when the street was illuminated by flashes of lightning. Thunder boomed like big bass drums. The windows rattled at each outburst.

A sense of euphoria enveloped her. She loved listening to storms, and tomorrow she was going to see her father.

When it was her turn in the bathroom she emptied half a bottle of bubbles into the tub. Sinking in up to her ears in the aromatic suds she closed her eyes and hummed a tune.

After her bath, she had almost finished combing out her hair when she heard a soft knock.

"Haven?" Kara called. "Jennie needs to see you as soon as you're dressed. She says it's important."

What could Jennie want? She threw on a fresh sweatshirt and jeans. When she opened the door, steam followed her into the bedroom.

Kara, wrapped in a pale blue bathrobe, lounged on her bed, a magazine cradled in her hands. "I've got some extra magazines here, if you're interested."

"Thanks. When I get back I might take you up on the offer."

The lights flickered and went out.

"Well, that's just perfect. I just get myself settled for the night with a good magazine and now this."

"Here," Haven said, "I'll get my flashlight." She made her way carefully to where she supposed the desk to be. Feeling for her pack, then fumbling with the clasp for a minute, she pulled out her flashlight and switched it on.

She went back into the bathroom and returned with a pack of matches and a votive candle which she lit and placed on the nightstand

"I'll be back in a minute." She followed the beam of her flashlight down the stairs to the lobby. Jennie was standing with Liz at the front desk, the area lit by a propane lamp.

"You wanted to see me, Jennie?"

The counselor took her by the arm and steered her over to the couch in the lobby. "Have a seat."

Something was definitely wrong.

Jennie's eyes looked troubled. "Your dad's been in a car accident, and he's been taken to the hospital in Monroe. We don't know how bad it is, only that he was able to tell the emergency room personnel to call here."

"He's okay, he's not—" She couldn't finish. A strange feeling of unreality hummed around her head, as if she were floating above herself, watching the scene. Her stomach churned.

"We don't know any more about his condition," Jennie said. "The nurse who called had to get off the phone, and when we tried to call back for more information the phones weren't working." She took Haven's hands, as if trying to squeeze comfort into them.

For a moment, Haven stared straight ahead. *Think, Haven. How can I get to my father?* "How far is Monroe? Could we drive there, now? Does anybody have a car that I could borrow? I've got to get there and be with him."

"Hold on, Haven. Monroe is a long way, and that storm is really bad. We don't have any idea how the roads are and—"

The front door flew open, accompanied by wailing wind and cold spray. A patrolman stepped over the threshold hurriedly and shut the door. Haven jumped up. Liz and Jennie both hurried over to him, reaching him at the same time.

"How's it out there, Jim?" Liz put her hand on his arm. "Can you stay for a few minutes and dry out?"

The patrolman's uniform dripped all over the carpet. "Can't stay long, Liz. I'm just making the rounds making sure that folks stay put tonight."

Liz went to the front desk and returned with a thermos of hot coffee and a Styrofoam cup. She poured some and handed it to the patrolman who downed the hot coffee in seconds.

"Thanks, Lizzie."

Jennie turned and saw the look in Haven's eyes. "Sir, we've got a situation here. This is Haven Ellingsen and she's just finished our Ventures program. Her dad was driving up to meet her and got in a car accident outside Monroe. She's just got to get to the hospital there as soon as possible. Is there any chance that we could drive there tonight?"

The patrolman frowned and shook his head. "I'm sorry, ma'am. But it would be suicide to go out on a night like this. I've seen trees down everywhere, with downed power lines lying around on the roads. And I just got a call that the bridge is blocked by a mudslide. It'll probably take most of the night, maybe even most of tomorrow, to get that shoveled out of the way."

Haven's brain crackled like a burning fuse attached to TNT. There had to be an alternate route to Monroe.

The patrolman looked at her with a sympathetic tilt to his eyebrows. "We'll get those roads cleared and I'm sure you'll be able to get a car out of here, maybe by tomorrow afternoon. That is if the storm cuts out."

Heart punctured by his words, all the arguments drained out, and she sank onto the couch before her knees gave way. *Not again. Not my dad, too.*

Jennie sat and slid her arm around Haven's shoulders. "I'm

sorry. We'll just have to wait till tomorrow. Grant's got a Jeep, and I'm sure we could use it to get to Monroe."

Haven pressed her fingers to her chin to stop it from quivering. "What if he's really hurt? What if I don't get to him?" *What if I never get the chance to ask for forgiveness?*

"Come on," Jennie said. "Let's go gather some friends and pray about it. Go tell Kara. I'll go get the others. We'll meet in your room."

Ten minutes later, Jennie, Lance, Grant, Kara, Josh, and Latrice assembled with Haven in her room. Standing in a circle, holding hands, the group poured out their prayers. When they finished, they quietly dispersed to their own rooms. Latrice hugged Haven. With tears in her luminous eyes she said, "Everything's gonna be all right. You're in the Lord's hands and so is your dad. Remember what I've been telling you all month? 'He will cover you with His feathers, and under His wings you will find refuge.' Just wait and see what the Lord does." Latrice gave her another long hug, padded softly out of the room, and shut the door behind her.

Haven took out her pajamas and dressed mechanically.

"C'mon," Kara said. "You need to get some sleep." She turned down Haven's bed and patted the pillow.

"I just want to make this last entry in my journal."

Kara nodded and left her.

Haven opened to a fresh page and set her pen onto the paper. *"Dear Dad, I hope I get the chance to talk to you ..."*

Long after Haven had gone to bed the storm continued to unleash its fury on the village of Lily and the surrounding mountains. Haven tossed under the rumpled sheets. As if to accompany her mental turmoil, the wind howled, tearing at the hotel's siding like a bear, clawing an old wooden stump.

What if they didn't get the bridge cleared tomorrow? What if her father's condition was serious?

God, why is this happening? Why don't you stop this storm right now? You took my mother. Are you going to take my father, too?

Her father thought she hated him. She'd been showing him that for the past year. What if he died never hearing how she loved him? God couldn't let that happen. What if she never got the chance to ask him to forgive her for treating him so badly?

She flipped over on her side. Just being with her father might help him get better.

A picture of the rope line catapulted into her mind. She'd set it up two days ago, for her group to practice crossing the river, commando style. It was possible they hadn't taken the rope down yet. She wouldn't have the rappel harness but ...

The dimly lit pack, sitting by the closet called to her.

"We'll just have to wait till tomorrow," Jennie had said.

No. If she waited any longer, she might not get to the hospital in time. She pulled back the covers and set her feet on the carpeted floor.

She dressed, shouldered her pack, and pulled her rain poncho over. Tiptoeing down the hall, in case someone was still awake, she peeked over the bannister. No one. And no one at the front desk, either. One step creaked when she descended the stairs. She crossed the lobby and slipped out the front entrance.

Deep puddles from last night's downpour clogged the gravel parking lot and road. She passed Grady's Hardware, then Lily General Mercantile, next, a grassy vacant lot. Farther south, a couple of modest houses.

In another quarter of a mile she left that road and turned onto the logging road that they'd taken on the first day of Life Ventures. Wind driven rain lashed her face. All around her tall pines groaned, and limbs cracked, some crashing to the sodden ground. Lightning strobed the dark forest. But none of this was going to discourage her.

Another hour passed. It had to be at least midnight. Finally, she saw it. A slender line of rope glimmered through the rain like a spider's guy line. Two days ago, she'd strung it across the water for her last wilderness exercise. But the creek below had been transformed from a pleasant stream into a snarling, frothing beast. She shut off her flashlight and stowed it in her pack. The swirling waters would show no mercy if the rope failed. *Don't look down.* She clenched her jaw. *You've done it before. Come on. You can do it.*

She raked her wet hair away from her face. Grabbing the rope, she swung her legs up to cross her ankles around it. The weight of the pack dragged on her. Hand over hand she pulled herself across. The only casualty was her sweater, which she'd looped through the straps of her pack. It must have worked its way loose, and at an especially strong gust of wind, escaped. The sweater dove into the rock-strewn river where it was carried swiftly away with the current.

Nearly to the opposite bank, her feet slipped. *Oh, God, help me!* One leg dangled only a couple of feet from the angry river. She didn't have the strength to swing her leg back up onto the rope.

With a yell and one last burst of strength, she swung the last three feet, then dropped, exhausted, onto level ground. *Get under that tree. Rest. Get your breath back.* Under the cedar, she tucked her rain poncho around and under her. Even with climber's gloves, her hands burned from the ropes. She couldn't rest long. Her father might be thinking and wondering about her right now. He might be hooked up to an IV with nurses hovering around his bed. Maybe the doctors were consulting with each other about his X-rays or CT scans. A car accident could mean a closed head injury or trauma to his heart and other vital organs. She'd seen enough medical shows on TV to know that much.

Flashlight in hand, she jumped up and set off in a northward direction.

Once across the river, the paths and terrain on this side were sketchy in her brain. The map she'd studied showed that the river flowed from the northwest. It passed under the Lily Bridge. Beyond it, she could try to catch a ride going west.

It wouldn't have been easy going even in ideal weather. The way along the rain-swollen stream was uneven, slippery at places, clogged with debris and sometimes, thorny undergrowth. *Don't go away from the water. You'll get lost.*

Close to dawn a large concrete structure loomed through the mist. *It has to be the bridge.* She turned her face upward and let the rain wash down her cheeks.

As she approached, the lights and growl of engines warned her. Road crews worked to clear the mudslide just east of the bridge. Just past the noisy, beehive repair action sat a squad car, its headlights and flashers illuminating the bridge. The last thing she needed right now was to be spotted by a highway patrolman and picked up. Road flashers had also been set up on the east side of the bridge.

She clambered up the slippery embankment, clinging to any root, vine or stone that still held firm in the rain-soaked soil. A cold wind swept under her poncho and gripped her around the waist with icy hands. Teeth chattering, she hurried to get past the glare of lights.

Half an hour later, the rain and wind had diminished. A faint glimmer from the east revealed details of road, rock and tree that had been lost in shadow only moments earlier.

She should find a place to clean up a bit and have a bite to eat. It wouldn't do to try to hitch a ride looking like a drowned rat. A fallen log near the road invited her to rest. But just for a minute. Already, morning was breaking. A squirrel twittered a warning as she passed under the creature's tree. Mist from the damp earth and vegetation swirled upward. Soon the sun would burn away the lingering fog.

The small meal of trail mix and water only slightly dulled her hunger. She could eat later. The important thing was to get to her father as soon as possible.

When she stood up again and shouldered her pack, the fatigue she'd been ignoring dragged at her legs. There had to be a gas station somewhere near. People had to get gas without having to travel all the way to Monroe. And there had to be cars or trucks traveling up or down this road. She plodded along and strained her ears for the sound of anything motorized. Finally, a truck passed going east.

"That's good." She increased her speed. "If one's going east, maybe the driver knows that they're getting the bridge cleared and maybe a car will be going my way eventually."

A sign on a gas station storefront grew clearer with each step west. "Quick N Easy." She checked her watch. Seven o'clock. The store had just opened for business. She hadn't brought much cash with her since the bulk of her Life Ventures experience would be spent away from civilization. But she'd offer the entire meager contents of her wallet to anyone traveling toward Monroe.

When she entered the store, wind slammed the door shut behind her. The cashier inspected her suspiciously, her gaze sweeping over Haven's backpack, rain gear and muddy boots.

Haven eased the pack off her aching shoulders and set it down in front of the counter. "I got caught in a downpour." She held up her mud-smeared hands and smiled apologetically. "Mind if I leave my pack here while I pick up a few things?"

The clerk's face softened a bit. "Sure, Hon, I'll keep an eye on it."

Haven shed her rain gear, folded it and stuffed it into her pack. "Do you have a phone around here I could use?"

"Well, we got one around the corner outside, for the public, but I just tried it when I opened the store and it's still not working."

Haven frowned, then headed to the restroom to clean up. She scrubbed her hands and face and combed out her damp hair. Later, as she wandered the narrow aisles searching for energy food, a gust of moist cool air accompanied a weathered-looking cowboy type when he stepped through the front door. She paid little attention to the lively conversation between the old lady and her new customer.

When she rounded a corner with her basket, the man at the counter jerked his head in her direction. "Who's the doll?" He'd asked in a loud enough voice that it was obvious he meant to be overheard. His broad grin communicated she should be flattered.

Haven hurried down another aisle. Men like that always made her want to respond with something equally rude, even though she never did.

"Pretty sure she's not from these parts," the clerk said. "She kinda looks like one of those 'green' types. You know, the kind that are out there huggin' trees."

The man chuckled.

Hello? Did they think she was deaf? And would the guy never leave? It was getting harder and harder to ignore the man's stare. When she couldn't wait any longer, she dropped her last shopping item into the basket and approached the checkout counter.

While the clerk rang up her groceries, the cowboy slouched nearby, pretending to examine a pair of sunglasses. His attempts to examine her were so clumsy she had to restrain herself from returning the man's rude stare.

"That'll be twelve dollars and 38 cents," the clerk announced. "And I hope you got a real meal planned somewhere between these snacks."

Haven pursed her lips. Lots of older people thought she looked young enough for unsolicited advice. *Just ignore it. You'll be out of here in ten seconds.* She opened her wallet to fish out the exact change. "Oh, I'll be fine once I get to Monroe."

"That your home?"

"No." *Again with the personal stuff.* "I'm just meeting someone there." *Stop explaining.*

"That's a lotta miles," the man joined in. "Hope you don't need to get there soon."

She directed her attention to the clerk. "Well, is there a bus that comes through here?"

"Hardly ever see one, except for a charter bus now and then. That's for bringing those mental cases up to Lily for that camp thing they got up there." She sniffed contemptuously. "How 'bout you, Buzz? You ever seen any buses?"

Buzz scratched his unshaven chin. "No, but lotsa folks 'round here drive to Monroe once or twice a month, you know, to get things we ain't got here."

Buzz caught the troubled look on her face. "You really need to get to Monroe today?" He and the clerk both stared at her.

She didn't owe them her life's story. On the other hand, if she told them about her father …

"Well, hey," Buzz's face brightened. "I'm goin' to Hayfork." The man smiled, revealing crooked and missing teeth. "That'd get you a bit closer to Monroe. I could take you if you don't mind ridin' in a smelly old pickup."

She gave the stranger a quick once-over. The fact that he seemed to know the clerk well reassured her only slightly. She could wait for another ride, but it could be hours before someone else showed up at the gas station.

When she hesitated, Buzz dropped the sunglasses back into their display holder. "Okay, it's no skin off my nose if you don't wanna free ride." His eyes glinted as he grabbed his shopping bag and headed for the door.

This could possibly be her only ride to Monroe. "Mister? I'd like that ride, please."

"Well, okay then." He turned and smiled, not unlike the smile of the canasta player who's just picked up 'the' card.

She lifted her pack.

"Let's go." He held the door for her and followed her out. Out of the corner of her eye, she saw Buzz's unshaven lip curl into another snaggle-toothed smile. A chill lifted the hair at the base of her skull.

Chapter Seven

Out of the depths I cry to You, Lord; Lord, hear my voice.
Let your ears be attentive to my cry for mercy.
Psalm 130:1-2

Haven followed Buzz out to a mud-covered, work-worn pickup truck. "Climb in," Buzz called from the other side. "Just give that door a good yank. It kinda sticks."

He was already revving the engine as she struggled with the door, lifted her pack to the seat and climbed in after it. Buzz put the engine in gear and the truck jerked forward with such a jolt that she fell back into the ripped upholstery. She sat up and shot him an annoyed glance. But it didn't seem as if the man was aware of anything but the loud country music blaring from the radio.

As the truck roared along the storm-strewn road, Buzz dodged tree branches and occasional mudslides.

"I really appreciate the ride," she said over the music.

"What'd you say?" Buzz called back.

"I said, thanks for the ride," she tried, even louder.

"Oh, yeah, no problem." He turned the radio down a smidge. "I always like to rescue pretty ladies in need."

It could have been an innocent statement, but Buzz' look made her nervous.

His gaze swept over her again. "So, did your car break down or something?"

She stiffened, but tried to appear matter-of-fact. "No, I was camping with a group and when the weather got rough we all went home." Well, it was the truth.

"You sure don't look like the camping type to me."

"What do you mean?"

"Just that I picture a girl who'd be luggin' a backpack around as the tomboy sort. You look like the kinda girl who should be wearin' pretty dresses, havin' lots of dates."

"Oh." His comments made her uncomfortable, and in the close quarters of the truck's cabin, the man's rough appearance intimidated her. Maybe, if she didn't answer, he'd stop flirting.

"Yep," he continued, "I'll bet lots of guys are swarmin' around you. Is that who's meeting you in Monroe, a boyfriend?"

She slunk down into her seat, looked out the window, and pretended not to hear Buzz. They drove in silence for ten minutes, but she could feel his eyes taking her in.

"You sure got blonde hair." He reached out an index finger to touch her hair. "I'll bet it's natural, too."

"Hey!" She jerked away from him. What if she just asked him to pull over and let her out now?

Buzz pulled his hand away. "Okay, don't get scared. I'm not gonna do anything." He rolled his eyes, put his hand back on the steering wheel and muttered something to himself.

The morning local news came on and Buzz turned his attention to it. The report spent some time on the storm and its effects on local towns, then a commercial break for a local hardware store. Haven vaguely heard the news report. When Buzz frightened her, she'd slid her hand under the straps of her pack, gripping them for security. She was anxiously watching for a mileage sign for Monroe, when the report on the car accident arrested her attention.

"In other news, the storm has claimed the life of an Oregon man when his car spun out of control on Hwy 2 and hit a tree. The man was transported to Monroe Hospital where he was pronounced dead. And in an unrelated accident, a couple—"

Haven gasped and slammed her palm against the radio knob to silence the news. She broke into sobs. "I didn't make it. God, you did this." Her face contorted in an agony of frustration, anger and grief. Tears spilled down her face.

"Hey, what's the matter, girl? What happened?" Buzz slowed the truck, then reached over to try to steady her.

"Don't you touch me." She shoved her back against the cold metal door. "You keep away from me." Her view pixilated as tears mounted. "I've got to get out of here. Stop this truck now."

Buzz slowed to take a hairpin turn. Gripping her pack, she reached for the latch and shoved on the door.

"Hey, you can't do that. You tryin' to kill yourself?"

The passenger door flew open. Buzz grabbed at her arm, but she twisted free and tumbled out. She landed with a thump on the shoulder of the highway and rolled a few feet. Adrenaline surged through her limbs as she jumped to her feet, still clutching her pack, and galloped into the darkness of the tall ferns. The ground sloped away into thick forest.

Buzz's truck screeched to a halt. Seconds later the crunch of steps on gravel neared her hiding place. He peered into the woods below the road.

"Hey, girl. Come back. You'll get lost." He took a couple of steps onto the trampled path that her boots had forged into the undergrowth. Haven held her breath as the man approached. Eerie silence reigned "I wasn't gonna hurt you." He shrugged, and returned to the truck, rubbing his stubbled chin. In another moment, Buzz's truck screeched into gear and disappeared around the turn.

Guy set the motel phone back in its cradle. A soft knock alerted him, followed by the sound of a card swiping the key card lock on his door.

Joy limped into the room and set her purse down on the dresser. "Any luck yet?"

"Nope." Guy took a sheet of the Monroe Inn's stationery on which he'd recorded several numbers, folded it and stuffed it into his jacket pocket. When he stood up, his head pounded. He walked slowly to the window to check the weather. "They're saying Lily's phones won't be up and running till at least noon today. Too bad cell phones don't work around here. Haven's probably going crazy, stuck over there without any more news about our accident. Oh, I called the Jupiter car rental place, and they've got one mid-size available."

Joy sat in the chair he'd just vacated and lifted her wrapped foot, setting it gingerly on the bed.

"How's your head?" She stared at his forehead. "Guess a sprained ankle is better than a bad bump on the head when it comes to driving. Good thing it was my left ankle." The skin around her brown eyes crinkled into lines of concern as she studied him.

"I'm okay. ER doc said I'll need a few days before it's safe to drive, just to be careful."

He drew out the rental car information from his pocket and brought it to Joy. "Here's the rental info. They said they'd deliver the car about 9:30. I already told them you'd be the driver."

Joy glanced at her watch. "Good. That gives us enough time to get some breakfast. I'm starved." She chuckled. "Sitting in the emergency room for half the night sure works up a healthy appetite. By the way, the lady at the front desk said there's a good café down the road about a block. Then we can see about the car towing arrangements."

Haven kept a hand over her mouth to cover any breathing sounds. When Buzz's truck drove off, she stepped from the cover of the tall ferns and made her way farther from the road, deeper into the sheltering darkness of the tall cedars. As she walked, a curious cold numbness crept up her feet, traveled to her thighs and up. It invaded her torso, and froze her heart. For once, her brain was silent, all the conflicting voices of reason and passion and grief laid to rest, just like Buzz's radio. *You've got to sleep.* Wrapping herself in her rain poncho, she lay down and curled up like a child. She settled her head on her pack and fell into a dreamless sleep.

When Kara awoke, the sun shone bright. She'd neglected to

set her travel alarm clock and now it was nearly an hour later than she'd planned on sleeping. She turned over to wake Haven, but her bed was empty.

A knock on the door startled her. Jennie's voice called, "Hey, sleepy heads, you're going to miss breakfast if you don't get down here real soon."

Kara jumped up. "I'll be down in a minute." She threw on her clothes, ran a brush through her hair, and hurried downstairs. Following the aroma of coffee and bacon into the dining room, she seated herself at the nearest available place setting.

Josh leaned over and whispered, "So, where's Blondie?"

She smiled. It was evident to everyone that Josh had a crush on Haven. He had placed a sheet of paper on the plate next to his and had scrawled on it in large letters: THIS SEAT SAVED FOR MISS ELLINGSEN.

Kara scanned the room. "I thought she'd already come down. She wasn't in our room when I got up."

Josh sat back, with a slight frown. "Well, I've been here since breakfast began, and she's never come in here."

"You know, she was pretty upset last night about her father. Maybe she's still too upset to eat. I'll go look for her in a couple of minutes." She hurried to finish her meal.

After breakfast, she ran up to her room hoping to find Haven. Everything appeared exactly as she had left it a half hour earlier. Haven's journal still lay on the desk. But her backpack was gone and she couldn't remember if it had been there when she got up in the morning. She opened the closet door. Haven's luggage sat there, untouched since last night. "Now, why would she need her pack today?"

On her way downstairs again, she ran into Josh.

"Is she up there?" He had a small gift-wrapped package in his hands.

"Josh, I'm getting a little worried." She glanced back up the stairs. "Wherever she is, she took her backpack with her. I'm going to ask Jennie what she thinks."

They returned to the dining room but nearly everyone had finished breakfast and returned to their rooms. The kitchen door sat open and Lance's big voice boomed in animated conversation with one of the kitchen workers. She knocked on the open door and Lance's head appeared from around the corner.

"Kara," he greeted her with his usual energetic good humor, "didn't you get enough to eat?" But then he noticed the look on her face.

Josh stepped inside. "We haven't seen Haven all morning and her backpack is missing from her room. Jennie was the one who told her last night about her dad's car accident. We were hoping that maybe she knows something we don't about Haven being gone."

Lance put down his damp dishcloth and ushered them toward the hotel lobby. As they rounded the hallway corner, Kara collided with a tall man in a red plaid jacket, coming the opposite direction.

"Oh, Mr. Colton, excuse me." She backed up and edged behind Josh. What was it about the man that always made her feel like a mouse cowering in front of a cat?

Mr. Colton didn't seem to notice her. He stuck his hands in his pockets and smiled his toothy smile at Lance. "I was just … uh … checking with the desk if the paychecks had come in yet."

Lance shook his head. "Sorry, they won't be in till tomorrow afternoon. But, as long as you're here, maybe you can help us. Have you see Haven Ellingsen anywhere around the hotel this morning?"

"Haven? One of the Life Ventures students?"

"The young lady with the very blonde hair. 'Bout this tall." Lance indicated with his arm stationed chin high.

"Oh," Mr. Colton nodded. "You mean the one in Jennie's group. Last time I saw her was when the students were tearing down their tents yesterday."

Kara huffed and stepped out from behind Josh, finding the courage to speak. "Mr. Colton, we haven't seen Haven all morning and her backpack's gone."

"We're worried about her," Josh added. "She was really upset last night when she heard about her father being in a car accident."

Mr. Colton gasped. "What? Her father was in a car accident?"

"He got caught in that storm somewhere outside Monroe," Kara said.

Colton stared down the narrow hallway, and his mouth twisted as if he were seeing the car skid and run off the road. He turned to Lance. "That poor girl. How awful." He scratched his beard. "Is her father okay?"

Lance frowned. "We're still waiting to hear more about his condition. Haven wanted to get to him last night but the police said it wasn't safe to travel. We were planning on taking her to the Monroe Hospital later today … that is, if the roads are clear."

"Hmm." Mr. Colton's head lowered as if in thought. Then he jerked his head up, eyes narrowed, his mouth a straight line. He zipped up his jacket. "Do you think she might be trying to hitch a ride to Monroe?"

"I guess that's possible," Lance said. "But I don't know if the bridge is open yet. And there's no other way to get onto the highway going west toward Monroe."

Mr. Colton reached into his pocket and retrieved his keys. "I hope she's not trying to hitch-hike. Even a quiet place like Lily has its share of crazies. Have you contacted the police yet?" He strode toward the front door.

"Not yet," Lance said. "But if she doesn't turn up soon, we'll alert the police."

"Good," Colton said. "And in the meantime, I'll ask around town. I know tons of business owners in Lily."

"Thanks, man." Lance shook Colton's hand.

The big man nodded but looked grim. "Don't worry, I'll do what I can to locate her. She can't have gotten far." He hurried out.

Kara faced Lance. "Mr. Colton always scared me, but I guess he cares about the Life Ventures students more than I realized."

"I think he knows how easy it is to get lost around here." Lance pressed his fist to his mouth and shook his head. "We might need his tracking skills."

Guy kept an eye out for a public phone. They had passed two gas stations, and neither had working phones.

Joy nudged his arm. "Settle down. We'll get to Lily when we get there. And we'll get there quicker if we don't have to keep stopping at every phone."

"What else can I do?" He punched his thigh in exasperation and winced. "You've got the manly job. All I can do is watch the scenery go by." Haven needed to know he was okay. He shifted in his seat. Why couldn't they put a cell phone tower in these parts?

Joy shrugged. "You'll have plenty to do when we meet Haven,

plenty to say, too."

"Do you think she's still mad at me?"

Joy sighed. "I don't know. A month is a long time. Or a short time. Depends."

He sat silently, digesting Joy's words.

Joy's gentle face screwed into a thoughtful frown. "I guess what I'm trying to say is, up until Helen died you had a really good relationship with Haven. You raised her to know the truth about God and life. She's a very bright and talented young woman. And she has a heart for people. Sure, she had a rough semester at the University. Maybe it was too soon for her to take on all those classes after her mother's death."

He started to speak, but Joy held up her hand.

"But you didn't know that. She seemed fine at first. She even got through her finals okay."

He shook his head. "I should have brought her home from school way earlier. She'd have gotten back on her feet sooner."

"You don't know that."

"I know that she blames me for her mother's death. If I'd been there that night maybe—"

"Stop it, Guy." Joy put a firm hand on his arm. "When Haven recovers from her trauma she'll be able to see things more clearly."

They came around a bend and slowed to dodge a pile of dirt that had washed onto the road.

"She's going to come through," Joy added. "I know it."

He sat forward and stretched. "I think so, too. Hey, slow down. There's a gas station. I want to call the hotel and let her know we're almost there." They pulled up under the "Quick N Easy" sign and he jumped out. The phone was working. He left a message at the hotel front desk for Haven telling her he'd arrive by noon.

Twenty minutes later the rented sedan crossed the recently reopened bridge to the town of Lily. When the car pulled up to the Lily Hotel he noticed two police cars parked in front. A police officer and another man stood on the front porch watching them. Inexplicably, a chill ran down his back. As soon as he and Joy stepped from the car, the two men came down the steps and approached them.

It was the cold that roused her. The sun had traveled west and fog drifted in to thwart its warmth and light. Her body stiff, she pulled herself to her feet and glanced around. What direction had she come from? *It doesn't matter, anyway. I'm so tired. So tired of everything.*

She picked up her pack and wandered farther from the road. Somewhere down the hill, a river churned and splashed. As she trudged nearer, the unmistakable roar of a waterfall pulled her forward. The ground sloped steeply at the foot of the falls. She lowered her pack to the ground, and climbed down the bank, clinging to fir branches to slow her descent. She turned her face up and let the spray drench her face. *God, where are You?* The nearness and the sound of water had always calmed her, even comforted her when she had been troubled. Maybe at the water's edge she'd hear a soothing answer for her tormented and guilty heart.

Without warning, it came. Her Goliath. Thoughts thundered away. Coordination slipped from her fingers. Blood drained from her face and her lips went numb. Icy, invisible fingers seized her throat. Shut off her air. She clawed at the fingers. Her vision funneled. *Don't faint.*

Her body folded forward. Earth came up to meet her. Her hands splayed on the ground.

Revived enough to push off the wet soil. Vines caught at her ankles. She ripped her boots out of their clutches.

Chaos in her ears. Giant feet pounded the ground behind her.

Run! Get to the top of the falls. Outrun him.

She climbed. Scrambled up the slippery rocks, scraping her hands and knees. Tripped. Banged her elbow. Jumped back to her feet. Raced to outrun the invisible menace. Ragged breaths. Hers or the giant's?

Nearly to the top now. Her pulse hammered at her skull. Muscles burned, lungs ached.

At the top of the falls the river narrowed. The water slammed against three tall boulders. Sentinels. Protectors. She had to get there. Just beyond them, the water rolled over the edge and cascaded downward onto jagged rocks. She stepped to the first boulder and teetered at the edge, gasping for air.

Anything. She'd do anything to escape the giant. She swayed dangerously. A gray mist sucked at her. Goliath materialized. He clambered over rocks, leaped across the watery chasm. His immensity overshadowed her. A rush of icy air beat at her like the swift killing strokes of a demon warrior's sword. She raised her arms to protect her head. Goliath's talons pierced her flesh. The giant bent her body backward, over the falls. She couldn't breathe. Her knees buckled. *Death.*

When she opened her eyes, she saw gray sky and the tops of trees. The back of her head throbbed where it pressed into jagged granite. Her legs dangled over the rocks, and river spray wet the toes of her boots. For whatever reason, Goliath had retreated.

Sick. I feel sick. Fast heart rate, but no longer racing. Her brain had gone quiet, like always after a panic. If only God would speak now. But only a vague melody teased at her brain. Playing hide and seek in the roar of the falls.

"God, I just want relief and You can't even give me that. What good are You?" She waited. Maybe this time God would take pity, would communicate something, some comfort, some reason for the way things had happened. She waited a long time. Her breathing returned to normal. Her abraded hands and knees burned.

Still no word from God. So, all those nice things Latrice had said about God were a lie. God really didn't care. Because if He did, He'd see that she was desperately seeking Him and that it was time to do something miraculous. Something that would prove that He hadn't abandoned her.

She closed her eyes. Her young aunt's face took shape in her mind. Childhood memories flooded her brain. Joy's terrible car accident ten years back. They were the first inklings she'd had that God ignored her prayers. Joy wore a body cast for months afterward. Joy was beautiful, but now she'd always walk with a limp. And she'd probably never be able to have children. Some answer to Haven's prayers.

God had not prevented that horrible accident from happening. He hadn't prevented her mother's death. And He hadn't healed Haven of her traumatic memories and panic attacks either.

And now with her father gone, too, Joy and her grandmother were the only close relatives she had left.

She stared up into the overcast sky, seeing her father's face in the changing clouds.

The day was like a horrible dream that she couldn't wake up from. Her father, dead. Just when she'd decided to make things right with him.

What sort of person was she? *A lightning rod for death.* And who, of her remaining relatives and close friends, would be next?

Too horrible to think about. She jumped to her feet, brushed the dirt and pine needles off her jeans, and leaped across onto firm soil. Maybe she needed to stay away. Go far away where she couldn't hurt anyone she loved.

Chapter Eight

Like a broken tooth or a lame foot
is reliance on the unfaithful in times of trouble.
Proverbs 25:19

The shadows shifted. After her near-dive from the falls, she had climbed down the hill, retrieved her backpack and crossed the river. Hoping to clear her head and decide her next course, she walked aimlessly, crossing and re-crossing her path. Where would she go? Back to the University for her last year? It all seemed pointless now.

Her stomach cramped and her legs wobbled from going hours without food. But her hunger was nothing compared to her grief. After her mother died, she couldn't eat. Dad had gotten mad at her. "Eat, or I'm putting you in the hospital."

Who'd tell her to eat now? She leaned against a lodge pole pine, and pressed her face into the rough bark. "Dad, Dad! I blamed you for Mom's death. I said terrible things to you. And now I can't even tell you how sorry I am."

She turned and let her body slide down onto the soft dirt.

Wiping her face with her sleeve she gazed at her hazy surroundings. The breeze shifted and a mist chilled the air. Trees faded into tall ghostly apparitions, swathed in grays and charcoals. How often, on weekends away from the University, had she mixed these very hues on her artist's palette, attempting to portray the beauty and mystery of the Oregon coastline on a canvas?

"I'll eat. Not for me, but for you, Dad." She unfastened her pack and took out the sack containing her purchases at the Quick N Easy. Opening a box of crackers, she munched on a handful. She shivered. In the last hour, the temperature had plummeted. She needed shelter before the rains came. During her wanderings, she'd hiked uphill and now she was surrounded by high, level ground. Perfect for a rustic campsite. She reached into her pack and pulled out her tarp.

With morning, dampness had invaded every inch of her tent and clothing. Mosquitoes dove and danced about her face in an effort to collect their own breakfast. She swatted irritably at them, then pulled her hood down farther about her face. Lifting a flap of the tarp, she inspected the campsite. Her bag of food, far downhill, still hung suspended and apparently untouched. She retrieved her food and munched on her remaining protein bar. A night's sleep and a new morning shed greater light on her crisis. For the first time in nearly twenty-four hours she was able to see beyond her own grief and consider the ramifications of her wild flight.

Aunt Joy's face rose in her mind. What must she be going through, losing her brother and finding her niece missing, all on the same day? And what about her grandmother? And her friends?

She'd been crazy and irrational after learning about her father's death. Running off into the woods for a day and a night now looked ridiculous. She wasn't a lightning rod for tragedy. She would not attract more tragedy onto the heads of her loved ones just by being near them. In fact, they'd need her all the more after her dad's death.

She stuffed her supplies into her backpack and scanned her surroundings. She had a compass but hadn't taken her bearings since she'd returned to Lily the day before. Still, the highway had to be south somewhere.

She picked up the pack and started downhill, traveling as close to south as the terrain would permit. At least the drizzle had finally come to an end. Some parts of the ground not covered by vegetation sucked at her boots. Soon she had to stop and pry the muck off her boots with a stick before continuing on.

By now they'd be looking for her, and Joy would probably be going crazy, worrying and wondering what had happened to her.

For a long time—much longer than she had guessed it would take—she hiked, stopping periodically to clean her boots.

During her wandering, time seemed to have stood still. But now, glancing at her watch, her stomach roiled to think of Aunt Joy getting the news of her disappearance. She had to get back to Lily. To be with Joy. To rebuild her life.

And when she got back, she'd need to prepare for music auditions, and register for her next semester. She'd get back to piano lessons, and practice, and maybe some competitions—"

A path. She'd been walking right alongside it. But the thick undergrowth had hidden it from view. She stepped onto the packed dirt. If she'd seen it earlier, it would have saved a lot of time and energy.

Eventually the path turned steeper and narrowed into a series of switchbacks. When she reached the end of the trail, it deposited onto a dirt road. Her feet felt lighter already. The highway to Lily could be around the next bend.

She trudged along the road for nearly an hour, getting increasingly more hot and thirsty. The highway had to be near. It just had to be. The sun had long since reached its zenith and begun its descent. Her feet throbbed and her shoulders ached from carrying the pack.

She had stopped to adjust the straps of her pack when she heard the faint sound. Seconds later, she spied dust spun into the air by the tires of an approaching vehicle. The sound of a truck's diesel motor crescendoed up the rutted road. She lost sight of it on a curve and hurried to regain view of it. *Thank God.* The driver would stop and pick her up. She'd get back to Lily in minutes rather than hours. She'd explain to Jennie why she had disappeared at night in the middle of a storm. Lance and Grant and Jennie would have to understand how awful it is when you hear about your father dying. How you go a little crazy and do things without thinking.

The truck was coming around the last bend, maybe fifty yards away. She staggered out in the middle of the road and waved her arms. The driver applied his brakes. A man opened his door and stepped out.

"Haven, we've been looking all over town for you."

She halted and squinted in the light of the sinking sun until he moved forward into a shadow and she recognized the tall man.

"Mr. Colton." Her throat spasmed. Overwhelmed by the events of the past two days, even the past month, and seeing a familiar face, she broke down in sobs.

"It's okay, girl." Mr. Colton leaned over her and put an arm around her shoulder. "Now, you just take your time and tell me all about it, okay?"

She managed to calm enough to answer the man's questions in a small, shaky voice.

"So, you say your dad was killed in that accident? Are you sure?"

She nodded. "I heard it on the radio. Oh, God!" She groaned and slapped her hand to her forehead. Fresh sobs wracked her shoulders.

"I'm sorry, girl." He turned her toward him and let her cry into his chest. "Don't you worry now. You just climb into the truck, and I'll take care of everything." He led her to the passenger door, opened it, and helped her climb inside.

She leaned back into the seat and closed her eyes. In a few minutes—a half-hour at the most—she'd be in Lily and could begin putting her life back together.

Mr. Colton climbed in and started the truck. "You're safe now."

They bumped and tossed for the better part of an hour over rocks and deep sandy depressions, spitting dust and debris as the tires of Mr. Colton's Ford truck spun. She leaned close to the window and watched for any signs of civilization. Her wanderings must have taken her much farther from the highway than she'd guessed.

At last the road smoothed. A thick carpet of pine needles replaced the rocks. The truck climbed, then descended, and she was glad it was Mr. Colton who'd found her. He knew these mountains better than anyone. After what seemed miles they descended into a dark, narrow valley shadowed by tall pines and granite-like cliffs rising like shards of broken pottery along the northern banks of a small river. In the murky light under the deepening gloom of early evening, they pulled up and stopped in front of a log cabin. Immediately, the front door opened with a screech and a raven-haired little girl trotted out followed closely by a young man with equally dark hair. They both got halfway to the truck before spying Haven. The little girl halted, eyes large with surprise, and plopped her thumb into her mouth.

When the boy got closer, he stared at her. He appeared to be maybe seventeen or eighteen. He came around to the truck bed and peered in, then looked up at Mr. Colton with a questioning look.

Colton leaned his head out the window. "No supplies today, boy. Run inside and get Mama."

Haven clutched her backpack. The beginnings of suspicion and disappointment forged a sharp edge to her tone, "Mr. Colton, didn't you say you'd take me to Lily? Are we close to town?" Her stomach tensed. "Please, can't we hurry?"

As if in answer, the front screen door screeched open again, then slammed shut. Mr. Colton nodded in the direction of a tall heavy-set woman who had emerged from the cabin door. He climbed out of the truck and went over to speak to her. As he spoke, Mama turned and locked eyes with Haven. Her small eyes stared, and her slit of a mouth narrowed, sprouting lines down her chin like freshly raked furrows in a garden. Mr. Colton took her arm and leaned down to say something else to her. Haven couldn't see his face, but his words seemed to make the woman lower her head and tense her shoulders. He released her arm and set off around the west corner of the cabin.

The woman gathered her ankle-length, denim skirt and lumbered down the steps. She stopped to glare at the little dark-haired girl.

"Sarah, git on back inside and watch Rebecca."

"Yes, Mama," the girl mewed, but remained at her spot.

Mama approached the truck's passenger door. "C'mon, girl. Git on out and come inside the house fer a bit." She opened the passenger door and stood with her hands on her ample hips, making it clear that she did not expect to be disobeyed.

Haven pursed her lips. What would the woman do if she made her own point by refusing to budge? Why were they stopping at the house? And what was Mr. Colton doing? He had to know time was wasting. Everyone at the Lily Hotel would be worried and wondering where she'd gone. Maybe he was going to make a phone call first. Yes, that must be why they'd stopped here.

The boy came back out of the house and stood next to his little sister. Both gawked at Haven as she stepped reluctantly out of the truck. But when Mama turned and noticed them standing there, she roared, "Girl. Move! Did you hear me?" She made a threatening move toward the little girl. The boy grabbed Sarah and pulled her away from danger.

"Come on, Sarah," he hissed through clenched teeth. "You tryin' to git us both crunched?" With red cheeks, he hurried Sarah past Haven and mumbled without looking up, "She likes to sleep with her eyes open."

Despite the strange circumstances, Haven felt bad for the two children. The boy seemed acutely embarrassed. At the front door, he whispered something to Sarah and patted her on the back, then opened the screen door and gently pushed her inside.

"Jesse, you git around the side and help yer Pa," Mama barked.

"Yes, Mama." Jesse jumped off the front stoop and shot Haven one last glance before galloping around the side, after

Colton.

After Jesse and Sarah had gone, Haven examined the weathered cabin and the surrounding area. Cords of wood had been neatly stacked beside the house. A propane tank sat near the west end of the cabin. Besides a small wooden shed a short walk toward the west and the glint of some steel structure the opposite direction, there were no other houses nearby, no buildings, and no businesses that she could see. Disappointed and confused, she stared at the cabin.

Mama turned her attention back to her. "C'mon in here and set down." Opening the front door, she practically pushed Haven through the entrance. Inside, the cabin was dark and it took a while for her eyes to adjust. The odor of pine disinfectant took her breath away. Awful. She pressed her finger to the base of her nose.

Why hadn't Mr. Colton at least taken her down to the highway? She'd told him about her dad and the car accident. "Do you have a phone? I really need to call my friends. I've got to let them know I'm on my way. Please, may I use your phone?"

Mama steered her to a wooden chair. "Now, don't be thinkin' about no phone right now. You just calm down and set quiet fer a bit."

Mama stood close, almost looming over her, and Haven sensed the woman's tension swimming under the surface of her muddy grey eyes.

When she remained quiet, Mama went over to the kitchen area, reached into a cupboard and took out a canning jar. Pumping water at the sink, she filled the jar and handed it to her. "Here, yer probably thirsty after all that runnin' and cryin'."

A movement over to the far corner of the room caught Haven's eyes. In the dim light, she made out a baby playpen.

Through the mesh of the sides, blankets shifted slightly to reveal a chubby hand, then a round, cherubic face, flaxen hair and blue eyes. At sight of her mother, the infant whimpered for attention. Sarah moved away as her mother shuffled over to the crib. Mama lifted the baby into her arms, talking to her as only mothers do.

Meanwhile, Haven's eyes had adjusted to the light in the cabin, and she swiveled her head to take in the arrangement of furniture, which was scanty, and doors and windows. There were only two doors, besides the front door. The first was ajar. A bedroom. The other, she could only guess. No bathroom. And no telephone that she could see. Her heart sank.

After waiting for what seemed an eternity, she spoke up again. "Ma'am, I really do need to make a phone call. You see, when I heard that my dad was hurt I ran off without thinking, trying to get to the hospital and I've been gone way too long. They're really going to be worried about me and where I am. I've got to let them know I'm on my way."

Mama put the baby back in the playpen, turned and looked at Haven. Her mouth smiled yet her eyes stared, unreadable. "We don't got a phone here, girl, but we'll take care of you. Don't worry; we got it all under control. Why don't you go and git cleaned up some? You look all dusty and dirty. Pa and I'll figger out where to take you."

The woman grabbed an old towel from the kitchen table and led her to the sink. "There's soap in that dish there and while yer at it, you might as well git them muddy boots off and I'll git 'em clean. Don't want them tracking dirt all over my clean floor."

After Haven stooped to unlace and step out of her boots, Mama took them and disappeared out the front screen door.

She washed her face and hands with the homemade bar of

soap, and tidied up her clothing as best as she could with the damp towel. When she finished, she moved over to the window and peered out. Mr. Colton and the woman were talking. Mama handed her boots to him and he headed in the direction of the shack she'd seen when they first drove up.

Darkness arrived prematurely under the shadows of the south-facing cliffs and tall pines. Mama, after handing off Haven's boots, returned and began meal preparations. "Well, as long as yer here, you might as well make yerself useful." Mama handed her a vegetable peeler and ordered her to the table.

Haven opened her mouth to bring up the "getting to a phone soon" subject, but held her tongue when the woman's angry eyes brushed over her once again. No, she'd wait until Mr. Colton showed up. It was clear that Mama was not the kind of woman who encouraged arguments or discussions. Not only was she a large, shapeless, looming woman, but her moods loomed also; an oppressive glower hovered over the room. No wonder the two dark-haired kids seemed so fearful of her.

Mama plunked a basket of potatoes down onto the table with instructions to peel and slice eight large ones. While Haven peeled, Sarah played with the baby. She lay on an oval rug by the fireplace, balancing the baby on her legs, bouncing and chanting an old nursery rhyme. The baby squealed and chortled as Sarah spun and bounced her. Between bounces, Sarah studied Haven. But every time Haven raised her eyes from her work, the girl dropped her gaze.

Mama, her face a study in scowls, cut up a large piece of meat into slivers. She fried them quickly in a skillet, then dropped the pieces into a simmering pot of broth and onions. Her mousey blonde hair, streaked with gray, was tightly pulled back into one long, thin braid. Loose strands hung around her plain, round face and she intermittently blew the hair away from her eyes and mouth as she worked. In spite of the bad atmosphere and her hostess' manners, Haven couldn't ignore her hunger.

She worked to peel the potatoes as fast as possible. When Mr. Colton came back inside, and the family all had dinner, then they'd go. Even though it had been a bad enough drive when it was light outside, they'd have to take her back to the Lily Hotel some time tonight. She'd been gone almost forty-eight hours. If she didn't get back soon the Life Ventures people would probably call the police. What a mess that would be. And her grandmother and Joy ...

She glanced over at Mama, who moved from stirring the soup pot to rolling out dough for biscuits. The woman seemed totally engrossed in her thoughts as she frowned and muttered to herself.

Jesse came through the front door. He'd taken his shirt off and his lean, brown torso glistened with perspiration.

Mama slammed her rolling pin onto the counter and glared at the boy. "You git yerself out and take a bath, quick. You can't be cleaning up inside with the girl here, you moron." She came at Jesse with a kettle of hot water and the boy retreated out the door instantly. Muttering to herself again, she followed him out, letting the door screech and bang behind her.

Haven got up and tiptoed to the window. Jesse picked up a large old-fashioned tub, the kind she'd seen used in movies about pioneer life. He took it around the side of the cabin. Mr. Colton pumped well water into a gallon jug.

"Psst." Sarah's eyes, big with alarm, swiveled to the kitchen table. "Quick," she whispered, "Mama's coming back."

Without knowing why, Haven scurried back to the table. Seconds later Mama returned with the kettle, setting it back on the wood-burning stove for reheating.

"Are you done with them potatoes?" She took the bowl, dumped them into the soup pot, stirred and tasted the broth, added more pepper, then plunked the pot lid on.

"You keep yer eye on that pot and tell me when it's ready, girl." Mama walked toward Sarah. "Hand me Rebecca." She took the baby into her arms, carried her into the bedroom, and shut the door.

Sarah glanced at the closed bedroom door before getting up. She crept over to the table and regarded Haven with solemn eyes. "What's your name?" She stood at a distance as if not sure if Haven were friend or foe.

Maybe the little girl knew how far they were from Lily. Haven cleared her throat and smiled at Sarah. "My name is Haven and I'm twenty-one years old. I think I've heard that your name is Sarah but I don't know how old you are."

"I'm almost nine."

"Well, almost-nine-year-old Sarah, do you go to school around here and do you have any friends who live nearby?"

"Pa and Mama teach us. We have books, and they read them, and then Pa asks us questions. Pa and Mama read the Bible a lot, and then they tell us about God and people and stuff. Jesse knows how to read some."

"How about your friends? Do they come around here to play or do you go to their houses?"

"I play with Jesse and I have a doll. Do you want to see her?"
"Yes, but—"

Too late. Sarah jumped up, ran into the other bedroom, and returned with a bundle, cradled in her arms. Carefully, she pulled back the thin blanket to reveal a hand-made cloth doll. Its face had been crudely drawn in with indelible marker. Thin strings of black yarn sufficed for her hair and her dress was cut from old green canvas.

"This is Elizabeth. I named her that 'cause it's the most beautiful name I know. Don't you think so, too? Maybe when we get to be friends you can hold her sometime. I gotta put her back now. If Mama sees me with her, she'll take her away 'cause I'm not supposed to play with her now."

Sarah jumped up, and ran back into her bedroom. When she returned, she sat down at the table next to Haven and studied her again. "Why are you here?"

"It's kind of a long story, Sarah. I got lost and saw your dad, and he said he could help me, so here I am. I hope he can take me to Lily or somewhere close, so I can get back to my family."

"Oh," Sarah murmured. "Who's Lily?"

"Oh, Lily's not a person. Lily's a town not too far away. I've got friends there who will be worrying about me if I don't get back soon. Do you think—?"

Just then Jesse appeared at the front door, hair wet, wrapped in a blanket. His cheeks reddened again when he saw her. He kept his head averted as he hurried past toward the bedroom door.

Sarah jumped up and trotted to the kitchen. She climbed a stepstool, reached into a cupboard and pulled out bowls and spoons for the soup, and a plate for the biscuits. She set them all on the table.

Mr. Colton came through the front door and clomped over to the kitchen sink to wash his hands.

He's back, finally. Now we can hurry up and eat dinner and then get out of this miserable place. Haven rose from the table and hurried over to him. "Mr. Colton, could we drive into town as soon as everyone has had dinner?" Mr. Colton had probably called the hotel from some neighbor's place and told them they were on their way.

"It's too dark, girl," he said, not even looking up from his hand-washing. "The lights don't work well on the truck. We'll have to wait till morning."

Chapter Nine

A lying tongue hates those it hurts,
and a flattering mouth works ruin.
Proverbs 26:28

"We can't go until morning?" Haven asked.

Mr. Colton's words struck her gut like the kick of a horse. She put her hand on the counter to steady herself. "But you said ... you told me you'd take me ... look, Mr. Colton, I can't wait till it's light outside. My friends and—"

"If Mr. Colton says it's too dark to travel, then it's too dark." Mama loomed behind her, holding Rebecca. "You got two choices, girl. You can stay here tonight, and we'll take care of things tomorrow. Or you can skedaddle and run around in the black all night. A few more hours ain't gonna kill anybody."

"I-I-I thought," Haven said, a combination of spunk and intimidation warring in her bones. She ran her fingers back and forth against her bottom lip. *Think, Haven. How can I make them see sense?* Colton's words left her reasonless and wordless, as if boulders had avalanched and pinned her brain.

Mama whisked the pot of soup off the wood-burning stove

and onto the table. The family took their places. Jesse, dressed in clean clothes, slunk forward and sat next to Mama, head down, ears red.

Mr. Colton moved over to the table, not even looking at Haven. "Mama, make a place for the girl right here." He indicated a spot on his left.

"C'mon," Sarah said. She took Haven's hand and led her to the place next to Colton. Without any other options, Haven took her seat. Mama held the baby girl on her lap. Haven looked around the table. At Mr. Colton's place sat a large Bible. When he opened the book, Mama, Sarah and Jesse lowered their heads and closed their eyes.

In a slow, chanting voice, he intoned, "I am reading from the Holy book of Ruth. 'But Ruth replied, 'Don't urge me to leave you or to turn back from you. Where you go, I will go, and where you stay, I will stay. Your people will be my people and your God my God. Where you die, I will die, and there I will be buried. May the Lord deal with me, be it ever so severely, if anything but death separates you and me.'"

Haven sneaked a look at Mr. Colton's stern face. In spite of the crookedness of his nose, the man was handsome. Funny at this time that she should notice that. Her father was dead, and here she sat in a small wilderness cabin, having soup with complete strangers. Her breath caught in a prelude to tears. But Mr. Colton gripped her hand to silence her. He turned his face upward and prayed in a loud voice, "Oh Lord, we thank Thee for the blessing of food and shelter. We thank Thee for our children. For Jesse, for Sarah. And for this little one. Grant us the wisdom and strength to train up this poor sinner according to Thy Word, so that she will walk in Thy ways and grow to be mighty in the faith. And may she come to say, like Ruth, 'May the Lord deal with me, be it ever so severely, if anything but death separates you and me.'"

Colton looked down. "As I declare it, so it shall be."

Mama and Jesse and Sarah repeated, "So shall it be."

Mama drew Rebecca closer to her big chest and kissed the child's downy head.

Then began the strangest repast Haven had ever taken part in. Mr. Colton dipped a ladle into the pot and dished the soup into bowls. As the bowls were handed down to each member at the table, a low murmur of voices accompanied the clinking of spoons. She watched, bewildered. Sarah nudged her spoon, her eyes communicating that she should join the meal. Haven picked up her spoon, dipped it into the broth and brought it to her lips. Just as she was about to sip, she glanced up to catch all eyes wide in horror. She froze.

"You gotta say a word," Sarah whispered.

"A word?"

"You know, a word from the Holy Bible before you can eat. You gotta say a word every time you want to take another bite. Okay?"

"Okay." She looked across the table and found Jesse staring at her. He dropped his gaze immediately. "Sorry."

A word. From the Bible. Really weird. She lifted her spoon. "Joshua."

Sarah's shoulders relaxed. Mama smiled and Mr. Colton looked pleased. The meal continued, a combination of slurps and holy murmurs. Some words brought loud "Amens" from the group when one of the children came up with a new word. How they kept track of old and new words uttered during the meal mystified Haven. Occasionally, Jesse or Sarah seemed to be stumped, and the Bible was handed over for fresh vocabulary. When the last bites of soup had been consecrated by holy words, she hurried to push her agenda again.

"Ma'am, Sir, have you decided how I can get back to Lily tomorrow? The police are probably looking for me by now, and my family will be crazy, worrying about what happened to me."

"I thought you said your daddy was dead." Mr. Colton leaned so close to her his big head filled her entire field of view.

"I-I said that my mom and dad are both gone." She fidgeted with the small gold cross hanging on her neck. "But I do have an aunt and—"

"Don't git all excited now," Mama said. She stared at her husband while drumming her fingers on the table. "We'll take care of everything tomorrow when it's light out. No use frettin' about it now. God's people always do what's best."

She stood up to collect the dishes and spoons on the table, and Haven moved to help her. Mama seemed to be in a better mood now, and she smiled at her. "Well, thank you fer yer help. Yer a good worker."

After they had washed and put away the dishes and thoroughly scrubbed the table and chairs, Mama hung up the dish towels and called for Sarah.

"Here, you, go put some fresh sheets on Jesse's bed. The girl will be in yer bedroom tonight. Jesse, you can sleep on the couch."

Haven took a breath. "Ma'am, would it be okay if I got my pack? It has all my clothes and other things I might need."

The woman dismissed her request with an impatient wave of her hand. "It's been put in the shack for the night and the children don't wanna go out there in the dark to git it." She put a work-worn hand on Haven's shoulder and her voice gentled. "Anyway, what would you be needin' at this time of night? You got all the things you need right here. Clean night things and a clean bed. S'all you need."

Mama steered her to the second bedroom where they found Sarah in the middle of making Jesse's bed. Mama reached into a bureau drawer and pulled out one of Jesse's tee shirts. "Here, put this on. It should be nice and roomy fer you."

Haven waited for Mama to exit. But the woman stood with folded arms, and watched her.

"Is there a place where I can change?"

"You can change right here." Mama's harsh tone jolted her. "We don't got any secrets between us females. Just go ahead and git them things off and don't be so sissy."

Haven bit her lip at the woman's angry tones. Determined to maintain some dignity, she faced the wall as she pulled off her clothes. As soon as she dropped them and pulled the tee shirt over her head, Mama swooped them up and carried them out of the room.

Sarah had already climbed into her bed, so Haven switched off the light, made her way to the other bed and slid under the covers. Too tired to think or worry anymore, she was just slipping into slumber when the door opened and Mama's ample silhouette filled the doorway.

"Girl, what's yer name?"

"Haven, Haven Ellingsen."

"Hmm, I don't like it."

The door closed and silent blackness enveloped the room.

When Haven woke, dawn had broken, but the house was still silent. Sarah's bed was empty. Haven crept to the door and carefully turned the knob, easing the door open a crack, and peered out. Relieved to find no one stirring, she crept toward the front door. Halfway there, a soft sigh made her freeze. Sarah slept, snuggled next to her big brother on the couch. Haven continued toward the front door, and grimaced when a floorboard creaked. And worse, she'd forgotten about the screen door. It screeched, opening and shutting. *You've just tripped the alarm. Get going, quick. Maybe they're heavy sleepers.*

She hurried through the chill morning air. Today she'd be back in Lily. She'd get her pack and her boots and clothes, and be ready to go as soon as Mama and Mr. Colton got up. She just hoped they didn't sleep late.

When she got near enough to see, her stomach clenched. What? Someone—probably Mr. Colton—had padlocked the door. Why in the world would they need to lock a shack way out in the woods? She glanced over her shoulder. Such strange people. Did they think animals could open doors? There was one window close to the door. She wiped the grime from the glass and peered into the dark interior. Mostly garden tools and stacks of wooden crates. But in the far-left corner, she could just make out her backpack and her boots. Mr. Colton wouldn't be too happy if she broke a window and climbed in. Did it count as trespassing if it was her things locked inside their property?

"Anything I can help you find, girl?"

She whirled around. Mr. Colton stood a dozen feet away holding a shotgun at his side. His tall, powerful form and stern expression robbed her of movement. Her heart pounded as if it would pole-vault from her chest. "I was … I need … I mean, I was looking for my clothes and I'll need my pack when we go this morning."

The man's eyes narrowed. His gaze darted from her hair and her face down her body and bare legs. Then he averted his eyes.

She shivered in her cotton tee shirt and crossed her arms over her chest.

"You sure are fired up to get out of here." He pointed toward the cabin with the barrel of the shotgun.

Heart still pounding, she obediently turned back to the house. Mr. Colton followed like a mountain lion after a deer. When they stepped back inside, the entire family had been roused and Mama had begun preparations for breakfast. The aroma of strong coffee filled the great room. She had mixed dough for biscuits, and a basket of eggs sat next to the stove.

Jesse sat on the couch, putting on his shoes. When he looked up and saw Haven, his gaze riveted to her legs. Mr. Colton made some kind of gesture at him, and the boy immediately jumped up and hurried out the front door.

Mama stomped into her bedroom and returned with a long denim dress similar to the one she was wearing and thrust it at her. "Here," she said with a tone of disgust, "put this on. It's kinda big fer you but you can cinch it in with this belt. I imagine yer wondering about yer clothes. They're in the dirty pile. No sense washing 'em and hanging them out to dry last night. We can git to 'em after breakfast."

Haven glanced over at Mr. Colton. He stood by the front door, still gripping the shotgun, but kept his gaze turned to the far wall.

Mama growled, "Git it on quick so the men folk don't have to look at a half-dressed woman." She grimaced at Haven's bare legs.

Haven's cheeks turned hot. Without another word, she hurried into the bedroom to change. Without her own clothes, there wasn't any use arguing with Mama. Better to get this whole morning over and done with and then she could climb into Mr. Colton's truck and head on down to Lily.

When she returned, dressed in the oversized garment she asked, "Would you mind if I got my pack and boots out of the shack now?"

"First things first, girl. Gotta get breakfast on, then we can figger out what to do." Mama brushed past and resumed her preparations for the meal.

Jesse must have been waiting outside near the front door. As soon as Haven had changed, Colton opened the door and ushered Jesse back inside.

Haven stood in the middle of the room, fidgeting with her gold cross. Again, Mr. Colton and Mama, Sarah and Jesse seemed to regard her as if she had simply melted into the fabric of the family and taken her accepted place as big sister, oldest daughter.

Mama bustled past her again. "Put them plates on the table," she directed, pointing to the kitchen counter. "Sarah, go git some water." She shoved a pitcher at the girl.

Jesse headed over to the kitchen sink and pumped water to wash his hands. The boy watched Haven under dark, frowning eyebrows. In another moment, they had all come to the table.

Mr. Colton caught Haven's eye and nodded at the space next to him. For a second she was tempted to shout, "No!" then stomp her foot, and storm out the front door. There'd be more Bible reading and more prayer and then another slow, slurping, murmuring meal. And it'd be noon by the time they were finished and cleaned up. And meanwhile, by now there'd be police combing Lily and the area, questioning people, maybe putting her photo on the local news. Humiliating.

Still, the truck would get her to Lily quicker than walking. She frowned as she marched over and plunked herself down next to Mr. Colton.

Mama took her place, holding little Rebecca in her lap. As Mr. Colton took up the Bible all activity ceased and all heads bowed and eyes closed. This time he read a brief passage from the book of Jeremiah: "The Lord will roar from on high; He will thunder from His holy dwelling and roar mightily against His land. He will shout like those who tread the grapes, shout against all who live on the earth.

The tumult will resound to the ends of the earth, for the Lord will bring charges against the nations; He will bring judgment on all mankind and put the wicked to the sword, declares the Lord."

Colton closed the Book, raised his eyes to the ceiling, and prayed in a dramatic and archaic fashion, "O God, Thou remembers how Thy humble servant lived among the sinners; how his eyes grieved to see their rebellion and their wrongdoing. Thou has told him to flee to the mountains where he can remain pure. And now, God, Thou has shown Thy mercy to this little child, entrusting her to the righteous instructions and chastisement of Thy holy servant. I thank Thee. Thy servant will keep her safe. Separate. Untouched by filthy hands."

He placed the Bible on the table. "As I declare it, so shall it be."

"So shall it be," repeated the family.

Haven glanced over at the baby, sitting on Mama's lap. Why in the world did they keep calling that sweet, little baby girl a sinner? She couldn't have been more than eight or nine months old.

Colton poured coffee for Mama and himself, and passed the

biscuits, butter and eggs. Again, the murmur of holy words accompanied the meal.

But just as they were finishing up, the sound of an approaching vehicle and the squeak of hot, dusty brakes made the entire family stop in the middle of raising forks to their mouths. Mama darted a nervous look at Mr. Colton. Haven jumped up, but the man put his giant hand on her shoulder and pressed her back down.

"Everyone, settle down. I'll see who it is." He stood and stuffed his hands into his pockets. "It's probably old Martin, coming to pay a visit. He said he wanted to borrow my … jig saw." Mr. Colton stared at the front door as if he were trying to see through it. "He lives up the canyon a few miles. Kind of a crazy guy, though. I'm the only other person he tolerates. Hates kids. Cusses at them. Don't let him see any of you through the window."

Mama pushed back from the table and pressed baby Rebecca to her bosom. Her beady eyes blinked rapidly. "C'mon, children. Let's hide in my room. Dade, don't open the door yet." She herded Haven out of the kitchen along with Jesse and Sarah. "Hurry, hurry now," she hissed. "Git in there quick."

Just as Mama was closing the bedroom door, Haven glimpsed Mr. Colton stepping out the front door. A Jeep-type vehicle had pulled up to the front of the house, its motor running. A dog barked once.

"Mama," Jesse whispered, "why'd we have to hide? I never heard that old Martin hates—"

"Hush, you." Mama's face turned fierce. "Pa knows what's best. Not another word."

She put Rebecca on the bed and stood with clasped hands, rocking and humming, gaze fixed on the bedroom door. Sarah peeked through the curtains, but the window was facing the wrong direction. She pulled the curtain back as if trying to see around the corner. Haven moved toward the window at the same time Jesse did, and they bumped into each other. Jesse's cheeks turned pink, and he retreated to his original position by the door. Haven was just turning from the window when she caught a blur of movement outside. A German Shepherd dog ran by, nose to the ground, followed by a young man wearing a striped jacket. Clearly emblazoned on the back of his jacket were the words, "Search and Rescue."

Haven whirled around. Mama hovered behind her, staring at her, meaty hands clasping and unclasping. Their eyes met and locked. In one split second, all the events—the conversations, the Bible readings, the prayers, the locking up of her boots and backpack, being forced to hide in the bedroom—burst over her consciousness like a sickening wave of realization. Mr. Colton and Mama planned to keep her here. A cry burst from her lips. She dashed for the door, but Mama lunged and grabbed her.

Mama clapped her hand over Haven's mouth.

Haven tore Mama's fingers away from her lips and yelled with all her strength, "Help. Help. I'm here … help!"

Held fast, her eyes registered a blur of Jesse, standing frozen, his face contorted as if in agony.

Haven tried to shove the large woman off. "You can't keep me here. They're looking for me." Mama's rough hands muffled Haven's screams. "Don't you know this is kidnapping?"

They bumped into a dresser, lost their balance and fell onto the floor, locked in a hateful embrace. Mama clamped her hand over Haven's mouth again. Her bulk and height held Haven trapped between the door and bed frame. Haven gasped and fought to get out from under the woman's fearsome weight. With her legs pinned, she clawed at Mama's strong arms and tried to bite her fingers.

Mama let go for a second. She reached for something. Lifted it high above their heads. An iron doorstop. She slammed it downward.

An awful sound: iron impacting flesh. For a second, Haven couldn't comprehend it. She opened her mouth to scream. No sound came out. Her forehead erupted in blood. It poured into her eyes and splattered onto her fingers. Everything was red. Nothing but red.

Then it was black.

Chapter Ten

Enemies disguise themselves with their lips,
but in their hearts, they harbor deceit.
Proverbs 26:24

The next morning, Dade debated the merits of going into town and asking the counselors at Life Ventures if they'd heard anything more about Haven Ellingsen's disappearance. He needed the information, but it might look suspicious if he asked too many questions. On the other hand, as the local tracking expert he could offer his services to the Lily police. That way, he could nudge the outdoor investigation far away from his cabin.

On his way down the hill he turned on the radio. When the news report came on, he pulled over and idled his truck so he didn't miss a word of it.

"Local police are investigating the disappearance of a twenty-one-year-old Oregon woman. Haven Ellingsen vanished sometime in the early morning hours of July 6th from the Lily Hotel. The woman had just completed a course in wilderness survival led by the local organization, Life Ventures, Inc. A spokesperson for the investigation, Detective Angela Romerez, said, 'Foul play is not suspected. However, search and rescue teams have joined us in the investigation.'

Haven is blonde and blue-eyed, 5'4" tall, and weighs 110 pounds. Anyone with information on Haven's disappearance or whereabouts is asked to contact local police."

Nothing he didn't already know, except the name of the Detective. Dade pressed the accelerator. He could be at the Lily Police Station in less than a half hour. The sooner he volunteered to help with the search, the better.

He'd had his doubts that the girl's father had actually died as a result of the car accident. There had been nothing on the radio or in the Monroe Sentinel about Haven's father's death. But when he entered the Station, a middle-aged blonde man—a civilian, obviously— was talking to two police officers. The resemblance to Haven was striking.

Dade strode over to them. "Excuse me, Officer Lohan," he said, glancing at the officer's name tag. "My name's Dade Colton."

"Oh, yes, Mr. Colton, we were about to put in a call for you."

Dade almost gasped, but caught himself. Perspiration broke out on his forehead. "You were?"

"You have a reputation in this area for being an expert in tracking. We hoped you would be willing to help us."

Dade took a deep breath and exhaled silently.

Officer Lohan turned his head to indicate the blonde man standing beside him. "This is Haven Ellingsen's father."

Dade reached out and gripped Mr. Ellingsen's hand. "I'm so sorry about this, sir. I'll be happy to assist you and the police in any way I can."

Mr. Ellingsen nodded, his expression grim. "I appreciate it."

"We're just about to launch another search," Lohan said. "If you're able to start right now, I can call over to the Lily Hotel. There're about fifteen volunteers waiting to go out with us".

"That's fine." As long as the helpers didn't get ahead of him and mess up the clues he intended to 'find.'

Mr. Ellingsen raked his fingers through his pale hair. "I'm never, ever going to stop searching for Haven. She's smart and spunky. She's a survivor." He balled one fist and punched it into the other palm. "She's out there, alive, somewhere."

Dade nodded. *That's right, Daddy, she's alive. But you'll never find her.* "Okay, let's get going."

When she awoke, she was lying on a bed. She did not know where she was. Everything looked blurry. She started to lift her head but pain stopped her. Reaching up, her fingers traced a great swollen gash at her left temple. Blood had dried and clumped in her hair. Any movement made her head throb unbearably. She closed her eyes and lay very still.

She slept for long periods. Occasionally, she awoke to blurred faces bending over her, making sounds. Sometimes her body was handled, and it hurt. A rough, wet cloth scraped over her tender forehead. She heard someone crying when they handled her. Then she would be alone again and sleep.

Sometimes the room was light and other times, dark. Eventually her vision cleared. When it was light, the woman would come in, prop her upright, and spoon liquid into her mouth. She wanted to ask her who she was, and where she was, but words didn't come.

' One morning the brown-haired man came into the room and bent over her. He uttered a strange sound, "Ruth ... Ruth."

She tried to form her lips into the sound's shape. "Ruth," she tried in a weak, raspy voice.

The man smiled. "Ruth." He trailed his big hand down the side of her face.

"Ruth," she rasped again. What did "Ruth" mean?

She lay helpless in her bed, listening to the sounds of activities outside her bedroom. She managed to sit up without that awful throbbing in her skull. The brown-haired man came into the room, lifted her and carried her into another larger room. He set her down on an old sofa, and propped her body with blankets and pillows. All day she sat and watched the people move around the room. Sometimes, one of them would come near her and make sounds at her. And she would smile and nod.

Light times melted into dark times, and dark times into times of light. Her limbs got stronger.

The woman made mean sounds. Then she shoved. And slapped. It hurt her head. How could she tell the woman to stop? Did the people think she understood all of their strange sounds?

Mealtimes were hardest. When she tried to make sounds like the others did, the man stared at her with a strange look. The boy sometimes glanced at the cruel woman with a hard expression in his dark eyes. Then the cruel woman would make more ugly sounds.

Dade watched the girl carry a load of freshly scrubbed clothing and bed sheets into Sarah's bedroom. Considering how bad the girl's wound looked, it was a wonder that not being able to talk was the only bad thing to come from it. Or, maybe it wasn't such a bad thing.

The girl opened dresser drawers and put the clothes away.

Mama's iron doorstop might just have turned Ruth into the perfect woman; she didn't talk back, and she didn't ask questions. When he was a little boy, Mother Jane always told him, "Tommy, the way to keep your father happy is to say "yes, sir or "no, sir. Nothing more, nothing less. That way, you and Father both win. It's a little game we play."

After many days, Ruth spoke one word. "Jesus," she said during the noon mealtime. She had said it softly, not as a curse. Dade raised his eyebrows and put down his fork. He spoke to her, but she obviously couldn't understand him. She said, "Jesus," again. And when he smiled, she smiled back.

Mighty worrisome that a word had returned to the girl. And why that word? With that word, most likely, more words would follow. Did she remember where she had come from? Or who had injured her? The head wound had made her stupid—what a lucky accident. Even more stupid than Mama. And he'd been able to control her for several years now just by a few ambiguous Bible verses and some imaginative rituals involving extreme cleanliness, and "magic" words at mealtimes. Religion came in mighty handy. Maybe if he trained Ruth now before her mind recovered he could stop the questions, the thinking, and remembering.

Mama wouldn't allow her to go outside unless accompanied by the boy, and even then, only when the truck was gone. It wasn't too bad when the boy went with her to fetch meat from the shed. He seemed to like to talk to her. He waved his hands and pointed at things, as if it would help her understand what he was saying.

But once back inside the cabin the boy seemed to disappear. The tall man became the center of everyone's attention. Mama bustled. Sarah helped. The man called her Ruth, and taught her to call him Dade. He kept her busy with little things, mostly fetching a book, or a tool for him. Or wiping a dusty spot on the wall or the floor. Of course, the sounds coming out of his mouth made no sense. So, he took her hand and led her to the thing he wanted, or the thing he wanted cleaned. Then he stood over her and stared while she cleaned. She was never free of his attention. When Dade watched, Mama scowled.

Ruth couldn't decide which was worse: the way Dade stared at her, or the way Mama was always looking for a chance to yell at her, or shove her. One morning, Mama took Ruth over to the sink and made her put her head down into a bowl of warm, dark liquid. The dye made her once light-colored hair a dark, dull color. Mama dried her hair and combed and wove it into one long braid. Afterward, she examined Ruth's hair and made a grunting sound.

"Better. We can't … men-folk starin' … cause you got light hair."

Night-times were better. The man and the boy would bring out musical instruments. And then Mama and Sarah and the baby would sit and listen.

She couldn't name the instruments. Dade played the one with the loud, twangy quality. He played well, and his voice was strong and deep. Alone, the instrument sounded too loud. But when the boy played along with his instrument, the music was pretty.

She had been listening to Dade and the boy for several weeks when many words started to come back. Aside from the names of each family member, and a handful of simple words, the rest of their speech sounded like gibberish. But as Dade and the boy, Jesse, sang each evening, more and more words formed in her mind. She wanted to tell them how much she loved the music, how it brought words back.

When Jesse looked down at her, seated across the room, his dark eyes looked so sad that she half expected tears to flow down his cheeks. One evening he sang,

> *"The water is wide, I cannot get o'er*
> *and neither have I wings to fly*
> *Give me a boat that can carry two*
> *And we shall cross, my true love and I."* [2]

As Jesse sang, a door in her mind opened. Words, images, musical tones and scales flooded that part of her brain that had been silent for weeks. She brought her fingers up to trace the wound on her forehead. She remembered standing in a row with other young women, singing. A man, wearing a dark suit stood in front of them, his arms outstretched, moving to the sound of the beautiful music. His face expressed the sentiment of the song's text.

"Oh, love is handsome and love is kind,
Bright as a jewel when it is new,
But love grows old and waxes cold,
And fades away like morning dew."[2]

The words sounded familiar, like a book read many years before and only partially recalled. The music touched her heart with sadness.

"... and fades away like morning dew," she softly mouthed the tune. Tears stung her eyes and she closed them and tried to summon once more the vision of the singers and the director. *"And fades away like morning dew."* She replayed the words over and over in her mind. How beautiful those words were. How beautiful to hear and understand. She tried to form her mouth to more phrases, rocking her body slightly to the rhythm in her head.

When she opened her eyes, the entire family was watching her.

"Look, Dade." Mama gestured toward her.

The boy played a few more bars of the song, but this time he did not sing. Ruth crept up to the two men and sat down at their feet. Reaching up, she touched the strings of Jesse's instrument. "Dew," her throat hurt from days of silence.

Jesse looked up at his mother and said, "Mama" and "I do?" That much, she understood. She touched the strings again, trying to communicate her eagerness for him to continue singing.

Jesse sat forward and spoke something to her. He played a few more bars of music, then added the vocal part. His face flushed when she stared at him, and his voice became softer still when she joined him on some of the phrases. Although rusty, her voice stayed on pitch and the tune and some of the words came faster and surer with each repetition.

At last Jesse stopped and looked over at Mama, his face

triumphant. Ruth caught some of his words. He'd said that she was "not dumb," and that she had a "good voice." She smiled at Jesse.

Mama stood up with a "Harrumph. Tomorrow … read … Holy Scripture … her. Then … see."

Dade said, "No more … time … bed."

Everyone stood up. "Yes, Sir."

She could feel Dade's eyes on her when she stood up and followed Sarah. At the door to her bedroom, she turned and glimpsed a trace of something in his expression she didn't like. It made her afraid.

Dade watched Ruth follow Sarah into her bedroom. After she shut the door, he placed his banjo back into its case and returned it to its secure spot in the back of the broom closet. Just as he shut the closet door, a memory broad-sided him in its intensity and clarity. An ancient hatred welled in his chest as his father's voice came alive in his brain. He hurried outside the front door, and clutched the porch banister. Once the memory began to play in his mind, there seemed to be no stopping it until it had run its ugly course.

"Jane." Judge Boone's booming voice echoed throughout the first floor of the house. "Show yourself, woman."

"Hush up, Tommy," Mother Jane whispered as she huddled with him in the broom closet in the dark corridor off the kitchen in the old brick house on Lindon Street. She held him close. They hardly dared breathe. Father's drunken steps stumbled past the closet. A shuddering spasm shook Tommy's shoulders and he put both hands over his mouth to silence a whimper.

Mother whispered, "He can't hurt us if we don't make a sound." She stared at the sliver of light at the bottom of the door.

"Thomas Dade Boone. If you don't show yourself right now, I'll go upstairs and bust that new banjo of yours into a million pieces." Father's rage-filled voice made the decorative plates on the kitchen wall rattle.

Awful silence. Tommy imagined his father waiting, maybe listening for the slightest rustle that might betray their hiding place.

The man's heavy step tromped up the stairs towards the bedrooms.

Tommy tried to hold back a shuddering sob. "He's going to break my banjo. I've got to stop him." He struggled to free himself from his mother's firm embrace.

"Hold still," Mother Jane said. "I got money stashed away. If he takes it away, I'll buy you another one."

"But he takes away everything I care about."

"I know," Mother soothed, kissing Tommy's brow. She wiped the tears from his cheeks. More silence. Then the squeak of Father's brass bed. "There now," she took a deep breath, and relaxed her hold on her son, "he'll sleep it off now. We won, this time." They stood up and stretched their cramped muscles. Mother eased the closet door open and peered around the corner before she let Tommy come out. They tiptoed toward the back door.

Once outside the big, brick house he hugged his mother tight. Tears splashed down his cheeks. "I hate him, I hate him."

"Shh, little man," Mother Jane bent over him and stroked his hair.

"Let's run away, Mother. I'll take care of you from now on. I'll mow lawns and sweep and run errands. I'll make sure Father doesn't hurt you again. You'll be safe."

"He doesn't mean to hurt me, Tommy. It's just when he drinks, that's all."

"Why don't we tell the police that Father hits us?"

"Oh, Tommy, you must never, never tell anyone. He's an important judge. It'd be awful if people knew. Promise me you won't tell." She bent down and put her hand under his chin, lifted his head and gazed at him with so much love that he dropped his gaze. "Promise me."

"I-I promise. But just don't make me promise to love him. Cause I won't. Ever. He's a bad, bad man."

One morning, after breakfast, Dade and Mama held a whispered conversation in the kitchen. Ruth shuddered when he looked over at her. He pointed to the Bible sitting on the kitchen table. Mama didn't look happy. Then Dade put on his red jacket and strode out the front door.

After the breakfast dishes had been cleared, washed, and stored, Mama summoned her as well as Jesse and Sarah to sit at her feet. She settled on the old sofa and opened the Bible. As with Dade, when the Holy Scriptures were approached, Mama's voice and manner changed.

"Now children, I shall read from the Holy Book about Lot and the towns of Sodom and Gomorrah. We'll see what the Bible says about the heathen and the ungodly people who refuse to listen to God's warnings about the coming judgment. She read: "Then the Lord said, 'The outcry against Sodom and Gomorrah is so great and their sin so grievous that I will go down and see if what they have done is as bad as the outcry that has reached me. If not, I will know.'"

Mama read the rest of the account of how the two angels rescued Lot and his wife and two daughters from God's judgment of fire and brimstone.

"So," Mama said, "you see why I've always said it's so important to stay away from the ungodly ones who live down in them towns. Yer Pa's mother was a good religious woman, but she and Pa's father lived in a town. And even though Judge Boone went to church, he was an evil man. He sat there in that church pew just fer show, pretendin' to read his Bible. But the town got a hold of his soul, tempted him. So, he went after liquor and cheap women. Just like Lot and his wife. They didn't see how terrible their sin was when they was living with them wicked people in Sodom. And finally, God had to send his angels to pull 'em outta there."

"But Mama," Jesse said, "didn't Abraham ask God to spare the whole city if there were even ten righteous people livin' in it? So maybe Abraham knew that there had to be some good people livin' in the towns."

Mama waved her hand impatiently. "Jesse, weren't you listenin' when I read that story? Don't you remember that God couldn't even find ten righteous people? It's just as I'm always trying to teach you; there ain't any good people livin' in towns or cities. Soon as people git together and start hobnobbing with strange folk, bad things start comin' from it."

Ruth understood some of Mama's words, even though the woman's strange accent confused her. She also caught the wary tones of Jesse, and the little girl's frightened body language. What did they know about Mama's religious beliefs that she had yet to discover? Mama used the term, "ungodly ones," and the woman's disapproving face and voice showed hatred.

"And," Mama continued, shaking her head, "Lot's wife really didn't understand about the evil in towns 'cause, when they was runnin' away from Sodom, she looked back, wishing she was back there. So, God killed her."

Mama took a deep breath. Sitting back in her chair, she put her finger on a paragraph in the Bible. "Anyway, you gotta understand the Holy Scriptures the right way. God wants His people to stay away from the ungodly ones. If you go and stay in one of them places, sooner or later it starts to work its evil in you."

She closed her Bible. "That's enough reading fer now."

The children stood up quickly.

"Jesse, I need you to help yer father with the roof problem. Sarah, you can help yer sister clean out the cupboards."

Jesse pulled on his sweatshirt and headed for the front door. Mama loomed over Ruth, hands on hips. When Ruth took too long standing up, Mama lunged at her, grabbed her hair and shoved her in the direction of the kitchen.

"You stupid little mouse, git going!"

Ruth stumbled and almost fell.

"C'mon." Sarah grabbed Ruth's hand, gazing up fearfully at her mother. She led her to the kitchen area.

Mama stomped into her bedroom and slammed the door.

A tear dripped from Ruth's cheek, and she wiped it away.

"Don't cry, Ruth. Mama doesn't like it. Here, we gotta take out everything in these ..." Sarah pointed to the cupboards. " ... and wash them real good." She handed her a dishcloth and filled a bucket with hot water from the kettle on the wood-burning stove.

Ruth wiped her eyes as she looked at the closed bedroom door.

Images of another bedroom burst into her mind. A blue room with a white door. A lovely bed with a little grey cat curled up right in the center. Sunlight poured through an open window. Eyelet curtains fluttered in a gentle breeze.

Words from a verse of scripture played in her mind. "Lead me to the rock that is higher than I. You have been my refuge, a strong tower against the foe."

She jumped, when Sarah tugged at her elbow, and forced her concentration back to their task. They pulled out all the cans, bottles, spice containers, and odds-and-ends found in kitchen shelves. She recognized some of the labels. "C-or-n. C-orn. Corn," she said. Then, "Su-gar."

Sarah helped her pick up the items, one by one, and asked her to read the words. "Yer saying them," she squealed with delight. "Yer learning to talk again. Here." She picked up a small jar. "What does this say?"

Ruth examined the words carefully, tracing them with her finger. "Vanil-la."

When Sarah smiled, Ruth leaned over and kissed her on the cheek. A noise came from Mama's bedroom and they quickly resumed their work.

"Mama," Sarah whispered in a warning tone.

"Mama," Ruth repeated in a similar tone.

The little girl giggled, but not loud enough to be heard behind the bedroom's closed door.

Ruth fell asleep that night repeating "Lead me to the rock that is higher than I," over and over in her head. But she didn't sleep well. She dreamed that she was an infant, lying in a crib. A gentle voice called her and she turned her head to see a dark-haired woman with deep blue eyes. The woman leaned over the crib railing and gazed at her with sweet intensity. Her face seemed filled with concern. "Don't stay too long, my child." The dream haunted her in the morning.

What did the dream mean? Anything at all? Throughout the day, the beautiful woman's face came to mind.

Other, more troubling thoughts pressed in on her. As language returned, disconnected names and faces swirled through her brain. Were these real people that she had once known? She knew, or sensed, that she was not really a part of Dade's family but couldn't go beyond that feeling. A vague, disturbing sensation haunted her. She needed to be somewhere else. But, where?

Mama's harsh treatment urged her to remember. Even the name, "Ruth," erupting from the strident lips of Mama made her want to shout, "Not my name."

As her mistrust and dislike of Dade and Mama grew, so did her determination to hide the recovery of her speech. To all in the family, she'd regained a few words, names and phrases, nothing more.

Jesse was flattered that Ruth had taken such an interest in his singing and playing. What a beauty. Eyes as blue as a mountain lake on a cloudless summer day. When Pa wasn't around he showed her how to hold the guitar and where to place her hands, then later, how to play chords and scales. She was a fast learner.

He had to be careful. Pa always seemed to lurk nearby. He had to be careful not to touch Ruth or look into her eyes. Once, he'd stared at Ruth for a second too long. The next morning Pa had caught him outside and taken his belt to him.

If only he could be alone with Ruth. He wanted to bring out his secret stash of poems and read some of them to her. He'd always had such beautiful words, but there was no one to share them with. He'd find a time when Pa was gone. Then he'd get the notebook he'd hidden down by the river. She'd listen to him read and her big, blue eyes would brim with tears. Then he'd take Ruth in his arms and kiss her beautiful mouth. She'd know how he felt, what he thought of her. Maybe, in the future there was the possibility of Ruth as his bride. If they could get away. Even Dade's metal-tipped belt and hard fists couldn't keep him a boy forever.

As the guitar lessons continued, Ruth discovered the brain-healing wonder of music. She couldn't help smiling during music time. Each time she sang, more words and sentences burst into her thoughts. While Jesse taught her how to play, "Eensy, Weensy Spider" on his guitar, lyrics from songs she somehow knew ran through her head. Still, she needed to hide the reason for her joy. Better to leave them all ignorant and off their guard.

Bedtime was her opportunity for planning. It was then that her unhappiness and her hopefulness tortured her the most. Smarting from Mama's cruel words, shoves and occasional smacks across her wounded head, she struggled to contain her anger and hurt. Words came in stammering speech. "You b-be calm, you, w-w-whoever you are." Tears flowed down her cheeks and her mouth trembled. Oh, to be able to scream in protest at her treatment. She looked over to make sure she hadn't woken Sarah with her muffled crying. "I-I know my name not Ruth. Quiet. Quiet. Quiet. You k-know you can't think good w-when you feel hurt. You g-got to think clear and-and you got to keep your wits. Don't l-let them know what in head. Don't l-let them have suspicion you want get away or they start watching you c-closer."

Her chest heaved. "No. D-don't cry. Get hold of yourself."

The words and melody to an old hymn ran through her mind. "When peace like a river attendeth my way. When sorrows like sea billows roll; whatever my lot, Thou hast taught me to say, 'It is well, it is well with my soul.'"

How did she know that song? "Please, God, help me remember why I-I know things. I know I'm n-not supposed to be here. But I don't know wh-where I belong. How I know You? I-I-I so lonely and scared. Please h-help me, God."

Chapter Eleven

There is a way that appears to be right,
but in the end, it leads to death.
Proverbs 14:12

The front door stood open and Tommy waited just outside for his mother.

"I hate that dress." Father growled at Mother Jane as she picked up her purse and car keys in the front hallway. "I don't want you running errands downtown dressed like that. You look like something from the nineteenth century."

"But Bartholomew, I'm the church organist. And I teach Sunday School. Everyone expects me to look respectable." Mother smoothed the front of her high-necked cotton blouse."

"Respectable? Bah. As a judge, I've got a reputation, too, and I don't want people laughing behind my back because of my wife's old-fashioned attire."

Tommy peeked inside. His heart pounded at the sight of his mother and father in another argument.

Mother's face reddened and her eyes welled with tears. "I'm trying to make you proud, Bartholomew."

"Why don't you put on that sweet little number I got you for Christmas? You know, the one that shows a little skin up there." He pointed below his wife's neckline.

Mother Jane opened her mouth to say something, then stopped herself.

"That's right. Don't argue with me. I don't want to hear about the church and women's beauty coming from within. I'm a man and I want my wife to look as good as the girls down at Bailey's Club."

Father chuckled at Mother's shock. "You think I don't know what those girls look like? I've been there lots of times. Did you think I'm always working late? Try putting on a little lipstick and fancy up your hair. Then maybe you'll see me more often in the evening."

Mother turned around, sobbing, and ran upstairs.

Three or four times a week, Dade would load up his truck with tools and a big metal tool box and disappear down the canyon. He'd be gone most of the day. And when he returned with supplies, Ruth was not allowed to go out and help bring them in. Sometimes, when he returned he'd bring back boxes of canned goods, flour, sugar, oil, and other household supplies.

She dropped the dish rag she'd been using at the sink to scour the big soup pot and crept over to the window. Mama and Jesse and Sarah had gone out to help unload groceries.

Mama lumbered up the porch steps with two large bags. Ruth dropped the curtain and scurried back to the sink. The screen door screeched open as Mama shoved her body through and let it bang behind her.

Mama dropped the bags onto the counter, stopping only long enough to check on Ruth's progress. Ruth focused on her task, neck tense, and scrubbed hard at the already-clean pot. As long as she appeared busy, Mama ignored her. The woman returned to her groceries. Ruth relaxed a little. She rinsed the soup pot and set it in the dish rack to dry.

Rebecca started to cry and Mama put one last item into the cupboard. "Ruth, put the rest of this stuff away." She pointed to the bags and then the cupboards and gestured putting the items away.

Mama headed for the bedroom, leaving Ruth a few quiet minutes to speculate some more about Dade and his weekly trips. Where did he get all those supplies? Was there a town nearby? Something was down that road.

Another frustrating thing that hindered her chance to explore the cabin's surroundings was that she was not allowed to wear shoes even when making a trip to the latrine. Was this to prevent escape? She'd pondered on this, at first. But now she was sure. But how did Mama and Dade suspect she wanted to get away? The woman kept her indoors, busy from morning till after supper, padding about in her knitted socks, cleaning, cooking, baby-tending and sewing. No free time. No chance even of wandering down to the river and a quick peek to see where it led.

After breakfast and morning chores, Mama gathered Ruth and Jesse and Sarah, as usual, at her feet while she opened the big Bible. Turning to the book of Micah, she read with hushed reverence: "All peoples may walk, each in the name of his god, but we will walk in the name of the Lord our God for ever and ever."

Mama looked up from the Book. Her mouth worked wordlessly, and an expression of triumph lit her eyes. "Children, when I met yer Pa, he told me to git away from the badness in the towns … git away before God's judgment come down on them. So, I packed everything we needed to live, shook the dust off my feet and headed for the mountains with my man and you two little ones. And here …" She shook her finger. "… the air is clean, the water is pure, and so is our Scripture."

Mama put her hand to her chest. "And I'm gonna make sure my children ain't touched by any filth. Don't ever think about going near them towns down there. I think I'd rather see you children dead and buried than fer you to go and join with them people and learn their ways. It makes me shake to even imagine God's judgment on you if you turn yer backs on the holy ways we been teaching you."

Sarah sat motionless, her dark eyes expressing both fear and awe. Mama preached for a long time.

Ruth understood all that was said and her mouth itched to point out how Mama's cruelty didn't match her holy words. But she pressed her lips together. Staying a dummy might help her escape sometime.

Mama sent Ruth and Jesse out to the metal shed to get some deer meat for supper. He turned the key in the padlock and led her into the windowless room that contained the freezer, a generator, storage shelves, a worktable, and barrels of something she couldn't identify. The long afternoon's scripture session, sitting in one position had made her back throb. She rubbed her spine and looked up at Jesse.

"Sore … you?"

"Me? Aw, it's not so bad. You just git used to it after a while.

Are you okay?" He pointed toward her back.

"Sore," she pronounced slowly, smiling shyly. Then she tilted her head at Jesse. "Mama … Sarah." She made a slap gesture. She looked up at him, trying to make herself understood without using any more words.

"Jesse, not." Again, she made the slap gesture.

"Oh, I see what yer sayin.' Mama doesn't hit me. Well, she yells sometimes. She'd never hit Pa or try to boss him. That'd be like hittin' God." His face screwed up in horror and he shuddered. "She hits Sarah a lot, and she hits you sometimes." He studied her face, as if trying to understand. "I guess she doesn't hit us 'cause …'" He looked down at his feet, his dark eyelashes hiding a look in his eyes she was beginning to see more and more. "… well, because we're men."

Jesse was definitely attracted to her. And even though he was sweet and handsome, she didn't want him to feel like that.

"I don't think Mama thinks a lot of girls," he said. "I think she respects big, strong people and most of them happen to be men. Maybe it's 'cause she knows they can hit back."

He paused and frowned. "I'm not sure how much you can understand of what I'm sayin' but, if you can, I want you to know that I don't like how Mama and Dade treat you. Not at all. We're— me and Sarah—we're family, and we have to take it. But you …"

Jesse threw a nervous glance back at the door. He hurried to open the freezer. "We gotta git that meat and head on back."

That night, Ruth planned. It would be difficult. Every move of hers, even a trip to the outdoor latrine was supervised. To get past Jesse, sleeping on the couch, to climb out the bedroom window at night: each posed its own problems.

She turned over to watch Sarah sleep. It looked as if she might have an ally in Jesse. He was becoming more at ease, and his concern for her touched her. Still, she'd have to be a lot surer before she trusted her plans to him. Mama and Dade intimidated him, and he might not like the idea of her leaving.

Dade was her greatest fear. He hadn't hit her yet, but he seemed to enjoy taking full advantage of his height, standing so close to her that she would have to tilt her head far back to see his face. Then he would pronounce her name in his deep voice, green eyes staring down at her with that strange look, and issue his order. And if she did not understand, he would engulf her hands in one of his big, rough ones and lead her, trembling, to her chore. Dade had taken Jesse or Sarah outside when they forgot some chore or failed to listen attentively when he read from the Scriptures. When they returned, even though they restrained their tears, they bore red marks and bruises. It was bad enough that Mama shoved and hit her. She didn't think she could take it if Dade beat her. Just the way he looked at her or stood so near and watched her was awful enough.

Even if she managed to escape the cabin, she'd have to get far away before she had a chance of outrunning the man and his rifle. He was also an experienced tracker. She'd heard him tell the family stories about how he had followed bears or cougars into the canyon and brought them down with his rifle. One of the cougar pelts hung on the wall above the couch.

She ended her planning with a prayer to the God that she vaguely remembered. Was talking to God something she used to do? Maybe someone had taught her about Him.

Dade pressed the pillow into his ear to muffle the sound of Mama's snoring. Just ten feet away, behind a wall, Ruth slept. Her long hair would be spread out about her shoulders. Maybe her mouth was parted slightly as she breathed the silent sleep of a young woman. The moon would travel across her window and its beams would fall on her rosy cheek.

Ruth seemed to be settling into the family life. Her silence was reassuring. If she couldn't talk, then she probably couldn't think. And maybe if she couldn't think, she wouldn't remember her father, or the abusive life he had rescued her from. He wasn't sure how much she understood of his mealtime sermons. She had been listening for three weeks. Mama's Bible lessons, too. Just the tone of Mama's lessons would be enough to warn Ruth of dangers that lurked when he was not around. Ruth needed him. Any woman with a father like hers needed him.

His own father used to say there wasn't much good to be gotten from religion, except to keep one's reputation above repute. But there were many more benefits, the greatest of which was filling weaker minds with fear. Keeping Mama and Jesse and Sarah and Ruth afraid. Afraid to leave the cabin. Making them feel the need for his protection. His control. No one was going to take them from him.

And once the other cabin was ready, Ruth would become the wife she should have been nearly two decades earlier.

In the mid-morning, instead of the usual house chores, Mama surprised Ruth by telling her she had a job for Jesse and her. How wonderful to be out of the dark, depressing cabin, out in the sun and pine-scented cool air.

They carried hoes, a rake and shovel past the chicken coop and out to a small sunny field approximately fifty by fifty feet, all wired and posted to keep out the animals. There were rows of remnants of potatoes, carrots, small greens that might have been some kind of lettuce, and strawberries.

"Here," Mama ordered, "turn this section over, git all the weeds out and rake it smooth. Gotta git things ready fer more planting. I'll be back in an hour to see how yer doing."

She turned and trudged back down the path to the cabin.

Ruth watched until Mama got out of ear-shot, then turned and regarded Jesse. Just how much could she trust the boy with the truth of her restored language ability?

"C'mon," he motioned, "let's start over here." He handed her a hoe and gestured toward the ground.

"Like this," he picked up the other hoe and started working the soil. "See, you do the same thing over there."

"There?" she repeated, pretending to be unsure of Jesse's instructions.

"Here," he pointed her over to her section of ground.

His hands and feet were large, too large for his teenaged body, like a gangly puppy that was going to be big when it was all grown up.

"You do it like this," he grunted as he chopped and tugged at the soil with the tool. He handed the hoe back to her and pointed back at the ground.

She took the hoe and made a few small, clumsy strokes.

Jesse rolled his eyes. "No, you gotta really reach out and hit the ground hard." He took the hoe again to demonstrate, using all his strength, then stepped back, handed the hoe to her, and pushed his sleeves farther up his lean, hard forearms.

"Like this?" She made exaggerated strokes, grunting just like Jesse. She stopped and grinned at him.

Jesse eyed her curiously. "You're not dumb, are you?"

"Not dumb." She put her finger in her mouth and crossed her eyes.

They started laughing. Then Jesse put his finger up to his mouth. "Shh, we gotta be quiet or Mama will come out and watch us. She doesn't like too much laughing. Says it's 'frivolity.'" He put his hands up in the air in a gesture of mock horror.

She laughed again, which made Jesse beam. Gripping her hoe, she started in on her work. Jesse found a spot a dozen feet or so down the row and followed suit. They were quiet for a while.

When she stopped to rest and stretch her neck and shoulders, she spied the boy staring at her. "Jesse? Jesse?"

Jesse blinked. "Oh, sorry. Must've been daydreaming." He gripped his hoe and thrust the blade into the soil. "Yep, just thinkin' about lunch. I'm hungry, aren't you?"

He moved to another part of the vegetable patch and picked up a rake. "Hey, do you wanna do some more guitar today? I think yer ready to try some folk songs. You got all yer major and most of yer minor chords down, so why not?"

She tilted her head as if his words were hard to understand. "Okay." She went back to work. It was troubling the way Jesse stared at her when he thought she didn't see. She moved on to another weed-infested row. What if Jesse started liking her so much that he wouldn't let her get away? Maybe he'd been so carefully brainwashed by Dade and Mama that he thought like them, about the towns and the people being so evil. What if she showed him that she could talk and understand everything, and then he went and told Dade her plans?

She'd descended so deep into her thoughts as she chopped at the weeds that she didn't hear Mama's step. She jumped when the woman spoke.

"Well, well, now that's not too bad. You two have done a good job. Just git them last bits of weeds over there in the carrots and then you two can go git cleaned up fer Bible time." Mama turned and headed back for the cabin and called over her shoulder, "And Jesse, don't forgit to put the hoes and other things back where they belong."

When they were done, Jesse collected the garden tools and headed for the wood shed. Ruth took her time returning to the dark cabin. The sunshine kissed her shoulders and she hated to leave its light. She lingered for a minute by the chicken coop, cooing and clucking at the hens. But when she left the coop and neared the corner of the cabin, voices coming from Mama's open bedroom window made her halt. Mama's voice was muffled, and she couldn't distinguish her words. But Dade's were much clearer. His angry tone made her shiver. She flattened herself against the wall and strained to hear.

"We've been through this before, Brenda. I'm warning you, don't get me riled or you're going to feel my fist again. You hear me, woman?"

Mama choked out a "Yes, Sir."

A momentary silence followed. Then, "You can't have children. And I'm not about to steal any more kids from the state of Kentucky. It's too risky, and anyway, I want some that are really mine." Dade's voice became especially clear as his shadow passed the open window. Ruth held her breath.

The next time Dade spoke, it sounded farther away. "The boy's not ready for a wife. And I've got plans for Ruth."

She tiptoed away from the cabin wall and back onto the path. Entering the cabin noisily, she tried to appear nonchalant. Dade came out of the bedroom. His cheeks were flushed from his argument with Mama, but he quickly composed his face. He took his rifle down, and barely glanced at Ruth as he passed. When he stepped outside, he met Jesse at the screen door.

"Go get your sister. It's time for Bible."

"Yes, Sir."

"I saw her playing down by the river about ten minutes ago."

Dade's boots clomped down the porch stairs.

Mama stayed behind her bedroom door for a while, and when she did finally come out, Bible in hand, her face was puffy, her eyes were red, and there was an ugly welt on her cheek.

Chapter Twelve

Hear my prayer, Lord;
let my cry for help come to You.
Psalm 102:1

Jesse stood in the shallow part of the stream, absent-mindedly casting his line into the deeper water. Ruth. So dainty. So little. Her head only came up to his chin. What would it feel like if she leaned her head on his chest? What did she think of him?

It made him angry that Pa watched him so closely anytime Ruth was near. Why did the man have to be so suspicious all the time? And why did Mama have to put that brown dye in Ruth's hair and make her wear those awful, long, baggy dresses? Still, she was about the prettiest thing he'd ever seen and she moved like a magical creature.

He'd watched her that morning as she moved about the garden, turning the soil, raking the ground smooth, and sometimes stopping to close her eyes and turn her face up to the sun. And when he said some funny things, it made him feel wonderful to see her smile. The girl had such pretty laughter and her blue eyes sparkled. Her teeth were white and perfect, and her mouth …

He closed his eyes and imagined his hands caressing Ruth's face. He was almost a grown man now. He could get a job down the hill somewhere. And take Ruth with him.

In the evening before supper, Mama sent Ruth out to the metal shed for venison. She'd been sent out alone. They'd even given her the key. Why? Maybe Mama and Dade were at last relaxing their vigilance over her whereabouts. So, it had been a wise decision to keep her mouth shut and play dumb. She looked over her shoulder. How far could she make it in the dark and without shoes if she chose to bolt for freedom? How much could Dade track in the dark? Besides Dade, there was the problem of the terrain: the cliffs and to the south, the river. She'd gotten only glimpses of both natural features during the morning's hoeing and gardening. She looked up and scanned the jagged line of granite until it disappeared behind pine and fir. She doubted she could climb the cliffs. And if she tried and then got caught halfway up needing rescue from the very people she wished to escape? Horrible.

The road was the most logical escape route, but how far could she get that way before being caught? What about the river and following it out of the canyon?

She sneaked down to the river, stepped down onto the bank, and studied the fast-flowing water, inches from her feet. No, she'd have to know a lot more about the river before she tried that. It wasn't the right time. She needed help.

She glanced up at the path. A breeze stirred the stray hairs around her face and neck. She brushed them away, then turned back to the river. Exhaling a long, lung-emptying sigh, she watched the course of the river.

"Ruth."

Dade startled her so badly that she pitched forward. She would have fallen into the river if he hadn't reached out quickly and yanked her back.

"Mama wants that venison."

"I-I-I." *No! Don't talk. Play dumb.* She pointed at the water clumsily. "Th-th-the river. Pretty river."

His hands closed on her shoulders and he leaned close. "Yes, it's a nice river. Do you want to go in that river? It's very cold. Very fast." On 'fast,' he nudged her forward.

A panicked yelp burst from her lips. Stomach churning, she jammed her fists against her mouth. *Don't talk. That's what he wants.*

His hands still gripped her shoulders, but he hesitated, like a cougar with a bunny in its jaws. Thinking? Maybe—like a cougar— he was sniffing and turning his head, swiveling his ears, staring, tail twitching. Trying to decide what to do with his prey.

He'd come up on her as silently as if he had padded paws. And now, after he caught her, he was playing with her. Maybe hoping she'd do something to show she could comprehend. Where was he looking? Down at her? Across the river? She didn't dare turn to look at him.

"Come with me." He took the key from her hand, then gestured for her to follow. Was he finally going to punish her as he did Jesse and Sarah? At the shed, she stood behind him, knees trembling, while he unlocked the door. She should run away, dash down the hill and throw herself into the river. Even the danger of the frigid water and the cutting rocks seemed less threatening than the big man.

Run, girl.

But her body simply wouldn't obey the command. Dade pulled her inside.

She barely touched her food that night, still jolted by her encounter with Dade at the shed. She focused on her plate. She looked up once and found Dade staring at her. After that, she didn't dare look up again. She prayed that supper would end quickly.

The next morning, she and Jesse hiked once more to the garden, this time to spread manure and work it into the soil.

"You okay, Ruth? You haven't said much of anything this whole morning."

She didn't look up from her work. She paused to try to frame a child-like reply.

"Dade. Not like me."

Jesse came nearer. "No … no, he likes you just fine. He told me. He said yer real nice. He said you'd make a good wi—". He swiped his hand over his mouth. "No, what makes you say that?"

Her eyes met Jesse's dark ones. The boy's face reddened right away.

"Scare Ruth."

Jesse shook his head. "Aw, you must not understand something he said or did, that's all. Yer like his daughter. He just wants you to be okay." He touched her shoulder. "Don't you worry. Everything's all right. You just keep doin' everything they tell you and you'll be fine. He just wants you to learn to be righteous and good."

"Jesse good?"

He stepped back, and his face registered confusion. "I … I, what do you mean?"

"Help Ruth, yes?"

Jesse seemed to focus inward. He drew a deep breath and gave her a nod. "Sure, I guess I'd help you. I'm not sure what you mean by help, though."

She crouched down over the soil again. Maybe he'd think further on her few words.

Jesse whispered, "One thing you gotta know about Mama and Pa … see … I know you think it's Mama who gives all the orders. It just looks like that. I mean, Mama can be kind of mean and ornery, that's for sure. And Mama does most of the scripture teaching and preaching. But it's Pa who tells her what to think. And he gets his direction straight from God. Now, Pa acts real nice, most of the time. He's real quiet so you never see when he gits mad 'cause it's only him and the person he's mad at when it happens. He's the real boss, and he don't take any crossing, not even from Mama. Even she's scared of him. Just keep obeying him, and don't back-talk him, and he'll be nice."

That night it was cold. Ruth followed Sarah into their room and closed the door. After dressing hurriedly, she slipped into her bed.

"Goodnight, Ruth," Sarah whispered.

"Night." Ruth turned over and pulled the covers over her

shoulder. Wearied from her many chores, she soon fell asleep.

Sometime later, she startled awake. Someone had come into the room. The rustle of clothing announced the movement of an approaching body. She jerked upright and stared. Moonlight outlined the shape of a tall person. "Wuh?"

A hand pushed her down. It covered her nose and mouth.

"Just lie still and listen," Dade ordered. He leaned close so he could whisper.

"I've seen you look at that river like you wished you could sail away from here, from me. And if I thought for one minute that you were anything more than a dummy, I'd chain you up. So just put getting out of here out of your mind, because it isn't going to happen. There isn't a town or a relative or lawman or anyone else who could hide you from me, because I'd find you. Wouldn't matter how long it took. And don't think squealing to the police is going to help you. I'll kill you and anyone you tell about me."

His hand pressed down harder on her face. "You belong here and nowhere else. You get me, girl?"

Her breath puffed in and out through a tiny airway between his fingers. She clawed at his hand. *Air. Need. Air.*

He shifted his fingers, just enough. "Of course, you can hardly talk and you probably don't understand a word I'm saying. But, just in case you really can talk and you're fooling us …"

He removed his hand, and she gasped for air. The moon's rays caught the gleam of his teeth as his mouth spread into a gloating smile. He searched her face for a long minute as if hoping she'd speak and give herself away. His breath on her neck made her skin prickle. Finally, he straightened, and turning without another word, stole silently from the room.

Her next few days passed as if in a haze. Overwhelmed with

numbing fear and hopelessness, words escaped her and music did not come into her head. As if she'd reverted to the mental state shortly after her head injury, she roamed the dark cabin again like a mindless animal, a beast of burden plodding in front of its master, wanting only to avoid the snap and sting of the lash. She kept her eyes down and moved quickly to accomplish any directive Mama hurled at her. She avoided Dade's presence, and shuddered anytime he turned his watchful eye on her.

Gradually, after many days, she recovered from the fearful encounter with Dade. He said no more to her, only watched her when she seemed occupied in one of her many chores.

She hid her defiance and anger when Mama was rough or cruel. That could be endured for a time.

She had felt relatively safe once everyone was in bed for the night. Those hours had been all hers, for sleep, for praying or planning. But now, even those precious hours had been stolen from her by Dade's night-time intrusion and threat. What would stop him from coming into her room any time he wanted for further intimidation? With one hand covering her nose and mouth, he'd effectively communicated how easy it would be to snuff out her life.

She'd have to continue playing the dummy. The stakes were too high even to trust Jesse.

Daytime became the new time for thinking and planning. After all, cooking, cleaning, washing clothes, sewing, pumping water and carrying it from place to place didn't require much brain power. Dade seldom bothered her anymore while she did her regular chores. He was either gone somewhere with his truck or working somewhere outside the cabin. And when Mama called her and Jesse and Sarah to the daily scripture lesson, she could arrange her face and position her body in just such a way that she appeared to be listening, if not comprehending. It gave her an uninterrupted hour to think through the various difficulties she'd have to surmount in order to escape.

What could she do about Dade? Overpower the man? Impossible. Disable him? Possibly. But how? Outsmart him? Only if she kept her wits about her, and convinced him she didn't *have* any wits. Unlike Mama, Dade wasn't dense. At mealtimes, he watched where she looked, he watched her reaction to something Jesse or Sarah or Mama said. Did he suspect that she understood all that was said? And if he did, would he forever be one step ahead of her?

She stopped playing guitar. What was the use when thoughts of survival were the priority? Even Mama and Jesse didn't prod her to play. Lately, Dade and Jesse had been spending a lot of time outdoors hammering and pounding and sawing. One day, she'd tried to gesture a question to Jesse about what they were building, but he muttered something unintelligible and walked away quickly.

Obviously, Jesse was avoiding her, but why? And why did he look so resentful when Dade wasn't looking?

Ruth tried to get a better look at the new log structure any time she was allowed out, but Jesse or Dade always seemed to be nearby. One afternoon, after dumping a pail of water in the garden, she got off the path and pushed her way through the thorny berry bushes and undergrowth for a look at the new building. It looked like another cabin with a chimney. She crept closer and looked around. Dade was nowhere in sight. She pushed the door open and stepped inside. The room stood empty except for a wood burning stove against the inside wall. Near to it another door led to ... a bedroom? She nudged that door halfway. It opened noiselessly.

Why would they need another cabin unless Jesse was going to move out and live here? That would make sense since the baby couldn't live in her parents' room forever. And Jesse was growing up.

But if Rebecca moved into Sarah's room, where did that leave her? She had no answer and no more time for speculation. She backed up and turned to sneak out of the cabin. But just then the bedroom door swung open the rest of the way. She gasped when Dade stepped into the doorway. His hair brushed the top of the doorframe.

She tried to run, but her legs refused to move. Dade seized her and pulled her to him.

His mouth twisted. "Didn't I tell all you women not to come nosing around this place?" He gripped her arms in an iron-like vise, and bent over to fasten his gaze on hers.

"I-I-I –"

"What makes you think you can get away with disobeying me, girl?"

His deep and enraged voice swept thought from her. *Oh, God, help me.*

"Apparently, you think you can challenge my authority."

Dade dragged her into the smaller room, clutching her so savagely that she screamed in agony.

"I had planned on acquainting you with this place a little later on. But since your female curiosity has made you forget my orders, I'll let you spend as much time as you want here. And if you even poke your head out this door until I say you can, I'll chain you to the door. Now sit down there and think on your sinfulness and rebellion."

He shook her, like a grizzly clamped on its prey, then thrust her roughly down to the floor, leaving her whimpering and wiping tears from her face. He stomped out and slammed the door.

She sat for some time, still reeling from her encounter with Dade. How could she wrap her mind around his cruelty? Her heart hammered. What if he came back and beat her, or worse? For a long time, she gazed up through the window, rubbing her bruised arms. The sun traveled down toward the unseen horizon.

As night fell, the temperature in the room dropped. Hunger pangs twisted her stomach. There was no lantern and no fuel to light a fire in the stove. And anyway, Dade might come and hurt her if she moved from her spot on the floor.

Did God care? "He keeps saying that wives and children are supposed to obey." A tear trickled down her cheek, and she wiped it away fiercely. "But wh-what gives him the right to grab me l-like that and throw me onto the floor? And Mama hits and shoves me and c-c-calls me names. God, please help me."

Through the open window an owl hooted far off. There were other night sounds too. Was Dade out there?

She repositioned her stiff body on the cold, wood floor. A sob tried to push upward. *Don't cry. Dade will hear.* "God, I k-know that Dade and Mama want me to believe th-that You are as harsh and hard as they are. But, God, I know th-that You're not like that. I-I don't remember how I know that. I just do. Please protect me from Dade. I'm so afraid of him … what he m-might do. Please keep me safe. H-help me to escape some time. Amen."

The moon's soft rays invaded the small room where she huddled. Its light slowly advanced across the wood floor. And just as slowly, a calm and logical resolve penetrated her soul, giving her fresh hope. In order to assuage Dade's anger and suspicions, she must double her efforts to appear entirely submissive. She'd act as though she were in awe of him. She'd keep pretending not to understand. She'd keep her eyes reverently lowered in his presence. She'd smile shyly.

But she must not talk.

Ever since the time at the river, he'd been watching her even more closely. He'd say things to her to try to get her to talk. Testing her. Trying to see just how much she could think and reason. But she had to play this game of silence, of stupidity. Whatever it took, she must survive. She'd play the dummy long enough to make him think she'd always be slow and wordless and unable to plan an escape.

It was a frigid night and the temperature in the cabin plummeted. Dressed only in a long cotton skirt and blouse, she hugged her knees and tucked her hands inside the folds of the material, trying in vain to warm herself. She unfastened her braid and spread her hair about her shoulders. Her breath turned to vapor and she shivered.

Sometime later, she heard the cabin's front door open and close. She held her breath when the bedroom door glided ajar by an unseen hand. Dade's tall silhouette filled the open space. He carried blankets and a lantern, dimly lit. Setting the lantern on the floor, he spread one of the blankets, then sat and covered himself with the others. The flickering light of the lantern exaggerated the height and width of his shadow against the log walls. It grew, diminished, and shifted like a menacing phantom. Dade said nothing. Only watched.

Her shivering had become almost uncontrollable. Her teeth chattered. She clung to her knees. So, this was what it was like to freeze to death. If only the cruel man would allow her to return to the big cabin and her own bed. In spite of her obvious suffering, his face showed no pity or forgiveness.

The night wore on, as did her torture. But speaking or pleading would only prolong her punishment. How she knew that, she didn't know.

Finally, Dade took an audible breath. "Ruth, have you repented of your rebellion and disobedience? Are you ready to receive my forgiveness?"

She raised her head. Tears spilled and ran down her quivering jaw.

He got up and came and stood over her where she cowered against the cold walls. What was he going to do? Dade shook his head. "You can't win, girl. I'll always be one step ahead of you."

Don't answer him. She lowered her eyes and bit back choice words.

"Get on your knees." He waited, and when she did not respond, he gestured to make her understand his command.

She rose slowly.

"And kiss my feet." He pointed to the toes of his boots and his lips spread into their familiar hateful smile.

No. I won't do it. You monster. If only she could fling herself, screaming, on the man and claw that smug grin off his face. Her throat ached with rage at this humiliation. But she was no fool. Dade had just offered her a test, and she would pass it. Shaking with cold and helpless fury, she pulled herself onto her knees and lowered her face to his feet.

Dade crouched and gathered her in his arms. She didn't try to resist. Cradling her like a baby, he carried her back to the blankets. He sat and continued to hold her, covering them both with the still warm blankets. For a long time, he rocked her, singing softly: "My dove in the clefts of the rock, in the hiding places on the mountainside, show me your face, let me hear your voice; for your voice is sweet, and your face is lovely."

In the early morning, she awoke and found herself lying on the floor, wrapped in a blanket. Dade sat nearby, still watching her. Grateful to be alive and untouched, she stayed still until Dade spoke.

"Ruth, get up and go back to your room."

She slipped out from under the covers and hurried back to the main cabin and the soft warmth of her own bed.

"Drink your milk, Tommy. The school bus will be here in ten minutes."

Mother Jane turned wearily back to the stove and flipped the eggs over. She lifted the pot of coffee and poured a cup, then set it on the table in front of Father.

"Will you be home in time for Tommy's school program?" Mother slid two eggs onto Father's plate. She looked more tired than Tommy had ever seen.

Father bit into the eggs. "Can't. Got business tonight." He ignored her hurt expression.

"But I told you about his program weeks ago, and you said you'd be there." She set the frying pan onto the burner and faced the stove. "Can't you skip Bailey's for just this night?" Mother's voice had taken on an edge.

Father took a long swig of his coffee, as if he hadn't even heard her.

She whirled around and her slender fingers alternately

pinched and smoothed the fabric of her apron. "Did you hear me, Bartholomew?"

"Did you hear me, Bartholomew?" he mocked, making his voice sound thin and nasal.

Mother Jane lifted Tommy's lunch box and handed it to him. "Go on, Tommy. Run on down to the bus stop." She hurried him to the kitchen door and gave him a kiss before turning her attention back to her husband.

Father stuffed the last bit of eggs in his mouth and stood up. "I don't know why I even bothered to come home for breakfast."

Mother's face contorted with uncharacteristic anger. "So, why did you? You could have slept in at your girlfriend's place."

Father looked surprised that she had dared to talk back. He slammed his fists onto the table and glared at her.

"I've put up with your drinking and your fists 'cause I was taught to be a good wife."

"That's right, woman, so shut your trap before—"

"Before you hit me? Okay ..." She thrust out her face and her voice trembled. "... hit me. But I'm not putting up with adultery. The Scriptures say I don't have to."

Tommy hadn't left the house. He'd hidden near the kitchen doorway, clutching his lunchbox, watching the awful anger between his mother and father. Father's chair scraped back against the tiled floor. Tommy scurried to hide in the hall closet. He pushed his body behind the thick cover of hanging coats.

"I drove down there last night ... to Bailey's," Mother hissed. "I saw you getting in the car with that woman. So, you just go to work. Then go to the bar tonight and see your lady friend. But when you finally decide to come home, Tommy and I won't be here."

Father laughed. A horrible, mean, cruel sound. "Nobody runs out on me and gets away with it. I've got a reputation to keep up, and my wife isn't going to ruin it by deserting me. I know everyone in the county, and I know everything about everyone. So, no one's going to help you. You won't get far."

Mother started to cry. "I won't stay with a man who breaks his wedding vows."

Tommy heard movement, then Mother's hurried steps into the front hallway.

"Where are you going?" Father roared. Sounds of a scuffle. Car keys. The front door opening. Two sets of feet tramping out the door. Mother crying. Father cursing.

No. Mother Jane's leaving. She's going without me. Tommy thrust his body out of the closet and ran outside. Mother was running toward the car. Father stood at the foot of the steps, hands on hips, with a face like a thundercloud.

"Run. Run, Jane." Father taunted Mother Jane's fleeing figure. "Leave Tommy with me." His booming voice set off an alarm deep in Tommy's brain.

"But you'll come crawling back in a day or two," Father muttered as he looked down at Tommy. A cruel smile twisted his lip. He lunged for his son. Strong fingers gripped Tommy's shoulder.

Tommy stared upward at the narrow green eyes of his father. The old man's voice guttered with rage. "You can't beat me, Thomas Dade. I always win."

Tommy gasped. He twisted out of his father's grip and ran down the sidewalk. "No, Mother. Come back." He watched her car turn off their street. He could head her off if he cut through the Wyler's property. Then across Lilac Street, through old Mr.

Murphy's flower garden.

Tommy's breaths came fast and shaky, roughed up by the speed of his desperate race. Plunging across ditches, hurdling over fences. "Stop, Mother. You promised you'd take me with you. You said I could keep you safe from Father."

Running down Palmer Avenue, he wheezed. Lungs expanding, contracting. Heart pounding. His feet slapped the pavement like rapid little beats on a snare drum. Nearly to the bridge. It was a one-lane bridge. He'd run out into the middle. She'd have to stop. She'd open the passenger door and he'd jump in. She'd say, "Oh, Tommy, I'm so glad we're together. I'll never leave you. We'll go away ... some place where Father can never find us."

Father wouldn't win this time.

He sped across the railroad tracks, then down the little hill just above the river. The bridge. Mother's car hadn't even reached Palmer Avenue. He waited for two cars to cross the intersection of Palmer and River Road, then he scurried across.

Mother Jane's car reached the stop sign. She turned left onto the approach to the bridge. The car disappeared behind a long row of trees. He waited. The car was going fast. Much faster than he'd hoped. He hesitated. What if Mother didn't see him? She had to see him. She just had to. Tommy leaned his hands on the metal divider that separated the pedestrian walkway from the road. The car zoomed onto the bridge.

"Mother! Mother!" Tommy jumped the divider just as the car neared. He could see Mother's face now. It looked like she saw him. He ran out and waved his hands. "Stop, Mother, stop."

Tires screeched. The car fishtailed. He saw it in slow motion. It struck the right guard-rail, ricocheted to the left, spun like a top. Like a diver doing a weird kind of sideward somersault, the car flipped over and over, gaining momentum. Then the vault over the guard-rail. A second of awful silence, followed by the whoosh of a big air-filled thing as it struck the water. A sucking sound as water entered and dragged it downward.

"Ma-maaaaaaaa!"

Dade stood in the bedroom of the new cabin, staring at, but not seeing the rumpled blankets on the floor where Ruth had been lying. He closed his eyes and tried to thrust from his mind the horrendous image of his mother's death and the agonized echo of his own little-boy voice so many years ago. But even after twenty-eight years the events of that day remained forever seared into his soul.

Because he had killed his own mother, as surely as if he had turned the steering wheel that morning and sent her car plunging fifty feet into the river.

And because his father had won that time.

Dena Netherton

Chapter Thirteen

The prudent see danger and take refuge ...
Proverbs 27:12a

Escape was no longer merely a risky option. She would not, could not allow Dade to continue wearing down her will and her spirit.

On her knees that morning, furiously scrubbing the kitchen floor, she muttered, "God, h-he's not going to turn me into his slave." She checked to make sure Mama's bedroom door was still closed. "He th-thinks he can do whatever he wants to me and-and I can't do anything about it." She clenched her jaw so hard it hurt. "Throwing m-me around like a piece of meat and th-then freezing me. And making me kiss his feet." The more she thought about last night, the angrier she grew. "And w-what's next? What if he does something even worse next time?" *God help me.*

One morning, after breakfast, Jesse found Ruth as she gathered strawberries on the hillside above the cabin. He dropped down on his knees next to her.

"Ruth, I gotta talk to you real soon."

The urgency in his voice made her stomach tighten. "Here?"

"No," Jesse said. "Dade's not too far away." He craned his neck, as if trying to see if Dade was coming. "Can you come out of your room tonight?"

Her eyes widened.

"I know yer scared of Pa, but I gotta tell you something. Please, Ruth."

What could be so urgent? Her gut clamped. "I try, Jesse."

Jesse jumped to his feet. He looked back toward the cabin. "I gotta go." His lanky form retreated down the hill.

She leaned over and rested her hands in front of her. Jesse had something really important to tell her. About what? About herself? Did he know that she was planning to escape? Maybe he wanted to help her.

A shadow moved across her hands. She glanced up, and froze. Dade stood a dozen feet away, brawny arms crossed over his chest, staring at her with narrowed eyes.

How long had he been there? Had he heard Jesse's words?

Her body quivered as she lowered her head and waited. Would he seize her again? Drag her into the small cabin for more humiliation? His shadow traveled up her forearms, as if she'd dipped them in ink. Then, like a tsunami, it rolled and spread over her face. It stole her breath. She dug her fingers into the soft soil and gripped the dirt. *Oh God, oh God, help me.*

Seconds ticked by. Still inky hands. She held her breath until her lungs pleaded for air. Finally, she thrust her head forward out of the murk of his shadow, into the pure air and gasped for breath.

Play dumb, play dumb, play dumb. Reaching for the basket of strawberries, she plucked a berry with the other hand and dropped it into the basket. More berries followed. When she finally dared to look up, as noiseless as his shadow, the man had gone.

All day, as she performed her endless household chores, she mentally re-played Jesse's words. What if Dade had heard them? What if he already knew what she was thinking? No, he couldn't know. She'd been careful, very careful. She hadn't even communicated to Jesse that she was unhappy, let alone that she planned to run away. There was just that one time when Dade had sneaked up and caught her looking at the river. Since then she'd been careful to keep her eyes directed toward her tasks and away from the cabin door or windows.

Dade kept watching her. It wasn't like the dreamy expression in Jesse's eyes; she could deal with his teenaged crush on her. But the way Dade watched her was different. The lustful look in his eyes didn't match all his religious words. It made her wish that she had a weapon, just in case.

She lay in her bed and listened. Sarah's little chest rose and fell in a peaceful rhythm. Snoring came from the other bedroom. That didn't guarantee that all members of the household were asleep. She had memorized where the floorboards in her bedroom squeaked and knew just how to turn the doorknob silently. She wasn't sure how much whispering would carry. Slowly, she raised the covers and moved them away from her body. Slipping like a ghost from her bed, she glided to the door and eased it open. She held her breath and listened and listened. The muscles in her torso gripped her stomach so tight it nearly stole her breath.

Jesse's voice startled her, coming out of the darkness of the main room. She could just make out his shape sitting straight and still on the couch. She moved slowly over to him. When she reached him, he took her arm and pulled her over to the floor on the far side of the couch. They crouched there for a moment, waiting and listening. She opened her mouth to say something but he held up a warning finger.

"Shh," he whispered, "just listen."

Jesse brought his face close to hers. "About a week ago, I overheard Mama and Pa talking at night. I couldn't hear everything, but they were talking about you and me. I wasn't supposed to tell you about the new cabin Pa and me are building 'cause," Jesse hesitated, "I thought it was supposed to be ... well, that it was gonna be fer you and me to live in. But Pa and Mama were talking about how yer kind of hard to figure, and he said that you need a firmer hand, and that I'm not man enough and—"

Jesse broke off, either from embarrassment or anger, she couldn't tell.

She waited, trying to search his face in the dark, trying to control her impatience. Jesse breathed convulsively, as if fighting tears. Finally, he went on.

"Pa said that you need a grown man to husband you, that he'd git you to be a good second wife. He said that this was the answer to his prayers about having his own kids. He said, 'Ruth always wanted a whole lot of kids.' He said as soon as the cabin was finished they'd have the wedding ceremony."

"Ruth? Another Ruth?"

Jesse licked his chapped lips. "It's a long story, and I don't have time to tell you now. But it's something you gotta know about Pa. I'll slip you a letter, and then you can read it next time yer alone."

She put her face in her hands and shook her head back and

forth. "Why? W-why me?"

"It's got something to do with a bad thing that happened a long time ago."

"I ... afraid ... Dade. Help. Help."

"You're gettin' outta here." He gripped her hands. "I don't know how or when, but I'm gonna think of a way. It's gonna be dangerous, though. No telling what Pa will do if he finds out."

Jesse rose silently and pulled her with him. "You better git back to your room now. I'll talk to you again, soon as I come up with a plan. Go on now." He reached out to touch her shoulder, but stopped and withdrew his hand. She moved toward her bedroom and gave him one last, worried glance before closing her door.

She carried the pail of water down the path toward the vegetable garden. After setting the pail down at the edge of the rows of plants, she looked around and studied her surroundings. No Dade. No shadows. Still, she hesitated. The man seemed to be able to appear and disappear like a vapor. No wonder he was able to track down and kill a cougar.

She reached into her pocket and drew out the letter Jesse had slipped her. Unfolding it, she took a deep breath before she read:

Dear Ruth,

I hope you can read this letter. I will use easy words.

A long time ago, when Pa was only a teenager his father decided to get remarried. This was a few years after his mother got killed in a car accident. Pa went a little crazy after his mama died so his father moved them out to the country. I guess he figured Pa would do better if he could roam around the woods and hunt. Also, I think his father was ashamed of the way Pa turned out and wanted to hide him.

Anyway, his step-mama had a beautiful daughter named Ruth. She was little and blonde, just like you. Pa fell in love with her, and I think she kind of fell for him too. Pa's father was a real bad guy and used to beat him. I guess Pa figured his father would beat Ruth, too. He already blamed him for the death of his real mama. So, they sneaked out. They planned to take a bus somewhere out west. Pa's father caught them at the same bridge where his mother had died a few years earlier. There was some kind of fight, and when Pa realized that he wouldn't be able to protect Ruth from his father, he threw her off the bridge. She drowned. She was only sixteen. Pa was seventeen. When the police asked him why he killed Ruth, the only thing he said was, "So my father wouldn't win."

The law put him in a hospital for mental patients. He was there for a few years. Then he disappeared. Pa got far away from Tennessee and sort of reinvented himself. He learned to talk like he wasn't from the south. Even worked his way through college.

You're probably wondering why I know this much. One day, a few months ago, when Mama got beat by Pa, she was so upset that she told me about him.

It's bad enough that Pa is the way he is. But one time before you came here, when we were having dinner, I remember him saying that it's always better for a kid to die than to be with a bad father.

Somehow, he sees you and starts treating you like you're the other Ruth. He thinks he's in love with you just like he was in love with Ruth. He's going to marry you, and you'll stay with him and have a family, just like the first Ruth wanted. And he'll make sure you never go back to wherever you were before he first saw you. He thinks that if anyone or anything gets away from him, it's like his father is "winning" all over again.

And here's the thing that I'm really scared about. If you try to get away, he might do to you what he did to the other Ruth.

I hope you trust me enough to help you get away. You're going to need help because Pa is real smart.
Your friend, Jesse.

The next morning during breakfast Ruth had to work at making her face look empty and stupid. But Jesse acted overly nonchalant, and she worried that it might make Dade suspicious. She kept her eyes down for most of the meal and softly murmured words from the Bible with each bite.

During breakfast cleanup, Dade came out of his bedroom and slipped on his jacket and work gloves. Standing at the front door, he whispered something to Mama, touched his hair and looked over at Ruth. Mama nodded and whispered something back. Then Dade stepped out.

Mama stood at the door and watched her. She frowned even more than usual, the lines around her mouth and eyes accentuated by a parade of obviously negative thoughts and emotions. Ruth looked down and pretended unawareness. Her neck tensed when Mama approached.

Mama seized Ruth's one large braid and fingered it.

"Ruth, yer hair's getting dull. We gotta put some more dye in it today. Put the kettle on to boil."

Mama clomped noisily into the bedroom to retrieve her hair coloring supplies.

Ruth longed to be able to see her reflection in a mirror. She'd been denied that privilege since the first coloring, weeks ago. When she had asked to use the only mirror, in Mama's bedroom, she had been roughly sat down on the floor and treated to a lecture about female vanity and the waywardness of her soul. Later, when no one was in the main room, she had sought out metallic surfaces in the house—skillets, pots, and tableware. But most were so scratched and dull they proved useless for reflective purposes. Only the knives, regularly sharpened, yielded a clue about her appearance. Blond roots peeked out of the top of her head. Why couldn't Mama leave her hair to be whatever color it was? She wanted to ask Mama but she'd probably give her another "female vanity" lecture.

Mama returned with towels and a jar with some dark, dried plant stems and roots. Using a sharp knife, she sliced the stems and roots into thin shavings and placed them into a bowl, adding some tea leaves. She poured hot water over the mixture and waited for it to steep. After the water had turned a dark brown and had cooled, Mama ordered her to strip off her long dress.

Baby Rebecca started to cry in the next room and Mama dried her hands on a towel. "Put yer head in the bowl, Ruth, and keep it there 'till I git back."

Mama was in her bedroom for a long time, feeding and changing the baby. The steam from the hot hair elixir wet Ruth's face and neck. Something about its aroma aroused a memory. Sitting at a table with a small, beautifully decorated cup in her hands, sipping tea and savoring the sweet fragrance. She must have been a young girl because her chest was still flat and her hands were tiny. Across from her sat a man with pale, blonde hair and a kind face. He smiled at her and his blue eyes crinkled affectionately. He held a small slip of paper in his hands. "May I read your fortune?"

Tears stung her eyes, and without thinking, she cried out, "Dad!"

Mama came to the door, holding Rebecca. "Ruth, did you call me? "

Remember, you can't talk. "Y-yes, Mama." She pointed to her head. "Hair?"

Mama lowered Rebecca into the playpen. "Well, let's take a look at yer hair and see if it's dark enough. Here, just lift yer head so I kin see the top. Hmm." Mama pushed the dark hair around near her scalp. "Good," she grunted. "It's a nice dark color. Oughta keep you fer at least six more weeks."

"Here," Mama grabbed a towel and shoved it at Ruth. "Dry yer hair good."

Then Mama took a wide-toothed comb and set about with rough hands to detangle Ruth's long hair. When she finished combing, she pulled it all tightly to the back and wove it into another braid. "Okay, you can git yer dress back on." And Mama watched with barely disguised animosity as Ruth pulled up her faded dress, and buttoned the front.

For the rest of the day Mama put her to work scrubbing the doors and windows, inside and out. Sarah stayed busy playing with the baby, and Mama retreated to her bedroom with a headache.

What was Jesse doing? She'd had no more communication from him since the letter. Had he come up with a plan? She started work on the outside of the windows and peeked around the cabin corner from time to time. Dade moved about through the trees. Sometimes she could hear him sawing wood or pounding nails. She had paused in her work, trying to see where Dade had gone when Jesse's voice close by startled her. She started and nearly fell off the short ladder she'd been using to reach the tops of the windows. He reached out to steady her but she jumped down quickly.

"Ruth, can you drive?"

"I-I don't remember if I learned."

He looked surprised when she answered. "Well, never mind, 'cause if yer not sure, I'll bet you don't drive a stick. And you'd have to be real good at a stick 'cause Dade's truck is hard to start."

"Jesse, do y-you drive at all?"

"No, Pa never showed me. I watched him sometimes but to be able to start that noisy truck up quick enough to git goin' before he could come on out with his gun … I don't think I could do it."

Jesse looked over his shoulder. "But I've been thinking. One way would be to take the road and git off of it as soon as you come out of the canyon. Or, if I can git at the truck without them catching me, maybe I could put a nail in one of the tires or something. But even if I could hurt the truck, and you took off on foot, Pa can run a lot faster than you."

When Jesse saw her hopeless expression, he whispered, "The only way we're gonna git you away is to do it at night when everyone's asleep. There's a backpack and boots in the shed. It's got clothes and stuff in it that used to be yours before you came here."

She stared at him.

"I'm sorry, Ruth. Pa said he'd beat me within an inch of my life if I ever told you about how you came here."

"It's okay, Jesse. I-I can understand w-why you had to keep your mouth shut. But if-if that pack is locked up in the shed, h-how can I get it? I'll need it and the boots to get far. I can't run very far with j-just these socks on my feet. Also, if you help me, h-how's it going to go for you with Dade?"

"I know. I thought of that, too. I can git them and break the window in the shed so it looks like you did it to git in."

"I've tried to open m-my bedroom window, but it's stuck. And even if I could, Sarah would probably hear me. Oh, and what about the front door? No one could s-sneak out without the whole house hearing the door screech."

Jesse smiled. "Here." He pulled out a small container of grease. "This should take care of it. Only, I'm not gonna put it on the hinges till after everyone's in bed. Don't wanna make Pa or Mama suspicious." He stuffed the container back in his pocket.

"Jesse, y-you're a wonder."

He loped away without another word. She grabbed her rag and started up the ladder once more, hope lightening her step.

Later that afternoon, as she had almost finished scouring the outside of the front door, Dade did it again. "Ruth."

This time she didn't allow herself to jump or appear startled. *How does he do that?* her mind screamed. She turned around to find him towering above her. *Meet his eyes. Smile shy-like. Look down at your feet. Keep your shoulders hunched over a bit.*

"That's a good job you're doing here, Ruth." His voice sounded almost gentle. "Well now, I've never seen the windows look nicer. Pretty soon I'll be having you do some cleaning in the new cabin."

He ran his hand over her hair in a brief caress and she restrained a powerful urge to shudder. Her smile trembled, and vanished as soon as he stepped around her and into the cabin. She fingered the scar on her left temple. That area throbbed whenever she experienced strong emotion.

As she helped prepare supper, Ruth noticed that Mama's behavior had changed. In fact, it had been several days since Mama had hit or shoved her. She seemed almost subdued, even sad.

What did the large woman feel about Dade taking another wife? Mama probably hoped Ruth and Jesse would be together eventually. It must have come as a shock to hear that she'd have to share her husband with another woman. But if she complained, Dade would probably hit her again.

Compassion stirred her heart, but then fresh memories of Mama's cruel tongue and stinging hand stifled that emotion. Just because Mama wasn't hitting her now didn't mean she had changed. Mama was probably just as mean and nasty underneath. But she was afraid of Dade. And now, Mama most likely would hate her more than ever. It wouldn't matter how nice Ruth was to her.

Right before supper was served, as the family was taking their usual places at the table, Dade swooped Ruth's hand into his and led her toward the head of the table. He motioned for her to stand next to him. Lifting up the large Bible, he read from the Psalms: "Blessed are all who fear the Lord, who walk in his ways.

You will eat the fruit of your labor; Blessings and prosperity will be yours.

Your wife will be like a fruitful vine within your house; Your sons will be like olive shoots around your table. Thus is the man blessed who fears the Lord."

Dade closed the Bible. "Tonight, I want to remind my wife

and children of God's promises to those who faithfully obey His commands. He told Abraham to leave his country and go to a land that He would show him. After Abraham obeyed God, He blessed him and promised to make a great nation from him. Now, God called us to leave our old land and to flee to the mountains. I'm claiming God's promise to bless us because we've been obedient. He's already blessed us with three children. And one day they'll help build our sacred community by having more sons and daughters."

"And now," Dade placed his hand on Ruth's shoulder, "God has also blessed the family with our sister, Ruth. We have taught her the scriptures and trained her to become a blessed woman by her hard work. I've been so impressed by her purity and obedience that I am ready now to give her the highest honor by welcoming her into the family as my wife. Through her we shall raise up a godly generation of true believers. The second house will be finished tomorrow and I shall take my new wife into her home then."

Jesse's mouth dropped open.

Ruth stared at Dade. A sick feeling dragged her stomach into the abyss. It was happening much sooner than she'd expected. Dade fumbled in his pocket, withdrew a gold ring and, before she could flinch, slipped it on her finger. Then, picking up a length of cord that had been draped over his chair, he wrapped it around both their wrists, binding them together.

If she protested, there was no telling what he'd do, especially as his family looked on. She forced herself to continue to gaze into his eyes, wearing a carefully rehearsed shy smile on lips that trembled.

In a deep and reverent voice Dade prayed, "Oh God, look

down with favor on this betrothal and, just as this cord symbolizes the binding of our bodies and souls, may Ruth, my wife be bound to me in this life and the next. Grant us fruitfulness as we seek to obey Thy will."

Dade pulled her bound hand toward him. Bending over her, he planted an ardent kiss on her lips. Then he released her.

"As I declare it, so shall it be."

He indicated that she should take her seat. Then he sat down next to her and prepared to serve the meal.

Ruth's cheeks burned with shame.

Everyone at the table sat in stunned silence at Dade's words and actions. Mama's mouth drooped lower than usual. Sarah looked confused. Ruth glanced up and caught Jesse's blazing eyes. Their communication was clear: tonight.

Chapter Fourteen

Whoever dwells in the shelter of the Most High
will rest in the shadow of the Almighty.
Psalm 91:1

After supper, Mama told Sarah and Ruth to clean up. "Ruth, you got a pile of clothes that need mending." Her voice sounded tired. She slunk into her bedroom and did not come out the rest of the evening.

When the supper dishes were all washed and put away, Sarah played with the baby. Jesse sat on the old sofa and whittled away on a wood doll he'd been working on for Sarah's birthday. Ruth stitched a ripped seam on one of Dade's shirts, and Dade took down his rifle for cleaning. Rebecca began to cry and Sarah lifted her and carried her into Mama's room.

Except for the "wic, wic, wic" of Jesse's knife and the clicking noises of the metallic parts of Dade's gun, the room was quiet. Ruth sneaked peeks at Jesse. He whittled away at a block of wood, brows knit in concentration. He had to be thinking up a storm. When she glanced up again, she found Dade studying her. Her lips trembled like a shy bride on her wedding day. He held her gaze.

He's trying to read my mind. Well, Mister, you're not going to read anything there but an empty head.

Her hands shook. She looked down at her sewing, took another stitch and pricked her finger. She tied off the thread on the seam and set the shirt down on the couch. Keeping her head down, she reached for another shirt, threaded the needle and began work on the sleeve.

Her heart beat so rapidly it made her feel faint. Trying to calm herself with deep, silent breaths didn't work. Dade had to have noticed that she was trembling. So many things could go wrong with their plan. Dade was a lot smarter than he let on. What if he knew what she and Jesse were going to do? What if he was just playing with them? And why, of all nights, was he cleaning his gun?

She pricked her finger again. Oh, if only the night could be over. She glanced over at Jesse. His legs were stretched out on either side of a basket, which caught the flying bits of wood. His eyes focused on his whittling and his knife moved in small, rapid downward strokes over the wooden figure. He had to be almost as scared as she was. What would happen to him if Dade caught him helping her escape?

The waiting was awful. The more she thought about it the more hopeless Jesse's plan sounded. She turned the shirt over for a few more stitches and stuck her finger again. This time it drew blood. She huffed and put her finger to her lips.

Dade chuckled. "Looks like you've got your mind on other things, Ruth. Well, I guess I can understand why."

He had put his gun back together and wiped down the barrel till it gleamed. Carrying it back to the mantle, he replaced the rife on its hooks above the shotgun "Now you're ready for the next big hunt." He put his hands behind his head and stretched his long frame.

He swaggered toward the couch to look down at her progress. "Better put that aside for the night, Ruth.

"Wuh?"

Dade sighed. He pantomimed putting down the shirt, standing up, and walking toward her bedroom.

"Jesse, you too. We've got a long day ahead of us tomorrow, getting the new cabin ready for Ruth."

Ruth gathered up the mending and dumped it into a basket sitting on the floor between the bedroom doors. Dade walked over and stood in front of her like a groom about to say his vows. When he reached for her hair and trailed his hand down its length, her breathing turned erratic.

Behind him, Jesse scowled and balled his fists.

"Goodnight, Ruth." Dade bent to kiss her, but she turned her head at the last second and his lips only brushed her cheek.

Reaching behind her, she turned the handle to the children's room and backed inside. Awful. Awful, also that she couldn't give Jesse one more look before she closed the door. But Dade had blocked her view. For all she knew his icy green eyes were still staring at the back of her door.

Sarah wasn't in the room yet, and that was a good thing. Jesse had promised to slip a pair of his old jeans into her drawer some time that day. She found them and slipped them on right away so she didn't have to make any noise later that night. Just as she was getting into bed, Sarah came in, looking groggy.

Poor little thing. She must have fallen asleep on Mama's bed. Ruth turned over and faced the wall. She didn't want to talk or have to explain to the girl about marrying her father.

Then began the hardest preparation for her flight: waiting. If only she could jump out of her bed and simply run out of the house. She had to wait for Jesse, had to wait for the all clear from him. But what if Dade was still up? *Stay still. Do you want to ruin your chance to get away? Jesse'll come when it's safe.*

Her gaze roamed about the dark room. She held her breath and listened. No snoring next door. Nothing. "God," she whispered, "you know w-what's going on here. You know that I-I have to get away from Dade. Please h-help me, God. Please keep me safe. Please guide m-me out there. And God, please help Jesse and d-don't let Dade find out that he helped me. Amen."

Jesse waited. At one point, he crept over to Dade's room and listened. It seemed too quiet in there. He judged it dangerous. He moved back to the couch. Another hour passed. Dade had to be asleep now. He pulled the tin of grease out of his pocket, pried the lid off and slid it under his pillow. Watching Dade's door, he stood up and inched his way toward the door. He opened his tin and applied grease to the hinges. Did he put enough on? He had to test it. Slowly he turned the knob and eased the door open.

"What are you doing there, Jesse?" Dade stood fifteen feet away.

Jesse nearly banged his head into the door. He spun around and clapped his hands to his stomach. "I-I don't feel so good," he moaned. Blood drained from his face at the sight of Dade's narrowed eyes. "I think I'm gonna be sick."

He had to make it an inspired performance. Doubling over—

to hide the tin of grease—and clutching his stomach, he threw the door open noisily, ran out and raced for the latrine. When he returned, ten minutes later, Dade was still standing there, waiting. His face still registered suspicion. Jesse wiped his mouth and hobbled over to the sink for some water. Taking a big swig of water, he gargled and swished it about in his mouth before spitting it noisily into the sink. He remained there, moaning and resting his head on the countertop.

"I think it's something I ate," he moaned again. "Oh … oh, I'm not done. I think I'm gonna do it again."

He staggered to the couch and lay down, making his breath sound labored.

Dade didn't move. Arms crossed over his chest, he watched Jesse with his head cocked to one side. He looked almost convinced. "I think I'll wake Mama."

"No," Jesse groaned. "Just let me lie here fer awhile. I'll be okay. But I might be sick again."

Dade hesitated. His gaze flicked from the couch, to the front door, to Ruth's door, and back to the couch.

"It's okay, Pa. I'll be all right. I can take care a myself." He closed his eyes and feigned exhaustion until his pa left. The bedroom door clicked shut.

Ruth waited only long enough to be sure that Dade was not going to return. Now was her chance. She startled Jesse when she appeared and glided silently over to him. Without a word, they made for the door. It opened without a sound. They did a fast tiptoe down the path, avoiding the noisy gravel on the road. She looked back only once. What she would do if Dade barged out the front door, she didn't know. The cabin remained dark and silent. Fifty yards from the cabin, Jesse pulled her aside.

"Wait here," he whispered. Seconds later he returned, lugging her pack and boots. He set them both at her feet. "There're lots a thing in there that you might need. I also put some jerky and biscuits in it ... and something else."

"Jesse, c-c-come with me. We can both g-get away from this madness."

"No, Ruth, I gotta stay with Sarah. She's too little to understand what's going on here. And I gotta protect her." The boy started to cry, and he muffled it in his sleeve.

"We'll see each other again, w-won't we? When things are-are better, when you do finally get away?"

"Hurry, Ruth." His voice broke. "Don't talk anymore. Git your boots on, and git away."

She threw her arms around Jesse's neck and kissed him on the cheek. "I'll see you again s-sometime. I'll never forget you."

She dropped to the ground and pulled on her boots. When she looked up, Jesse had gone.

The moon shone just bright enough that she could make out the path. She stayed off the road until she was sure the sound of her footsteps would not carry to the cabin. In another fifty yards, she set her feet on the rough, rutted road. She hurried to distance herself from the dark cabin and Dade. It had been many weeks since she had exerted herself hiking and carrying a pack and her breath came in ragged little gasps. "Oh, God, please let Jesse get back into the house without Dade hearing him."

An hour passed, then another, and still she kept hiking. She stopped once to listen for pursuit. Far off, the yip-yip of a coyote echoed in the stillness. The only other sound was her heart, thumping rapidly as she faced a night of uncertainty. Coyotes, bears, cougars. They were nothing compared to facing Dade.

The moon traveled across the star-filled sky. She crossed a log bridge and kept on the road.

An hour before dawn, Dade came out of his room to check up on Jesse. The boy lay quiet, looking as if the worst of his suffering had ended. He turned to go back to his room, but stopped and smiled. Ruth. Sleeping only yards away. He hadn't touched her. But now those months of self-denial had come to an end. He had worked hard to prepare a place for her, and today he would come to take his bride to her new home.

He had to look at her. He eased the handle to her room and entered. He thought he could just make out her graceful form resting quietly. He bent over and reached down to touch her …

When his fingers touched the empty blankets a snarl erupted from his mouth. Turning, he shoved the door against the wall, ran to fetch his rifle from the hooks above the fireplace, and rushed outside. Heart racing, he ran to check the latrine. Not wanting to believe what his heart feared, he ran to the shack and found the broken window and her pack and boots gone.

"No!" his agonized bellow echoed throughout the canyon walls.

"Come back, you dirty little—" His voice choked off. Shaking with rage and disappointment, he shot off two rounds.

"I know you can hear me. I'm coming after you," he roared. "You'll never be free of me. You hear me? Never." He shot the rifle's entire magazine into the darkness.

Miles away, Ruth heard the rifle report. It sounded like distant thunder. She quickened her pace. Almost dawn. She had to get off the road. It was where he'd expect to find her. But where to go? As she hiked, her mind played and replayed the words he'd spoken to her that night he'd almost suffocated her. She didn't doubt his capability to carry out his threats. But, terrified as she was of the man, the thought of putting someone else in harm's way that might shelter her was more horrifying. But who could she trust? The only adults she had known for the past three months had hurt, bullied and terrorized her. Mama had spoken of the unrighteousness of the people down in the valleys. Ruth didn't want to believe Mama, but what if she was right? What if she turned to strangers for help and they didn't believe her? What if they just thought she was a kid, a runaway, and let Dade take her back? She looked very young; Jesse had said she looked no more than sixteen or seventeen.

The thought pummeled her stomach. She bent over to retch. When she straightened, she wiped her mouth and cast about at the dark and strange wilderness. "God, I-I don't know where to go. H-help me."

Long buried words shot into her mind. A distant memory took shape as words and phrases formed on her lips. An image rose in her brain of a young black woman with a Bible resting in her hands. She smiled as she reached over to squeeze Ruth's hand. Her musical voice soothed as she read:

> *He who dwells in the shelter*
> *of the Most High*
> *Will rest in the shadow of the Almighty.*
> *I will say of the Lord, He is my refuge,*
> *My God, in Whom I trust ...*
> *He will cover you with His feathers*
> *And under His wings*
> *you will find refuge.*
> *His faithfulness will be*
> *your shield and rampart.*
> *You will not fear the terror of the night*
> *nor the arrow that flies by day ...[3]*

The image fled. Silence bore down and surrounded her with a powerful sense of urgency. *Get away. Get away.*

The sun's first rays filtered through the dark needles of the ponderosa trees, and some inner prompting turned her feet northward. He would expect her to go downhill. So, she would go up. The way was long and hard, and she was so tired. She stopped every few minutes to rest and catch her breath. At last, struggling over a high crest, she looked westward. A wide grassy valley stretched out below. She made her way down, then headed straight across. Halfway across she saw an elk and her calf and retraced her steps, giving them a wide berth. Following the periphery of the valley, she came to a shallow stream. Hoping to foil Dade's tracking, she crossed and re-crossed it, sometimes walking upstream for a quarter of a mile before exiting.

As soon as Pa grabbed his rifle and ran outside, Jesse bolted off the couch, pulled on a sweatshirt and jeans and ran into Sarah's bedroom to wake her.

Mama hurried into the room, pulling her robe around her ample middle. "What? What's got Dade so—"

She stopped when she saw Ruth's empty bed and Jesse's expression. Her mouth screwed into a mean, triumphant smile. "You helped her get away?"

"I had to, Mama. It wasn't right what Pa wanted."

"Maybe ..." Mama's mouth worked and her eyes flitted around the room. "Maybe she got away through the window?" Mama stomped to the window, unlocked it and shoved it open enough for a slender body to climb through. "Let's git on outta here."

Sarah and Mama followed Jesse out of the room. They huddled in front of the couch.

Jesse's stomach lurched when Pa's boots stomped onto the porch.

Pa stormed inside and moved like a cat for the kill. His eyes blazed. "How'd she get past you, Jesse?" Shoving Jesse up against the wall, he grabbed him by the throat. "It was your job to guard the door at night."

"Pa ... I," he gagged. "You know I was sick last night. I—"

Mama rushed forward with outstretched arms, looking helplessly at Jesse. "Dade, Sir, I think she got away through her window. Sarah said it was wide open when she woke up."

"No, No," Dade yelled and the whole family jumped. "I would have heard it open."

He turned silent, and Jesse tried to swallow against the man's grip. Pa's quiet was way worse than his rages. He released Jesse without warning and let him slump onto the floor. He turned and walked into Ruth's bedroom. Seconds passed, followed by the sound of the bedroom window sliding shut.

Still coughing and trying to catch his breath, Jesse cringed when Pa returned and looked at Sarah. He bent over her. "Did you help her?" He fingered his belt.

"No," Sarah cried. Her tender little mouth quivered, and tears ran down her cheeks. "I'm telling the truth. You gotta believe me, Pa. I didn't hear anything." She ran to Jesse, and he folded her in his arms. Pa's rifle lay on the kitchen table. Just a few feet away. How long would it take to get to it? And if he did, would he have the gumption to use it against the man he called Pa?

Pa straightened. He looked at Mama, and his mouth twisted. "You get in your room, now."

Pa followed her into their bedroom and kicked the door shut. Jesse hugged Sarah to him. Muffled shouting followed. Then the sound of slaps and Mama crying. Jesse and Sarah jumped up and hid in the other bedroom, watching through a crack in the door. Pa threw his door open and stomped to the kitchen cabinet where he stored the ammunition. He pulled his backpack out of the closet and stuffed provisions into it. Mama slunk after him, sobbing. "Don't go after her, Dade. You don't need another wife. Let her be. She doesn't want you."

"Well, I want her. I'm going to bring her back. No one leaves me and gets away with it."

Mama hurried behind him as he strode to the front door. Trying to caress him, she murmured, "Dade, stay with me. Yer my man."

He put his face down close to hers. His voice sounded like gravel. "You got it wrong, lady. You're my woman, but I'm not your man. Nobody owns me."

He shrugged her off and slammed out the door.

When Ruth couldn't walk any further, she lowered her pack and sat down next to the stream she'd been paralleling. She chewed on a long strip of deer jerky and a biscuit. *Thank you, Jesse, for thinking of food.* The sun had risen hot and bright and her shirt clung to her sweat-soaked back. A kind of euphoria enveloped her. She had actually gotten away. In the warm sunshine, danger seemed far away. *Unrealistic, Ruth.* Still, tracking her would keep Dade moving way slower than she was moving.

Enough time for a quick dip. She dropped her clothes and stepped into the slow-moving water. The coolness of the water soothed her aching feet. She soaked in the water a long time, scrubbing her skin and hair with sand. It would probably take ten more baths till she had completely removed the scent of Dade and the nauseatingly disinfected cabin. The gold band on her finger caught the sun's rays. *Eww!* She ripped it off and flung it into the water. She plunged her hand into the river sand and scrubbed her fourth finger until it turned red and raw. Out of the river, she let the sun beat down on her wet hair. She had to sleep, even if it was only fifteen or twenty minutes. She stretched out and closed her eyes.

Dade followed the road and looked for any signs of tracks moving off into the surrounding forest. The weather had been rainy recently and the moist dirt held many fresh boot prints. Crouching to examine another print, he traced the outline of the impression and placed his own boot next to it. No doubt about it, those were her boot prints. He straightened and smiled for the first time in six hours.

Ruth started awake. An ant had crawled onto her and was biting her leg. She slapped the insect off and sat up. The sun had traveled well past its zenith. Should she try to make a few more miles before holing up for the night? She reached into her pack and took out fresh clothes and socks and dressed hurriedly. When she rummaged further inside the pack she found a hatchet. She sat back on her heels. No wonder the pack was so heavy. Besides the food and clothing, she also pulled out a tarp, rope, a roll of fishing line and a couple of hooks, and Dade's flies, a sturdy knife, three bars of homemade soap and a container of salt.

"Thank you, J-Jesse. Thank you, God. Please take c-care of him and Sarah and little Rebecca. Lord, p-please help them to-to get away from those horrible people."

She shouldered the heavy pack once more. She'd put a few more miles between herself and Dade before making camp.

Dade crossed the log bridge. *This is too easy.* His mind conjured satisfying images of Ruth's surprised and frightened face as he ran her down and seized her. She'd head directly for some kind of civilization, but the weight of her pack would keep her hiking at less than three miles an hour.

He was breathing a little bit harder as his legs carried him at a boot camp pace. Ruth would never get to the highway before he caught up to her.

Then he halted. The tracks disappeared. He cursed, retraced 'his steps until he found the tracks again. They turned and headed northwest into the pine, maple and fir, straight uphill. Tracking would be more difficult, but not even the soft pine carpet could fool him. One broken twig, one overturned stone, the smallest indentation on the ground; these all betrayed her passage. He'd have her back within hours.

The way had been slower. Sometimes he had to retrace his steps before he found the clue that aided his tracking. He straightened occasionally to listen. He could be as close to Ruth as the next rise.

He bent to inspect a scuff of pine needles. "There. She came down here and slipped. But she didn't fall. She must have caught herself. Grabbed this branch. Broke it. Then she must've gone around this bunch of rocks. But then …" he placed his hands on the rough rock and searched the perimeter, "she stepped on the bare ground." He found another boot print and some other type of indentation. Probably her pack. She would have taken it off to rest. He looked up and spied the valley below. "Of course, she would have gone down there. It's a lot easier hiking." He headed downhill.

It took him much longer to follow her path down to the valley. She had back-tracked and turned circles in an attempt to put him off. In spite of his overwhelming desire to capture her, hunting a human—even a stupid one—fed his soul far better than the best meal Mama ever cooked.

He reached the valley and the fields of faded September grasses by late afternoon, almost losing her path several times. The darkening sky and the cold compelled him to stop and make camp.

Ruth went in search of a likely spot for her shelter. The sun dipped, a breeze had sprung up and the air chilled her. The tarp would not provide enough warmth this night. She needed to get up a ways from the stream, to a level spot out of the wind. What she needed was a young, downed tree she could build into a shelter. And if not that, then she could use the ax Jesse had stuffed into her pack. *"Don't build it too big,"* someone—maybe a woman—told her. But when? Someday her brain would stop resisting her search for memories. *"You want your body heat to fill the inside."*

In the end, she did have to use the ax, using up precious energy to chop it down and drag it over to a bigger tree stump. After removing some of the branches, she leaned the thick end on top of the stump and gathered up smaller branches to reinforce the sides of her shelter.

The process took her some time as she stuffed, wove and padded her shelter with as much pine boughs and vegetation as could fit. She covered the floor of her shelter with the tarp.

The temperature dropped as the sun slid down to the horizon. She stowed her food and the soap high in a tree many yards from her camp. Once inside her shelter, she ignored the wilderness sounds. *If a bear finds me, I don't care. Just let me sleep.*

The first rays of light woke her. The scent of pine clung to her hair and clothing. Hunger and that same sense of urgency she'd felt yesterday propelled her out of her shelter. She pulled down her food and munched on the last of the biscuits.

She returned to her camp and dismantled her shelter by dragging the dead tree back into the woods. She wouldn't give Dade evidence of her camping. She spread the boughs and grasses far and wide back in the meadow where she'd collected them. Putting her pack back together and checking once more that the area looked undisturbed, she headed upstream.

She continued to follow the river while watching the sun travel across the sky. Storm clouds had been brewing for the last hour and as she turned her face skyward to sniff the wind, the first raindrops smacked her face. *Get under cover. Quick now, before you get soaked.*

She pulled off her pack and crawled under the lowest branches of a massive spruce. It would have to do. There wasn't enough time to build another shelter. She dug around in her pack for her rain poncho and tarp. As best she could within the cramped space, she donned the poncho and spread the tarp over and around her.

When the clouds began to blow over, Dade quickened his pace. He'd found evidence of her movements down to the river and now the way was easier. Sometimes her tracks disappeared into the river, but he always found them again as he searched, heading upstream. At one point, next to the river, he found impressions that looked like a body had stretched out on the sandy soil. He ran his hands over the spot.

"It's only a matter of time now, Ruth. You can't go on like this forever. Sooner or later you'll get too tired and hungry."

A glint of yellow in the creek caught his eye. He squinted at the object, then cursed when he recognized what he was looking at. Ruth's wedding band. He waded into the water, plucked up the ring, and stuffed it into his pocket.

He stood up and adjusted his pack and gun. But just at that moment, clouds released their moisture on his head. He crouched under cover of the trees, pulled his hat farther down and waited for it to pass. He watched helplessly as the rain built in intensity, till torrents began to wash his clues away into the river. His jaw clenched, and he mumbled curses. By the time he caught up to her— tomorrow morning, most likely—he'd teach her what happens when a girl disobeys. He set about to make camp again and get a warming fire started.

Dena Netherton

Chapter Fifteen

For in the day of trouble
He will keep me safe in His dwelling;
He will hide me in the shelter of His sacred tent
and set me high upon a rock.
Psalm 27:5

Thunder boomed throughout the river valley. Wind hissed and roared through the trees. Occasionally, lightning struck a tree with a tremendous bang. It sounded like Dade's rifle. Rain trickled down the branches and ran in rivulets within the tree well. She scraped up dirt and spruce needles, forming little barriers to prevent the water from reaching her chilled body.

If only she could make a fire, even a small one for warmth. But Dade could be out there right now, hunting her. How awful, if he found her. She could survive without a fire tonight. Maybe.

The air turned frigid. Hail pelted the ground.

Night fell and the hail ceased. Snow came. She shivered and listened. The white stuff had blanketed her shelter and the surrounding woods, reflecting the dim rays of the moon and stars.

A little fire would be okay. She was so far away from anyone or anything. Mama had kept the wood-burning stove burning every evening. Right about now, Jesse would be bringing in more pieces of wood and setting them next to the stove. The wood smelled wonderful when it burned. She had put her feet close to the stove, when they let her. Funny how she could remember smells, but not people or places. Just thinking about wood smoke, she could actually smell it.

It had to be safe to make a fire. A small one. Just enough to warm her feet. They were so cold. She rolled onto her stomach and pushed herself forward. A branch shifted. Snow pelted her head and she brushed it off fast, before it could melt into her scalp. The air was cold, but not cold enough to freeze her sense of smell. A whiff, just a hint of smoke whispered in her nostrils.

"That's a real campfire I'm smelling."

Ruth came to full wakefulness, having not slept. She'd spent the night trying not to freeze. She'd wrapped every article of clothing in her pack under and around her body, then drawn her fleece hood down over her face and wound a shirt, turban-like, around her head. Slowly, the warmth of her body brought the temperature up in the small space under the protective, snow-covered spruce boughs. It was just enough to keep her alive, yet not at all comfortable. Every time the wind blew, tiny cascades of snow sifted down onto her from the upper branches of her tree canopy.

How much longer could she run? Barely sleeping, no more food. Dade maybe, or maybe not, tracking her. She dragged her pack and tarp with her into the white coldness. A faint glimmer in the east propelled tiny fingers of light into the dense, icy atmosphere.

She brushed the snow off her gloved hands and legs and studied her surroundings. "Well, I d-don't dare stick around if-if that campfire last night was Dade's. B-but if I don't eat s-something soon I'm not going to be able to go any further."

She bent over and massaged her stiff thighs. "I c-can either stay here till I freeze or Dade finds me or I can go look f-for food and put tracks all over the place for Dade to find. Or I-I can keep moving till I find a place where I can build a better shelter and maybe make a fire."

Ruth groaned when hunger pangs cramped her stomach. "It's either eat or freeze. I c-can last a bit longer without f-food but I can't without some w-warmth."

She trudged on. Her boots and inadequate socks plagued her toes and the icy air made her face ache. But this cold was preferable to that other cold night. At least she wasn't imprisoned in a bare cabin while Dade looked on, enjoying her torment. And even if she froze trying to get away, it was preferable to enduring the touch of Dade's hands running over her hair, or touching her in other ways it made her sick to imagine. She looked back through the white forest at the tracks she'd just left. They'd lead Dade right to her. But there was nothing to do but to keep on walking and hoping her wandering would lead her somewhere.

The sun rose and the air grew still. But the sky's dismal grey persisted. *Keep your mind quiet. Focus on listening.* She heard nothing but the crunch, crunch of her boots in the packed snow. Sometimes snow fell from a tree bough with a hiss and a thump, and her stomach lurched. She had to pace herself, conserve her energy, walk at a slow, regular pace, breathe evenly.

She had followed the river, more or less, for more than an hour when the snow started up again. A soft, silent, downy snowfall.

Not the icy, windblown snow of the night before. And the next time she looked back, the snow had begun to fill her tracks.

"Thank you, God."

"I've got to rest a while." She found a place to sit and let the heavy pack slip to the ground. Tiny snowflakes landed on her lashes. She blinked them away.

Her mind taunted her with memories of meals she'd eaten at Dade's cabin. Chicken and mashed potatoes, heaped on a plate. Gravy, too. Thick slices of bread with mountains of butter and blackberry jam. Strawberry pie. Steaming hot coffee. A warm fire.

"God, I've got to g-get help. I've got to trust somebody. They c-can't all be like Dade or Mama." She stood up, and the effort made her legs tremble. Lifting the pack was getting harder, too.

Trees—her only hiding place should Dade get within view— had dwindled, replaced by tall grasses and alder. When the ground grew boggy she was forced to move to higher ground away from the river. Steeper and steeper. Firs, pines and maples huddled close and thick undergrowth snagged her boots. She ducked and squeezed her way through the wet, green stuff. Occasional gullies blocked her way. *So steep.* Panting and feeling light-headed, she couldn't go any further. She had to find a safe, wind-shielded place for her shelter. Skirting the downhill side of a boulder, she stepped down onto a sloping, rectangular clearing. Her boots struck something hard and hollow. It made a *thunk* sound. She crouched to brush the snow away. Under the snow, a flat, square piece of bark emerged. She brushed more snow away and found more flat pieces of bark, arranged in a regular layered pattern. Midway down the clearing, to the left, another familiar object drew her forward. She bent to examine it, too. A metallic chimney. Beyond, a sharp drop of perhaps ten feet left her no more doubt; she'd stepped down onto the roof of some kind of structure.

Overwhelming relief flooded her mind. She retraced her steps, and scrambled down the hill she'd just struggled to climb. The cabin, resting on concrete posts, had been built so that its backside nestled into the rock wall she'd been skirting. Steep hills, covered with trees obscured the cabin's two sides. She had not spied the front of the cabin as she'd hiked up the hill. Because of the snow and the dense trees, if she'd labored ten feet higher up the ridge, she would never have discovered it.

She approached the door slowly. "Hello? Anyone th-there? Hello?" She knocked, waited, knocked again. "Can you hear me? Hello?"

She moved to the dust-covered window. Wiping away a circle of grime, she peered inside. A shaft of light, streaming from a small window on the right revealed little but a section of floor. She moved back to the door and turned the handle. Stepping into the darkness, she called out once more, just to make sure. She left the door open, waiting for her eyes to adjust. When she could see, the room presented itself in Spartan fashion. The back wall was constructed solely of rock and mortar. A single room with sparse furniture, a wood burning stove and a simple kitchen. She slipped her pack from her shoulders, pulled off her gloves, drawn forward by a collection of tins, boxes and jars sitting on the shelves. She looked back at the doorway more than once, half expecting the cabin's owner to return at any moment. What would she say about trespassing? Didn't matter. This was survival. No one would turn her out in the middle of a storm.

She read the labels and joyfully fingered the various containers. Opening a box of crackers, she tore into the wrapping and devoured half the box, following up with an entire jar of peaches. Satisfied at last, nourishment flooded her system. Exhaustion took over.

She didn't bother to make a fire. *Too tired. Gotta sleep.* She pulled back the covers on the single bed, fell into it, and drew the blankets over her head. "Thank you, God."

Dade kicked out the fire and shouldered his rifle. Although an experienced woodsman, he'd endured a cold, wet night. He stretched his back and rubbed his shoulders to work out the kinks from sleeping on the hard ground. He was hungry. Having assumed that both he and Ruth would long ago have returned to their home, he'd brought only the barest of food supplies.

"You're going to pay for running away, Ruth. No dumb little female turns her nose up at me and gets away with it."

But it appeared that she had gotten away with it. The more he thought about it, the more enraged he grew. He cursed her under his breath.

The girl was near. He could feel it. He'd found more evidence of her along the river. He'd doubled his speed. How Ruth had managed to elude him, a tiny slip of a girl without any intelligence or knowledge of the woods, mystified him. But at least she hadn't headed for civilization and her father. It would be much better for her to die in the wilderness than to go back to him.

He gazed upward. "Why are you letting Ruth get away from me? You can see that I can't let her go back to her father. He hurt her ... just like *he* hurt Mother Jane."

He turned back to the ground and searched for more signs of

Ruth. By mid-morning he encountered the boggy ground. That meant a lake was nearby. Ruth would have had to turn north to get out of the stuff. He made for higher ground. As he climbed uphill, the snow began to fall once more. Cursing his luck, he quickly searched back and forth for any indications of tracks before they were forever obliterated. It was difficult going among the dense trees and the steep ridges. More than once he slipped and had to grab hold of branches or slender trees for balance.

"Nothing … nothing." Where was she?

Suddenly comprehending that he'd lost, he vented his frustration to the white, silent world. "Ruth! Ruth! Where are you? Ruuuuuuuth!"

He turned back, supremely disappointed.

Twenty-five yards uphill, within the snug cabin walls, Ruth dreamed that a large grizzled wolf stood outside, howling its hunger and loneliness. She shivered in her sleep and turned over.

Ruth woke only when sunlight heated a slim section of her forehead. Her lashes fluttered and blinked in the bright beam. She put one arm up to shade her eyes. Turning away from the window, she examined her surroundings again. Her gaze continually returned to the door. Whose cabin was this? Where was the owner and why wasn't he here?

The door was closed, but not locked. She jumped out of bed, rushed to the door and pulled down the latch. Her heart thumped. She tiptoed to the window and peered out, half expecting Dade to be standing outside, leveling his rifle

She stood at the window for a long time and watched. But she had to eat, and that meant moving away from the window. Make a fire? No. Not yet. He'd see smoke from her fire for sure. There were cans of food she could eat for a while.

Water was a problem; there was none. Where was water and how would she get it without leaving tracks all over the place? But if someone lived in the cabin they'd have to be able to get it pretty quickly.

She crept to the window again. There was plenty of snow outside. She could get some quick and melt it. It wouldn't give her much, though. She remembered trying to melt some in her mouth when she was trudging along the river yesterday.

She had to chance it. She dressed and pulled on her boots. They were still damp from yesterday's flight. She picked up an old stainless kettle resting on the stove, then unlatched and opened the door slowly. She scanned the area. It really was very well hidden, this little cabin. The ground stretched out level for perhaps twenty or so feet, then descended gradually. The trees began at the point of descent. Two large shrub-covered mounds of earth appeared to have been placed, if that were possible, directly in front of the cabin. Could a person even see the small building from down the hill? It was almost as if it had been planned as a hideout.

She stepped out onto the small porch. The bright sun was beginning to melt the snow. Water dripped from the eaves. Well-worn paths led from the cabin to various locations beyond her view. Which path led to water? A trail wound to the east. She'd follow that for a bit. But it turned into a twisted uphill route, finishing abruptly at a cliff. She crept as close to the edge as she dared and looked down on a rockslide.

"Well, that's n-nice to know. Just what I've always w-wanted.

More rocks." She turned back, slipping and sliding down the steep path.

Another path pointed from the cabin directly south and downhill, but she was afraid to go down there. Dade could be down there, following her tracks from the river.

The other noticeable path led west. It climbed a rise, leveled, then descended. Once over the rise, the musical splashing and gurgling of falling water drew her forward. Whoever had lived here had trampled, a packed, level landing above the water. He'd pressed smooth, flat stones into the soil for more secure footing. She crouched and filled the kettle.

Snow fell in mushy dollops from the pines, sounding like the soft steps of a hunter. Grasping the kettle, she hurried back to the cabin. Once inside, she latched the door immediately.

This time she explored the kitchen in depth, pulling drawers open, examining knives, unmatched tableware and small cooking odds and ends. A ring of dried scum lined the middle of the kitchen sink. Whatever water that had been in it had long since evaporated.

"Come to think about it," she murmured as she studied the room, "everything's dusty, like whoever l-lives here hasn't been around for a m-month or two, maybe longer."

She pulled the chair out, sat down and rested her elbow on the table. A wood burning stove, a stocked pantry, bed, solid walls, even a secure latch on the door. What better alternative did she have?

"It's more of a s-sure thing than anything I-I can imagine at this point."

Without money and no other place to stay at least she'd be safe here for the time being, until whoever owned the place came back. Out in the forest? Dade or someone or something equally dangerous could be lurking.

But there had to be people out there somewhere who weren't bad. She imagined them during the day and dreamt of them at night, almost like she was remembering. But where were they? Were they real? And if she found people, could they be trusted?

Better to hold on to a sure thing.

She stood up and fingered her throbbing scar. Until she knew about herself, maybe started remembering who she was, this cabin would be her home.

She set to work cleaning the small room. It took her most of the day to sweep, dust, air out, tote water, and boil the water for washing and disinfecting.

There were several places on her way to the stream where she could view the river valley. It settled her stomach to know that she'd be able to see someone coming from a long way off. Someday she'd get up the nerve to go down to the river valley. Fish would be a welcome addition to her diet, but Dade might still be looking for her. She'd never forget his threat back at the dark cabin. Or Jesse's warning in his letter to her. Not yet. She would wait, watch and listen.

Three days passed without incident. She continued to clean, tote water and watch the river valley.

Two large, mysterious, steel drums sat against the back wall. What was in them? She pounded on them and produced a slightly hollow "wonk." Next, she tried to move them. Heavy, but not solid. She could hear and feel items shifting when she nudged the drums. There was no obvious latch or lock. She tried to turn the tops. They seemed stuck solid. She tried, using a couple of dish towels to cushion her hands as she wrestled with them. Finally, she noticed the small handle on the top. Tugging firmly, the lid popped off.

"Dumb, brain-damaged girl." She rolled her eyes. "Handles are usually there for a reason."

She reached in to explore the drum's contents. Lifting out bags of various types of pasta, she came to the containers of oatmeal, cornmeal and barley. At the bottom sat plastic containers filled with dried beans: lentils, split peas, navy beans, kidney and black beans.

She took a deep breath and tears filled her eyes. "Unbelievable. God, t-thank You. I asked You to help me, but th-this is more than I imagined. Thank You."

"And whoever you are who l-lives here, I promise I'll repay you for using your place and your food."

On the fourth morning, she took down the pair of binoculars and hung them around her neck. Ruth climbed the rocky outcropping just to the east of her cabin. As she perched at the edge of the precipice, she scanned the entire river valley. From here, if there were any other cottages or cabins, she'd be able to see them.

She raised the binoculars and made a wide sweep of the high hills above the river. "No smoke, no chimneys, no cabins, no roads." Disappointment squeezed her heart. "Nothing."

How far was she from a town? And who would've built a little cabin so far from other people? Maybe whoever lived here had also wanted a hideout or a refuge. Possibly, a hunter had built the cabin. But why was it so well stocked?

She was about to lower the glasses when movement made her focus more clearly on a spot halfway up a hill due south of the river.

She lost it for a second and swept east and west until she caught what she was looking for again. Her heart lurched. A man was hiking up the spine of a ridge. His back was turned away as he hiked southward. He wore a black jacket and his hair appeared to be black as well. He must have been athletic because even his backpack and rifle didn't slow him down as he hiked upward, over the uneven terrain.

So, there *were* people in these mountains. He might have hiked from some distance, but at least one other person was familiar with these woods. Maybe he was a hunter or just someone out for a day hike. She raised her arm over her head and took a big breath to yell across the distance separating her from the man.

Then he disappeared behind the ridge. *Come back, please.* She kept the binoculars focused on the spot, just in case. Seconds later, the man reemerged. Excitement and relief coursed through her. She raised her arm again, and opened her mouth to shout. But this time, the man turned to face her direction. He pulled the black cap from his head and raked his fingers through his sandy brown hair.

Short, brown beard, broad shoulders, long, long legs, hawk-like profile. He stopped to gaze out across the valley. Her breath cut in the middle of inhaling. Electric darts shot through her gut, her arms and legs. Dade raised his own pair of binoculars.

The shout died on her lips. She dropped to a crouch and scrambled like a squirrel behind cover of a large, jagged rock. Breathing hard, she pressed her back into the hardness of the granite and hugged her knees to her chest. Had he seen her? She didn't dare try to look. He might have his binoculars trained on her at this very moment.

"He's still hunting me," she whimpered. "Oh, God, please don't let him see me."

She lifted the strap of the binoculars over her head, rolled over onto her belly and flattened herself against the rough ground. To get a good look across the valley she'd have to expose her head and shoulders just enough to be able to raise and swivel the binoculars in a wide sweep. She wormed forward slowly, but kept her head low. With his binoculars, Dade might be able to see any movement. Once she peeked her head out from behind her rock, it took her several minutes to inch the glasses from her side back up to her eyes. Fortunately, clouds kept the sun from catching and reflecting any glare from the binoculars. She searched for Dade.

"He's not there." She swept westward. "No, not there either." She lowered the glasses and peered over the edge of the outcropping. There was no sign of movement down by the river. Or on the north side.

He could have gone behind a ridge again. She raised the binoculars and searched up and down the hills once more. Still no movement. Where had Dade gone? Had he seen her?

She waited and searched the hills again and again. She couldn't get up, couldn't leave. Not until she was sure. She grew cold and her body ached from holding her position. Clouds blew over. Cold rain smacked her head. But only when lightning struck nearby did she risk raising her body to creep backward. Back under cover of the rocks again, she sprang up and dashed down the steep path. Sheets of rain pelted her and she slipped several times on the slick trail. Once inside, she bolted the cabin door and did not risk a light or a fire for the entire night.

When Dade returned without the girl, Mama put on her best face while she tried to judge whether or not he was approachable. She called Sarah and Jesse and they took their places at the table. Placing a roast chicken before him, she hardly dared breathe. In stony silence, staring at the bird, his mouth formed the word, "Ruth." He took up the carving knife and thrust the point straight down into the bird's breast. Mama kept her head down, her back straight and her hands folded. She watched, under cautious lids as Dade prepared to serve the meal.

Chapter Sixteen

I will say of the Lord,
"He is my refuge and my fortress,
my God in whom I trust."
Psalm 91:2

When Ruth woke on the sixth morning she glanced at the backpack. She'd moved it next to the door while she was cleaning. Now it was time to take everything out and decide which items she'd be able to use during her stay in the cabin. She'd keep the pack full of supplies and near the door if she ever had to run from Dade again.

Dade's not out there. He had to have gone home by now. Go on, build a little fire. Your toes are going to freeze. She stuffed tinder inside the stove, lit it and added fuel as the fire got going. After breakfast, she pulled the pack over next to the stove where it was warm. Kneeling, she reached in and pulled out items, one by one. When she got near the bottom, her fingers identified the denim dress she'd worn the first night of her escape. Lifting the wrinkled and dirty garment out, she regarded it at arm's length, half expecting the dress to wrap itself around her and bind her hands and feet. She hurled it across the room. She'd deal with that later.

But it was impossible to concentrate. She glanced over her shoulder. *Breathing. I hear breathing. And wasn't the dress closer than the last time I looked at it? But it couldn't be.*

A cold draft flowed across the floor space between Ruth and the dress, carrying with it the scent of the dress: Dade's antiseptic cabin.

Ruth jumped up and stomped across the room. Seizing the dress, she ripped it from the neck to the waist. Buttons popped and clattered to the floor. Grabbing scissors from the kitchen drawer she attacked large sections of the dress. She laughed as she opened the stove door and shoved pieces of fabric inside. Watched the material curl, twist and blacken in the flame. *Yes, kill Dade. Sear that awful gloating smile right off his face.* She thrust more fabric into the overstuffed chamber. She was laughing so hard now she could hardly breathe. Smoke backed up and poured into the room.

"Dade's burning up. He's dying. I've killed him." Her laughing melted into sobs. Tears streamed down her cheeks and her gut heaved.

Dade was out there somewhere, trying to find her so he could beat her, or worse.

Or maybe he was desperately seeking her, calling her name in an agony of worry and grief. "How c-could I kill him?" Sobs shook her. "He-he-he was trying to help me be g-good and righteous. Maybe he really does l-love me."

She clutched the mangled dress to her chest. "I'm s-sorry. I didn't m-mean it."

She thrust the cabin door open and stumbled out onto the porch.

"I'll come back, Dade. I-I'll do it right now."

She ran straight down the hill, still clutching the dress. "Don't be mad at me."

She cleared the open space. Running too fast as she descended, she couldn't control her body. Leaping over plants and dead timber she lost her footing, tumbled and rolled several feet before coming to an abrupt and painful stop. Stunned, the earth and sky spun in crazy circles around her head and her ears roared. When she could move again, she went to brush off her face, but the hated dress was still clasped in her hand. "Eww, get away from me!" She bolted upright and flung it down the hill. Turning over, she crawled back up the hill, on hands and knees, not trusting her balance.

"What's wrong w-with me? Am I losing my mind? Dade's a monster. He said he'd kill me."

Once back inside the cabin, she sank onto her bed and covered her eyes.

Dade was bad, terribly bad.

No, Dade had tried to teach her to be good. Dade had fed and clothed her.

But Jesse had told her that Dade was evil and crazy. He'd killed that girl, Ruth.

She turned over on her side and cried. Crying would release her pain, right? But it didn't. Sunlight traveled across the room, then faded. Darkness arrived and still she huddled, clutching her blankets. Where was God?

Her own voice startled her in the dark room, as if another voice had spoken. "Could hell be much worse?"

She must be going crazy, splitting into two women. Dade was a good man. He'd taken care of her. Yes, he'd disciplined her, but only when she deserved it.

"No!" she yelled at the ceiling. The man was dangerous and

delusional.

But Dade had never really hurt her. He hadn't beat her, not like Jesse and Sarah, with a belt, or with his fists.

"Stop it. Stop it, you stupid, brain-damaged woman. The man b-beat Jesse and Sarah and Mama. He threatened you. He grabbed you a-and threw you around. He purposely terrified you. He f-froze you and humiliated you. He thinks he's married to you. He's trying to find you right now."

Dade is a good man. He reads his Bible.

Dade is crazy, evil.

Morning came. But it didn't help her get out of bed. The sun moved across her face, down the bed, across the cabin floor. Words stopped. When she stared at the ceiling, she saw only Dade and his gun and the hands that had almost snuffed the life out of her.

The next morning, Dade's image faded from the ceiling. She opened another can of beans and sat at the kitchen table, mindlessly chewing, gaze roaming the cabin walls. *Boxes. There are boxes under the bed. I wonder why I never noticed them before.*

She got down on her hands and knees and peeked under. Two boxes. One of them was easy to move. She slid it out. Pulled the flaps open. Just men's clothing. But maybe she could use the fabric for something else. She pushed that box back under.

The second box was way heavier. Once she got it out, there was a blanket folded on top of whatever was heavy. *I can use the blanket.* She set it on top of the bed.

Underneath—*thank you, God*— a collection of books. An

eclectic bunch. Whoever lived here must have been educated. Biographies, textbooks, American histories, a Shakespeare collection, two books on wilderness survival, several religious songbooks and some novels. Men's novels. Spies and government conspiracy types of suspense books. Close to the bottom snuggled a tin box. Would it be right to open the box and inspect somebody else's stuff?

It had to be. She'd slept in a stranger's bed, eaten his food, lived like the place was her own, for days now. She pulled the lid off and fingered the contents. Mostly family photos, a couple of letters, and a journal. It didn't feel right to read that. She closed the tin and stuffed it back into the box.

At the very bottom of the box sat a black, leather-bound book, its cover dull and scratched. The initials, G and D had been inscribed on the cover. She opened to the first page. "Holy Bible." She thrust the book away and wiped her hands on the bed covers. Dade and Mama had used the Bible to justify all sorts of harsh and evil things. She jumped up and paced the room, arms folded across her chest. How long would it take to burn if she pulled out each page, one by one, and fed them into the stove? She picked the Bible up, dropped it on the bed, picked it up again. Yes, it was true that Dade and Mama had twisted some of the scriptures to fit their strange view of the world. But that didn't make the Book itself bad, did it?

Open it ... to the middle. Wasn't that where Dade went for the meal-time reading?

When hard pressed, I cried to the Lord:
He brought me into a spacious place.
The Lord is with me; I will not be afraid.
What can mere mortals do to me?

The Lord is with me; He is my helper.
I will look in triumph on my enemies.[4]

She scrunched her eyes shut. "I want that to be t-true for me, too. I'm c-c-calling out to you, God. If You're really my helper, please help me. Keep me safe. Please don't let Dade find me."

Dade listened every day to the news on his truck radio. He also picked up a local newspaper whenever he went to town for a carpentry job. It had been two weeks and no information had surfaced yet about the girl.

She's still out there, then. There'd have to have been something in the paper if she'd been found. She's got to have found some place to hole up.

But then a disturbing thought entered his mind. What if she told somebody?

Told them what? She can hardly talk. Or think. Anyway, it was her word against his and Mama's, and who would believe a dummy that could hardly put two words together?"

He set the paper down on the truck's seat. But if she was still out there, why didn't he find her? What if an animal got her?"

His gut tightened at the thought of his beautiful Ruth mauled or killed by a bear or cougar. He thrust the thought far from him. No, he had tracked her, and she'd been moving just fine. If an animal had gotten her, there'd have to have been some sign. Blood, signs of a struggle or dragging or worse. There wasn't anything out there, just tracks and then that snow. She could still be alive if she managed to make it through that storm.

He slammed his fist down on the steering wheel. "She's alive.

When two weeks passed and Ruth didn't see any signs of Dade, she relaxed her vigilance. But only a little. She wanted to explore the river valley farther to the west. Early in the morning, she hiked down the hill. She met her stream farther down and jumped it. After half a mile of hiking west, she looked down. A small lake shimmered through the trees. A trout dinner would sure taste good. Could she catch one? Jesse had brought some home two or three times. He had even asked Dade one time if she could come along the next time he went fishing but had gotten an emphatic "No. Women need to be watched. You can't trust them away from their house work."

She picked her way down to the water's edge and examined the pebbly bottom. The lake was shallow for perhaps twenty-five yards, then dropped off into some unknown depth. She didn't see any fish, but they had to be hiding somewhere. Jesse had said that they liked to hide in shady spots, like under overhanging trees or rocks, or around logs.

She moved farther west along the shore, flushing ducks into the water. They paddled swiftly away into the deeper water, quacking indignantly.

The lake had looked small when she was coming down the hill, but it was taking her much longer than she'd estimated to get around it. Boggy areas along the shore forced her to backtrack and move away from the water. It would probably take her at least another ten minutes before she'd get to the western side.

When she finally did reach the far western end of the lake, the effort made her pant. Sounds of the river got louder. The ground rose steeply above the west side of the lake so that the river which fed it, cascaded noisily, boulders separating the flow into three or four ribbons before reuniting at the bottom.

The water was much deeper here. The river had gouged out a deep section. Should she try to cross the river farther upstream for more exploration? No, that would have to wait. She was too tired. And anyway, it was probably not much different on the south side. She'd come back tomorrow after she figured out how to make some kind of fishing pole.

She retraced her path. The roar of the river receded as she moved north. She hadn't gone more than a football field's distance beyond the boggy section when the voices jerked her to a stop. Men's voices.

Hide. Hide before they see you. She had only seconds to scramble for cover behind some bushes. They were coming the way she had just come, moving at an athletic pace, laughing and talking animatedly. She caught her first glimpse of the men through the branches. They were both young. The first was of average height with a wiry build and brown, curly hair. The second was several inches taller, with wavy, gold hair and a strong, muscular frame. He wore a trim beard, like Dade. His voice was deep, like Dade's. The men both carried backpacks, heavily laden. Speaking some kind of foreign language. The men passed so close she could have almost touched them. Their boots crunched the pebbles lining the shore, and she pressed her hand to her mouth to stifle the sound of her breathing.

The backpackers rounded the bend of the shore, and she lost

sight of them. *Run away. What if they see you?*

But what if they were nice? What if they could help her?

But she didn't know them. She didn't know anybody except Dade and Mama.

Well, Jesse was nice and he had helped her.

Still, wouldn't she want to make sure if they were okay before she went and trusted them?

She nodded in silent agreement with the warning words in her skull. *Move quietly. Keep your eyes focused on the direction they went.*

She had to be careful. What if they knew Dade and they told him they'd seen a girl out in the woods? What if Dade had gotten more people to look for her? Even if they didn't know Dade, they could still go back home and say they'd seen a girl all alone in the forest. And then someone might come nosing around, and she wouldn't have her hiding place anymore.

What if they tried to help her and Dade shot them?

Her gut burned, and her mouth turned dry. "Don't get ahead of yourself. You don't know anything yet. Just watch them."

The men hiked up and then down another ridge. They stopped at a flat, grassy spot. She stayed behind the ridge, and hiked up higher to get a good view of their camp-making. Hiding behind the shelter of fallen logs, she lay down on her stomach. Propped on her elbows, she watched, fascinated, as the thin, darker-haired man set up their tent. The big, yellow-haired one constructed a fire pit. He didn't have to go far to find dry firewood. After everything had been unpacked and set up, they sat down to rest on their camp chairs. They talked softly. Then the smaller man got up, took his fishing equipment and walked downhill toward the lake. The big one remained in his chair and studied a thick notebook.

The end of the show. She'd come back tomorrow morning.

She tiptoed across the ridge uphill from the campsite, moving slowly, avoiding anything in her path that might alert the man and make him look up. Once clear, she ran most of the way back to her hidden cabin.

Fortunately, the weather promised a clear and mild night. It was too risky to make a fire in the stove since the smoke might waft into the men's campsite. Better that they didn't know that anyone else was around, just in case.

She woke before dawn, dressed and waited at the window for the sun to do its push-back on the dark. She'd get another look at the strangers. But to do that, she needed to get into a safe viewing position before they woke up. They couldn't be like Dade. He terrified her ... on purpose. Those two men wouldn't be like that. They might listen to her and help her.

She positioned herself behind the logs she'd watched from the day before. The campsite was quiet except for the scurrying about of a chipmunk searching in vain for crumbs.

Then the walls of the tent moved. In another minute the tent flap unzipped by an unseen hand. The tall blond man stepped out. He stretched and ran his hands through his tousled hair. He set about to get the fire going again. Pouring water from a plastic container into a percolator, he added the coffee and set it above the fire. After a few minutes the aroma of the coffee reached her nostrils.

Watching him, a strange sense of longing invaded her soul. If only she could run to him and tell him about her situation. He seemed so strong, so calm, so sure of himself. Gentle. Maybe he would care. Maybe he would help her.

He moved about the campsite with quiet, purposeful actions.

His preparations seemed so mundane, so innocent. Hiding was silly. Yes, he looked like Dade, moved like Dade. But he didn't seem like Dade. Maybe it was time to reveal herself. Her mouth went dry and her heart drummed when she got up and sat on the log in full view. A ravine separated her from the tall man. He continued to busy himself with food preparations. He had set a pot next to the percolator and stood up to brush the dirt off his knees. Then he looked up and saw her. His handsome young face snapped to alertness, and he straightened. He took a step forward and shaded his eyes.

"Hey." He raised his voice to carry the distance. "Girl, are you all alone?" He took a couple of steps in her direction.

She bolted off her log. He strode closer to the ravine. He looked so much like Dade.

"Don't go. Hey ... wait. Come here."

He was fast, but seventy-five yards separated them. He had to go down before he could come up. By the time he reached the log, she'd already hidden herself. He bent and put his hands on the place where she had been sitting. He ran up the hill a little, looked about. But he was no tracker. He did not see her watching him from a tangle of bushes and undergrowth a stone's throw away. The man gave up and made his way back to camp. But he looked back several times with an unsettled expression. He met the brown-haired man halfway down and they exchanged foreign sounding words, the one questioning, the other explaining in hushed, troubled tones.

It was a long time before she felt safe to leave her hiding place and run back home.

She spent the rest of the morning looking out her window. What if those men decided to look for her and came up the hill?

Why did the big, blonde man run after her? Was he concerned for her? Or did he have other intentions? Impossible to tell. They looked like nice young men, but Dade had seemed nice at first, too, back at the dark cabin.

She punched her thigh. "Why d-did I let him see me? He's going to wonder what I'm doing w-way out here away from any town or houses. Now they're p-probably going to go back to town and tell someone about m-me. And Dade will c-come after me."

The thought shocked her brain like electricity. She jerked her head from point to point to point around the cabin like a trapped animal. The room seemed to shrink and tilt. In the darkest corner of the room, a darker, man-like form materialized. The thing grew taller and broader. Two green points of light pierced the shadow it cast. The glint of a brandished blade swung up and outward, its cold light streaked across the log walls. Chaotic noise pounded inside her skull. Her heart raced, and she gasped for breath. Nausea rolled through her gut like a lava flow. The giant spread and loomed over her, bending closer … closer. A grimacing grin opened to swallow her. His head accordioned inward, stuffing her nose, her gaping mouth with black mud. Sucking her downward.

No air, no scream. She withered onto the floor. *God help me!* She curled up like an unborn child and surrendered.

The morning after her panic attack, she prayed. Not much of a prayer. Simply, "Help me, Jesus."

The pain of loneliness was too much. A tight band seemed to have wound itself around her chest. Except for the tired plodding of her heartbeat, the silent room pressed in on her.

She stared at the walls of her little prison. *Give up.* The rafters of the cabin looked sturdy enough to support a body. One of the drawers held a coil of rope.

Then, there was the rocky cliff just to the east of her cabin. *Throw yourself off.*

No one knew she was here. She had no family. No one would grieve over her death.

God was a nice thought, but He'd never responded to her calls for help.

Dade was still looking for her. Maybe she could wander on back to his cabin and just let—

"Get up and praise Me."

The voice that had interrupted her came from inside her. But not from her.

Urgent, yet inaudible. She sat up and waited for more words, or some kind of explanation. But there was nothing more. Obedience born out of hope made her swing her legs around and place her feet on the cold floor. Would the voice in her head speak again? Still waiting, she crept uncertainly to the kitchen table where the songbook lay. Half expecting it to glow with a holy light, she picked it up and thumbed through its worn pages. But it was just an old songbook, smudged in places from a man's fingerprints, its pages dog-eared by repeated use. She selected a song at random, took a deep, ragged breath and sang:

> *Where can I go from Your Spirit?*
> *Where can I flee from Your presence?*
> *If I go up to the heavens, You are there.*
> *If I make my bed in the depths,*
> *You are there.*

If I rise on the wings of the dawn,
If I settle on the far side of the sea,
even there Your hand will guide me,
Your right hand will hold me fast.[5]

She stopped singing. Because she was not alone. As if the front door had been opened by an unseen hand. Someone entered, bringing with Him the freshest, purest air she'd ever inhaled. An invisible Presence of indescribable and transcendent sweetness approached, descended and enveloped her. In her mind, the Presence spoke "I love you. I have never left you. I've heard every prayer you prayed."

In awe, she fell onto her hands and knees, and wept, surrounded by Heaven. The Presence hovered only seconds more, pressing the consciousness of His love down into the deepest part of her spirit. Then He withdrew.

She wept for a long time. If only it could go on and on. "Thank You, thank You, Lord." She remained on her knees, worshipping, waiting, ready for more words from Him.

Chapter Seventeen

I will sing of the Lord's great love forever ...
Psalm 89:1a

In the days that followed, she continued to worship even when the dark shadow of isolation oppressed her. Fall skies darkened the days, but her soul grew lighter.

She kept the songbook opened on the table and sang from it each day. The Presence might return some day, and when He did, she wanted to be ready for Him.

One stormy afternoon, looking for something to occupy her time, she remembered the photographs. She lifted the small tin again and set it on the kitchen table. Picking up the photos one by one she studied them carefully. Some had been labeled on the back in a meticulous hand: Sandy, 16 years old; Kevin, 14; Shirley and I, Chicago. There were a few baby pictures, more of Shirley and one professional shot of "Gregory," obviously, the same man as in the picture with Shirley, except much older now, in a suit and tie.

Who were these people? Did they live here sometimes, perhaps in the summer? She picked up the picture of the family standing outside a big, brick house. The only label on the back was a date, "Christmas, 2000." There were only a few more photos to look at. Then she noticed the small black notebook. There were the initials again: GMD. She opened to the middle and read, "Business trip to Tokyo. I can feel a big bonus coming my way." She thumbed forward a few more pages. "September 16: Shirley's Doctor appt. didn't go well. More blood tests. Schedule appt. with Dr. Gregorio, the oncologist."

The next entry answered her question about Shirley's illness. "December 19: Picked up Sandy at the airport. Went straight to the funeral."

Some pages had been removed. Next, she read, "September 4: Drove Kevin to college. Going to miss the boy."

The next entries explained the presence of the Bible in the cabin:

Christmas: Sandy and Mike gave me a Bible. Can you believe it? Even put my initials on it. Young people always think they've got all the answers."

"February 12: Thinking about going to church. Why not?"

"March 2nd: Got baptized today. Sandy and Mike came to the service."

"September 16: Got the promotion and an award. More money, but more travel."

Several months passed before the man made another journal entry.

"May 16: Can't take the job anymore. Thought it would be so much better. There's got to be something more. Can't stand all the status hype. Life's nothing without Shirley. The kids are grown. Sick of stuff owning me. Sick of the company owning me. I'm out of here."

"June 5: Found the perfect spot for the cabin, right in front of a big rocky wall. No one's going to bother me here."

"August 12th: Kevin's helping me bring in the logs and other stuff. I knew that ATV would come in handy."

"September: The cabin's shell is up. I'll be moved in by end of this week. No stuff, nothing to spend money on, no frills. Just me and God."

"February 23rd: "God and I aren't speaking. I'm not going into town to church anymore. My church is right here in the forest. Anyway, they don't care about me, just my checkbook."

She turned another page, noticing another large time gap in the man's entries.

"September 5th: "Not feeling too well. I cough a lot. I think God's trying to get my attention."

"December 24th: "Kevin came up for Christmas. Brought tons of food supplies. Should last me close to a year. When he asked me about the cough I just told him I had the flu. He said Sandy and Mike are planning to come and get me for Easter."

"January 14th: Don't know what to do. Probably too late to see a doctor. I feel really sick and I'm coughing up blood. Got no appetite."

"February 11th: Hard to breathe. Don't know if I can make it to Easter.

"March 20th: Sandy: I love you very much. Kevin: I'm so proud of the man you've become. Mike, thanks for taking such good care of my daughter."

There were no more entries. She closed the small diary and tears filled her eyes. Where had the man gone? Was he taken home? Why would he leave the diary, then? Did he die?

So many questions clamored to be answered. She frowned as she traced her finger over the initials. "That poor man. He j-just chucked his whole world and ran away. And-and when he got sick there was n-nobody to help him."

What wouldn't she give for a loving family like Gregory's? She returned the diary to the small tin.

The woods seemed less forbidding. She explored farther from the cabin. Besides the trail that she had made down to the lake, she'd found no other signs that another human had passed anywhere near her hidden place. After her spirit-healing experience with the Presence, joy pushed her outdoors. Sometimes she raced to outrun her loneliness. But at other times, she ran to catch up with God on His morning rounds, following the path of the sun's first rays. Whipping around bushes, ducking under snow-laden branches, leaping rotted tree stumps, breathing the cool, mountain air. She stopped sometimes to break off a handful of pine needles, crushing the leaves to release the balsam fragrance on her fingers.

The box of books proved a great blessing. The words or illustrations stirred memories. Snatches of songs or whole orchestral compositions came back to her, which she hummed until the tunes ran out. Images jumped out at her while she read. Mostly images of young people with backpacks, hurrying to and fro outside impressive red brick buildings.

The book on wilderness survival techniques seemed familiar, too. Chapters on fishing traps and killing stones: why did the information seem familiar?

Her food stores would last for several more months. But still, it would be wonderful to add some fish or wild game to her steady diet of rice and beans.

Trapping and killing an animal? It made her shiver. Did she really have the stomach to kill an animal? But every time she went outside, a rabbit would zip out from near her front stoop and hide in the bushes. It made her hungry. The chapter on killing stones showed a man throwing and striking a rabbit. Of course, he made it look easy to hit and kill a small animal. She probably couldn't hit anything she aimed at. She'd have to practice a long time for any kind of accuracy. Still, it was worth thinking about.

The days grew colder and sometimes the snow remained for a few days. She had gone down to the river and collected an assortment of smooth rocks, heavy enough to be lethal if thrown with accuracy. Placing them in a basket, she lugged it up the hill and set it on the inside window ledge next to the door. In the late mornings, after she had finished with breakfast, toted water and done some cleaning, she practiced lobbing the stones at targets. She practiced until her shoulders ached. Someday that rabbit would be careless and she'd get close enough to throw a lethal rock.

The ducks down at the lake might make a good meal too. Hunger rumbled in her stomach, and she tossed the stone from hand to hand.

"I'll bet I c-could get close enough to try it." She went inside and grabbed her jacket. She returned up the hill two hours later, carrying her prize. She felt guilty, but also strangely exhilarated, because she had, through her own skill, brought food to her cabin. After the bird was plucked and gutted, she'd save the feathers for future use. Spitting the duck, she roasted it on the open fire in the fireplace. After weeks of beans, duck was amazing.

She kept the stove going nearly all the time now. The days

were growing short and after night fell, there was little to do in the dark cabin but read by candlelight. There was a box of candles in the pantry but if she used them up too quickly, what would she do later?

Something about the colder air and the shorter days made her want to light the candles even during the day. She couldn't explain the feeling. The crisp air and the scent of pine filled her with a sweet, indefinable longing. Lately, a memory had been teasing her, dancing just beyond her grasp. She remembered walking in a town, passing storefronts, gaily decorated, feeling the rush of air as cars whizzed down the street. Snippets of conversations tripped through her mind. Half-remembered faces tantalized her. Beautiful music floated through her mind. She hummed melodies throughout the day. Oh, how she longed to hear music. Maybe it would speed up the remembering.

The urge became irresistible: to see another human face, to hear another voice, to hear music. One gloomy afternoon, loneliness propelled her out of her warm refuge and onto the path that led west, beyond the lake. The way had become well worn; she had traveled this direction many times, longing for, but fearing human contact. She had always turned back at the same point, about a half an hour's hike up the river past the lake. This day she'd press on.

But an awful, shaky feeling jabbed at her heart when she hiked beyond her habitual end point. Snow had fallen recently. Not much. Just enough to make the path slippery, and leave tracks all over. But she couldn't stop. If she could see just one person, she'd go home and feel better.

When she had gone another quarter mile, cresting the top of the hill, a light peeked through the trees and the mist. *Check it out, but go slow.* She got close enough to see the house. It had been built on the very top of a hill. Its steep driveway descended around trees and bushes before meeting the country road. Lamps on either side of the house's garage had been turned on, illuminating boxes and folded blankets stacked to one side of the driveway. The sound of a motor made her duck for cover. A truck came within sight, backing slowly up the drive. "J and M Moving." When the truck reached the top, a man jumped out and shouted to his partner at the wheel. A big, black dog ran out, barking excitedly and a woman's voice yelled at it to stop. Seconds later, the woman, in a wheelchair, rolled herself out to the dog and grabbed its collar. One of the men came up to the woman, carrying a clipboard. The woman's voice rose angrily above the man's. Her tone came out harsh and nasal. The man shrugged and handed her the clipboard. Then the woman, still grabbing the dog's collar, wheeled herself back out of sight into the garage.

The other houses were pretty far down the road. Being in a wheelchair, the woman would have to have someone who took care of her.

The chilled air breathed cold down Ruth's neck, and she shivered in her fleece jacket. Snow began to fall. Time to get home.

Back at the cabin, she sat and warmed herself by the stove. Who was the woman on the hill? It didn't look like there was anybody else living there. She'd only seen one car. Of course, there could be a husband or children. Maybe she just didn't see them.

She set the lentils she'd been soaking in a pan onto the stove, added salt and some dried herbs and set the cover on the pan.

If the weather held, she'd go back in a couple of days. Maybe she'd be able to find out more about the old lady.

Maybe the lady would be friendly and offer to help her.

She wouldn't wait. She'd go tomorrow.

Ruth spent most of the following morning attempting to build a fish trap. All those packages of beans stored in the big metal drum would sustain her for months. But the thought of those little fish darting about the shallows of the lake and the stream below made her ambitious. When she finished making her contraption, she held a hollowed section of log, closed on one end and open on the other. Stuffed into the open end was a funnel fashioned from bark. It looked somewhat like the picture in the survival book. Well, it was worth a try. Maybe she'd get something.

She carried her trap down to the river, baiting it with anything a fish might find enticing. She set the trap into the water close to the bank and secured it with a couple of stones.

"There now, little fish. Swim inside and make me happy." She stood up, brushed the debris off her knees and inhaled the scent of pine.

What was the old woman on the hill doing today? Was she lonely, too? Did she have anyone else besides the dog to keep her company? Today, maybe, she'd find a way to introduce herself to the grey-haired lady. She turned and ran back up the hill to the cabin. Bounding inside, she grabbed the large man's coat and gloves hanging on the wall and pulled them on. She stepped outside and turned her eyes west once more.

When Ruth reached the house on the hill, lights lit up the interior of the house even though it was only early afternoon. An evergreen tree spread its foliage inside the big window. Colored lights decorated the tree. The old woman moved slowly nearby, placing objects on the branches. Music played. Ruth's heart squeezed. If only she had the courage to knock on the woman's door, maybe she could be sitting inside, warmed by the woman's loving arms, telling her story, hearing understanding, sympathetic, motherly words.

A dog barked. Probably the big black one she'd seen the other day. A wooden deck extended from the back of the garage and wrapped around the house. The back door on the deck opened, and the black dog came bounding outside followed slowly by the old woman, leaning on a walker.

So, the lady could actually get around without her wheel chair. She looked so frail, like a little breeze could blow her down.

The dog padded down the stairs and sniffed the ground below the deck.

"Hurry up, Beau," the woman called, watching from above.

Uh, oh. The dog's head came up, and his nose worked. His fluffy tail wagged high over his back, alerted to her unfamiliar scent. Ruth figured that she was well hidden from the woman's view, but the dog headed straight toward her hiding place.

She hunkered down. *Go away, dog. Go away. Don't sniff your way over here.* The jingling of the dog's collar grew louder as he moved around her bushy hideout. Ruth readied to face him. The dog snuffled to within five feet, then raised his head and looked at her, ears erect, tail held high and stiff.

"Hi Beau," she whispered. The dog tilted its head from side to side, regarding her with soft brown eyes.

"C-come here, Beau." She held out her hand. "Good boy, you're a good boy ... and you're so beautiful." Beau's tail lowered. He came up to her and sniffed her hand.

Beau barked excitedly, then bowed in typical doggie play posture.

"Beau, be quiet. Good dog. You'd better go back now. Go home. Good boy."

The woman called Beau again, this time with a certain edge. "Beau, come here … come now. What are you up to? You stop your sniffing. Come, Beau."

As quickly as he'd come, the dog turned and bounded away. His claws clattered up the wood steps and back onto the deck. In another minute the back door slammed shut.

She heaved a breath, stood up, and trudged back to the lake trail. Back in her dimly lit cabin, she ate her simple meal of beans and pancakes in silence, still picturing the old lady, the friendly dog, the lights and the beautiful music warming the house on the hill.

Morning frost sprinkled white over the trees and the front porch. Ruth donned Gregory's heavy winter coat and walked outside. Hopefully, there were fish in her trap down in the river, and then she could make a fried fish pancake for breakfast.

At the water, she crouched and pushed the rocks off her trap, lifting it slowly. Water poured out both ends. She peered inside anxiously. Small bodies flopped about within the confined space.

"Yes. Thank you, God." She picked up the trap and straightened. She'd open it up when she got back to the cabin. No sense standing around freezing.

As she turned to go back up the path, a movement upstream caught her eye. Something dark floated in the water. She squinted and tried to make out what she was seeing.

What am I looking at? Whatever it is, it looks dead.

But fifteen feet closer, there was no mistaking the object. Her gut wrenched. "Oh, no. Beau, it can't be you."

She ran down to the water's edge. The black animal floated limply. "Oh Beau, please d-don't be dead."

She dropped her fish trap and stepped into the frigid water. Wading in hip deep, she reached the still body. It was clear what had happened. The dog had gotten his collar caught on one of the branches of a dead tree partially submerged in the stream. Unable to free himself, he had probably struggled and fought the current until, exhausted, his nose and mouth sank under the water. The dog's lustrous fur waved in the current. She pulled the collar over his muzzle, lifted the head and stared into his glazed eyes.

The dog probably weighed as much as she, and it was a struggle to pull him across the water and onto the bank. Dripping and nearly frozen, she crouched above the animal and put her ear to his chest. No heartbeat.

"You c-can't be dead, you're so beautiful, Beau. I-I thought we were going to be friends." She shoved the dog's chest. Once on land, she'd be able to do more.

It was harder to do than she'd thought. The closer she got to the shore, the shallower the water, and the heavier the animal. By the time Beau was out of the water, Ruth's hands had turned into frozen stumps, and she was shivering.

"Breathe, Dog. Y-you've got to breathe. Please, God, d-don't let him be dead. Please help Beau ... please, God."

Nothing happened. Beau's tongue lolled out of his mouth like a red ribbon.

"No! You're the first friend I've had in months. You're not going to die on me." She slammed her fists down onto Beau's chest, then sat back, breathing heavily from her exertions.

A full minute passed. Ruth slumped onto the sand, and stared.

Then a loud belch followed by the sound of liquid being vomited from the dog's mouth. Coughing, choking and more vomiting followed.

Ruth flipped back onto her knees. "Come on, Beau. Come on. Keep fighting. Th-that's right, Boy, you j-just keep getting that n-nasty stuff out."

The dog's pupils were returning to normal. He whined in between coughing and vomiting. Both Ruth and the dog shivered in their wet skins.

After some time, Beau's breathing still sounded ragged but at least it was coming at regular intervals. He continued to cough and shiver.

Ruth's teeth chattered. "We've ... got to ... get back to the ... cabin."

She stood up, shivering uncontrollably. "Come on, Beau. We'll freeze if we d-don't get warm."

She had to drag him part of the way. When they got into her warm cabin, Ruth stripped out of her coat and clothes, pulled blankets off the bed and lay down next to Beau.

By evening Beau had recovered enough to move about the cabin and sniff its unfamiliar contents. He still coughed from time to time and he seemed much subdued from the energetic and playful dog she'd remembered at the house on the hill.

"What am I going to feed you? You're probably expecting a big hunk of m-meat. I-I could make you some pancakes. You might like that."

The little fish in the trap. She'd left it down by the river. "Well, they're probably frozen by now, it-it's so cold out. Bet you'd like them if I cooked them a little."

Gregory's coat was still lying in a sopping mud-smeared heap on the floor. She reached for the remaining sweater that hung from its hook. "Beau, I've got to leave for just a few minutes. Got t-to get those fish."

When she moved toward the door, Beau whined. She sighed and crouched down in front of the dog. "It's okay, Beau. I'll only b-be gone for a minute. I'm not going to leave you." She wrapped her arms around his furry neck and kissed his velvety muzzle.

She stepped out and hurried down the hill, pulling the sweater tight around her neck. By the time she returned up the hill with the frozen fish trap, she had started to shiver again. She could hear Beau whining and barking inside. When she pushed the door open, the dog greeted her joyously.

"See, I-I told y-you I wouldn't be gone long."

Ruth pulled out the funnel and reached inside. There were six small fish, all frozen. She quickly prepared them for the skillet. While they were cooking, she also mixed up a small bowl of pancake batter and added a pinch of dried herbs for flavor. When both were done, she wrapped each little filleted fish in a pancake and served half to Beau. She sat at the table, munching her fish sandwich, while Beau devoured his meal. When he finished, he nudged his bowl around. He looked up at her, wagged his tail, and licked his black lips.

She laughed. "Okay, you bottomless pit. But the f-fish is all gone. You'll h-have to be happy with just pancakes." She poured the last of the batter into the skillet.

After Beau finished the pancakes, she washed and dried the dishes.

"Now, Beau, where are you going to sleep? That bed's just not b-big enough for the two of us."

She pulled out the box of clothes and found the extra blanket for more padding. She laid it on the floor next to her bed. "Here you go, Beau." She patted the spot again. "This should be nice and comfy for you."

The dog immediately settled onto the makeshift bed. She stroked his soft head. "You're such a g-good dog. I wish I could keep you. M-maybe I wouldn't be so lonely. But I know where you belong, and it just wouldn't be right to keep you."

She blew out the candle and settled into her own bed. "I wish I knew where I belonged."

Chapter Eighteen

Blessed are the merciful,
for they will be shown mercy.
Matthew 5:7

Ruth woke to Beau's wet nose. When she opened her eyes, the dog licked her face and whined.

She got out of bed and shuffled to the door. "Now, don't go wandering."

Beau bounded outside. Ruth kept the door open a crack and watched the dog make his rounds in the semi light of approaching dawn. When he finished, he galloped back inside, joyously barking and dancing around her.

She crouched in front of Beau. "Oh, y-you are such a good dog. Yes, you are." Beau licked her face again, and she wrapped her arms around his neck.

"I wish I could keep you." She buried her face in his soft fur. Beau stood still and wagged his fluffy tail.

"Well," she stood up and patted his head, "I've got t-to get some breakfast fixed for us, and then I'll take you back home."

The stove had gone out several hours earlier. She stoked the oven, added tinder, and lit it.

With water heating up in a pan, she scanned the shelves for something to dress up the oatmeal that would be their breakfast. Dried apricots, cut up and thrown into the pan was the only thing her pantry offered.

When the oatmeal was ready, she spooned half of the mixture into a bowl for Beau, and poured more canned milk in to cool it. He finished his helping before she could even take a spoon to her own bowl.

"I-I don't know if it's the dried fruit, or just having you to keep me company, Beau, but I've never h-had a better bowl of oatmeal."

Beau licked his bowl clean again, and Ruth laughed. "Sorry, Beau, that's it for breakfast. But when I take you back, that old lady is going to be s-so happy to see you again that she'll probably give you s-something really special for dinner."

She caught a glimpse of herself in the mirror and frowned. "I-I've got to make myself presentable if-if I'm going to talk to an actual person today."

She scrubbed her face, brushed her teeth, and spent a long time combing her hair.

"Okay, Beau, l-let's go home to your lady."

They walked down the hill together. Beau sniffed and pushed his nose into any promising hole in the ground or niche in the boulders littering the hillside. When they reached the river, she rolled up her sleeves. Crouching at the river's edge, she placed her fish trap in nearly the same place as before and shoved river stones around to hold the trap down.

"That s-should do it. Maybe there'll be some m-more fish when I-I come back today. Now, where did I throw your collar?"

Beau whined. He sniffed the air, and his ears swiveled to catch something she could not hear.

"W-what's the matter, Beau? Do you want to st-stay with me?"

She checked the ground near the water's edge, finally finding Beau's collar. "Here, Beau, let's put this on you again."

She slipped the collar over the dog's neck. "Come on, Beau. I've got to get you home."

Beau followed her, his tail held high and the fur on his back raised. She scanned the other side of the river, body tense. The woods appeared normal. Quiet. Still. Maybe too quiet. Low growls resonated from Beau's throat. Ruth picked up a good-sized rock, then hurried in the direction of the lake.

By the time they reached the western shore, Beau had calmed down, and she breathed easier. She could use a big protector like Beau. Maybe when she delivered the dog, the lady would say, "Oh, that's okay. He can go live with you. I can see you love him even more than I do." Then Beau would prance and yip like dogs do, and follow her back home. And he'd sniff out any danger around her cabin and warn her when Dade got within one hundred yards.

Hah.

Without Beau, it might be better to go back using that other route uphill. Someone downhill wouldn't be able to see her through the trees.

She came in sight of the house on the hill. "Are you happy you're going to see your lady again, Beau?" She stroked the dog's soft ears.

At the boundary of the old lady's yard, Ruth's courage faltered. Her heart started to pound, and her hands turned shaky. It had been a long time since she'd talked to another human. *Don't talk gibberish when the old lady opens the door.*

She and Beau reached the driveway. Walking up the path to

the front door, her legs wobbled. "Go on, girl. Just keep moving. That's it. Go right up to that door and ring the bell."

She pushed the doorbell. Waited. Held her breath. Nothing.

Good. She let out all the air she'd been holding. But then the curtain next to the front door shifted. The door opened a crack. Beau barked and his tail wagged his entire body.

The old lady regarded her with a combination of distrust and ill temper.

"I-I brought your home, I mean, your dog home. I f-found him by the river and I—"

"So," the woman interrupted, leaning forward over her walker, delivering her words in a snappy, sharp tone, "I suppose you'll be wanting me to give you a reward for bringing him back."

"Oh n-no, Ma'am. I-I know … knew you … you be worry … your … dog."

The woman's dark eyes narrowed in suspicion. "Aren't you the girl I saw skulking around my backyard the other day, trying to play with my dog?"

Ruth took a step back, and swallowed. "I was … I-I …"

"Beau wouldn't have wandered off if someone hadn't lured him away. So, I'd better not see you hanging around here anymore. If you want to play with dogs, try going down to the pet shelter next time. Come on, Beau."

The woman opened the door wider, and Beau ran inside. Then she slammed the door shut.

Ruth stared at the closed door. Her eyes stung, then tears overflowed and washed down her cheeks. There would be no getting-acquainted, no warm friend-making today. She released a deep, shuddering sigh, and turned to retrace her steps.

At the top of the trail, just before it bent downwards, she

stopped to stare at the lonely way back to her cabin. "God, I tried to make a friend. Couldn't you have helped me out a little?"

It took much longer to get back to the cabin by the uphill route. She struggled through the dense trees and steep ridges higher up the slopes above the lake.

"Skulking." The woman said she was 'skulking.' Like some crazy, half human creature. Dirty and weird. Was that what she looked like to ordinary people? The scene played over and over in her mind. What had she done wrong?

Besides the obvious fact that you can't talk.

But I brought her dog back. She should have said thanks, at least. Why would she think I stole her dog?

She climbed down a ridge and then struggled back uphill. "I should have told her about finding the dog drowned in the river. Why didn't I tell her what happened? Why c-can't I talk when I get upset? Oh God, w-why am I like this? I wish—"

Bang. The blast of a rifle close by made her dive flat onto the ground. Scarcely breathing, she listened. Something large crashed through the undergrowth. She pushed up and crawled under cover of a spruce. More desperate panting, more crashing.

From farther downhill, a man yelled. "Dan, it went uphill. About two o'clock."

She froze under her hideout. A man passed within fifteen feet of her, heading east. She couldn't see him and dared not turn her head to try to find out where he had gone. He was breathing hard from the exertion of the uphill climb.

Dan's voice called back, "It's gone down the ridge. I can see it. It's down. Hurry up, Jimmy."

The sound of the man's movements receded into the east. Ruth allowed herself to breathe once more.

Great. Now I've got hunters surrounding my cabin. She lay still and listened for the men's voices. She waited a long time, just to make sure they weren't coming back. That had to be why Beau was so upset earlier. Dogs were sure handy creatures to have around. *Oh, Beau, I wish I could have kept you.*

She stayed under the tree for another half hour. Then she crawled out cautiously and studied her surroundings. She knew nothing about hunting. How long would the hunters spend with their elk or deer? Would they just take the head, like the one in Dade's cabin, or butcher it and take as much meat as they could carry?

She hiked higher up the ridge, moving slowly and staring in the direction the hunters had gone. The sun had climbed high. It had to be nearly noon. A squirrel chattered overhead and a raven flew nearby, its croaking call echoing over the valley. Normal.

When she got within fifty yards of her cabin, she tiptoed the rest of the way. What if the hunters had seen the cabin and looked around? What if they knew Dade?

When she came around the two big mounds obscuring the cabin she stopped. There were no unusual tracks and all seemed as it had in the morning. Yet, after the rejection by the old woman and her near encounter with the hunters, her brain felt like a rubber band that has been stretched to the point of snapping. The sound of the hunter's rifle had blasted Dade's tall, threatening form into the forefront of her mind. She hurried inside and bolted the door. She did not venture out for the rest of the day.

When Ruth woke the next morning, the room was unusually dark. She peered out the window. A storm brewed.

She settled back into her bed and drew the blankets close about her shoulders. Somehow, she remembered that she loved storms: the sound of the wind and the rain on the roof and windows, the snuggling in warm blankets, reading a good book and sipping dark coffee. The image of the blue room with the white trim and the small grey cat rose again in her mind.

There was no reason to go to the old lady's house anymore. She might as well spend the day reading and watching the snow gather. After the storm, maybe she'd look for another house down the road with a friendlier person.

At least I'm safe in a storm. Dade would be crazy to be out in this weather.

The next morning, a look out the window brought a gasp of delight. Her world had been transformed into a wonderland of snow-laden, glistening pines and firs, and deep snowdrifts piled against the two mounds and the walls of the cabin. Like stiff-beaten egg whites.

After breakfast, she went outside and jumped off the porch into a big snowdrift. Letting herself fall back into the soft powdery stuff, she laughed when the cold seeped through her sweater. A soft wind sent shimmering particles cascading down from the nearby pines, catching the sunlight, creating tiny prisms of multicolored gems.

Snowshoe hare tracks crossed and re-crossed the flat area just in front of the cabin. Someday, she'd find a way to get one. Rabbit would be way tastier than tiny fish.

One of the mounds in front of the cabin looked like a giant snowshoe hare. She jumped up. "I'm going to get you, Mr. Bunny, j-just you wait and see."

She gathered a handful of snow and packed it into a compact ball. "I see you over there, t-trying to make yourself look like nothing. You can't hide from me."

She lobbed the snowball and struck the *hare* directly in the heart. "Got you. What? Y-you're not dead? Prepare for attack."

She jumped behind a snowdrift, gathered snow and formed multiple balls. "Surrender or die." With a loud battle cry, she stood up and began her attack, pelting the *hare* over and over until her arms couldn't throw anymore.

She slogged through the snow to examine the little white hill. Her aim was getting pretty good. Tomorrow she'd switch to throwing rocks instead. Someday they might come in handy not only for hunting bunnies and ducks, but for protection.

Every day Jesse watched his pa's face. The man's green eyes smoldered with a crazed intensity. Pa spoke no more of Ruth within the dark cabin walls. He was even quieter than usual and Jesse tiptoed around him, afraid of his sudden and unexpected "holy" punishments.

He hid as much as possible down by the river, casting his fishing line. Everything had changed, grew darker in the cabin after Ruth left. Where had she gone? He dared not ask Pa or even bring up the subject. One day, he too would flee. But not yet. He had to have a plan not only for taking care of himself, but Sarah as well. He'd get away in a few months when he turned eighteen. He'd get a job and save up.

Maybe he'd find Ruth and warn her that Pa was still looking for her. The man hadn't stopped working on the smaller cabin, adding furniture and kitchen items. He had even finished the bed in the smaller room and added expensive-looking sheets, blankets and down pillows. "Things to woo his bride with," Jesse spat out. That Ruth didn't want Dade as her husband—didn't want to have his babies—obviously did not occur to his pa. During one of his supper-table rants, Pa said that it had become clear to him that Ruth had been led astray by "evil whisperings." Pa hadn't yet discovered who'd been guilty of filling Ruth's inferior mind with destructive messages. But he'd find out.

"Inferior mind," Jesse snorted. The girl's mind was anything but inferior. She had talent and spirit. She'd had the ability to see right through Mama's and Pa's preaching and strange ways. And her speech had been returning, though she'd hidden that to everyone but him.

A girl like that would never submit to Pa and his plans for her. Jesse clenched his jaw so hard it hurt. Even if Pa had actually married Ruth, did the man think she'd just give up and remain his prisoner? No, she would've gotten more and more words back. And eventually she'd remember everything.

And then she'd tell the police about Dade Colton—that he used to be Thomas Dade Boone from Tennessee. A murderer. She'd tell them about his little set-up in the woods.

But where was Ruth? And if Jesse found her someday, would she be happy to see him? Did she miss him as much as he missed her?

Chapter Nineteen

For this is the message you heard
from the beginning:
We should love one another.
1 John 3:11

Ruth opened the door and stepped out to test the weather. The cold struck her like a slap in the face. Maybe she shouldn't go out today. Besides, were any people in the old woman's neighborhood actually going to be out in this? It was even too cold for throwing rocks or snowballs.

She was just about to step back inside when she heard the dog's bark. A familiar deep-pitched 'woof, woof.' There it went again. The sound echoed throughout the silent valley. In another minute a big, black dog bounded into the clearing.

"Beau. What are you doing way out here?"

Beau trotted toward her. He stopped within a few feet of the porch and barked. She stepped off the porch and approached, but the dog backed away.

"Beau, what's the matter?" The dog held his tail high and didn't display his usual playful body language. "C-come here,

Beau."

The dog barked again and turned to race toward the edge of the clearing. When he reached it, he barked at her again. Clearly, he wanted her to follow.

She hurried back into the cabin, threw on her coat, hat and gloves, and grabbed her hiking stick. Beau waited just at the base of the porch steps, barking.

"Alright, I'm coming. But I-I sure hope your old lady isn't m-mean to me again when I bring you back."

Beau bounded away into the silent woods, but returned to her often. He would not let her touch him, jumping just out of reach any time she attempted to pat him.

The way around the lake was slick with ice. She used her hiking stick, thrusting it into the ice with each step. Her face ached with the cold. It took her much longer than usual to clear the lake and turn up the steep switchbacks toward the house on the hill.

When she came to the top of the path, the back portion of the old lady's house came into view. Her gut tightened. "Skulking." That's what the lady would say when she brought Beau back.

"Well, there's nothing I can do to avoid this confrontation." *Lord, please help the old lady see that I'm not up to anything bad. Help her to realize that I'm a nice person.*

Her boots crunched along the walk to the front door. Beau followed, barking incessantly. He took her coat sleeve in his teeth and tugged gently.

"What is it now, Beau?"

Beau tugged again, then released her sleeve and ran down the driveway. He turned and barked again.

"W-what in the world are you trying to tell me?"

Portions of the driveway were still covered with snow and

parallel wheel tracks—they must be the old lady's wheel chair—
headed down the hill toward the road. At one point, however, the
wheel tracks appeared to have skidded, then turned sharply to the
right. Now she understood. The dog plunged down the hill off the
side of the driveway. She followed as quickly as she dared,
slipping and sliding on the steep, snowy hillside. The wheelchair
lay on its side, halfway down the hill. A long, dark shape lay in the
snow. Ruth approached, heart in her throat, and crouched next to
the woman. She started to check for signs of life but stopped when
the old woman shivered.

Ruth touched her face. "Lady, can you hear me?" She brushed
the snow off the woman's head and shoulders and leaned close.

"Ma'am, c-can you move at all? We've got to get you inside
b-before you freeze." She gently prodded her. "Can you move your
arms, Ma'am?"

The woman turned her head and opened her eyes slightly. She
tried to lift her body, but sank back weakly. "Help me," she
murmured.

"Oh God," Ruth cried. "Help me help her. I'm not strong
enough to lift her and carry her all the way to the house."

She stripped off Gregory's coat and laid it flat on the snow.
Grasping the old woman by her shoulders, she dragged her onto
the coat.

"C-come on, Beau, you can help me drag her. Here, take this
sleeve."

Beau seemed to understand and took the fabric in his teeth.
She took the other sleeve and together they hauled the woman up
the hill. When they reached the walk leading up to the front door,
she paused to catch her breath. She could drag the woman up the
ramp and into the house but how was she going to get her into her

bed?

The woman was at least half a foot taller and probably outweighed Ruth by thirty pounds. She dropped to her knees and took a deep breath. "Ma'am, w-we've got to get you sitting so I can pull you up and carry you. C-can you help me? T-try to sit up. Here, I'll help you."

The old lady moaned with the effort, but she did manage to lift her body just enough, so that Ruth could pull her up the rest of the way.

"Thank you, lady. You're doing j-just great. Now, this isn't going to be pleasant, but I've got to p-pull you onto my back."

Beau's owner nodded and mouthed something Ruth couldn't understand. With supreme effort and a little help from the woman, she dragged her up and onto her back, then hauled her slowly through the open front door, and down the hall.

She found the bedroom, gently lowered her onto the bed, unzipped the old lady's boots and pulled them off. Then she drew the covers up and wrapped them around the woman's shivering body.

"Lady, I'm going to get s-some more blankets, and then I-I'll bring you something hot to drink. I'll be right back."

She found the kitchen, turned on the burner, put the kettle on, then ran back down the hall to look for extra blankets. After tucking them around her patient, she bent to check on her condition. Beau tried to push his nose into the woman's face and Ruth pulled him back.

"Here Beau, you can help make your lady warm." She patted the bed and Beau jumped up, and settled next to the old woman. "Now you stay there while I take care of things in the kitchen."

She returned to the kitchen and rummaged through cupboards.

There had to be tea or cocoa in the cupboards somewhere. There, good old Nestle's. She heated a small pan of milk, and added the cocoa and sugar.

When she brought the cocoa into the bedroom, the old woman's shivering had lessened. "Do you think you could sit up and drink this cocoa?"

The woman struggled to raise her body.

"Here, let me help you." She helped her sit up, propped pillows behind her, and handed her the hot mug.

"There's a hot water bottle in the linen closet in the hall," the woman whispered. "Would you fill it and bring it to me?"

"I'll g-get it for you, Ma'am." In a few minutes, she returned with the freshly filled bottle, wrapped in a towel. She pulled back the covers and settled the rubber container near the woman's chest. Then she stood back and watched her. Was the old woman more than just cold? Maybe she needed professional help.

"Ma'am, do y-you think I should get a doctor for-for you? You've taken an awful chill and that fall might h-have hurt you in-in ways we don't even k-know yet."

"No. No doctor," came the fierce but feeble response. "I don't want a doctor or anyone else in my house." The woman set the half-finished mug on the nightstand and slid back down sleepily. "Doctors. All they do is ... take your ... money. They don't care."

Ruth waited until she was sure the old woman was asleep, then sat close by. She dozed off, waking at each uneven breath or movement by her patient.

By the afternoon, the woman's sleep seemed peaceful and Ruth crept out of the room. She wandered the house restlessly. Should she call a doctor just in case and risk the old lady's ire? No, she would check on her in another half hour and make her decision then. In the meantime, she was hungry. Would the old lady mind if she fixed some lunch?

She tiptoed into the kitchen and opened the refrigerator to explore. *Grape jelly and bread.* She set them on the counter, then looked for a jar of peanut butter in the cupboard. She made an extra sandwich—just in case the old lady woke up soon—and stored it in the refrigerator.

She looked in the old lady's bedroom often, changing the hot water bottle, checking her skin to see if she had regained a normal temperature. By mid-afternoon, when she tiptoed into the bedroom, her charge had changed position and was gazing about the room. She looked surprised when Ruth entered, and then seemed to recall.

"How are y-you feeling, Ma'am? Is-is there anything I-I-I can get you?"

The woman propped herself up on an elbow and studied Ruth. "How did you find me?"

"Y-your dog came to my house and barked and barked until I knew s-something must be wrong. So, I f-followed him and-and he led me straight to you."

"Beau did that? I didn't think he'd be able to get help."

"Well, you've got a great dog there." Ruth looked at the big black dog still cuddled up to his mistress. "Yes, you are. You're such a good, good dog."

The dog's tail thumped the mattress.

"Oh, Beau," the woman laughed softly. She reached back until she found Beau's soft muzzle. "Have you been here all this time?"

"He helped me pull you up the hill, and w-when we got in here he jumped right up next to you. He h-hasn't moved since." Ruth came close. "Are you warm enough now? C-could I bring you something to eat?"

The woman settled back onto her pillow. Her dark eyes searched Ruth's face and a slowly emerging expression of wonder transformed her lined face. "Who are you and why are you being so kind to me?"

"My n-name's ... Ruth. W-we can talk more when you're feeling strong again. I made a peanut butter and jelly sandwich for you. W-would you like it now?"

"That sounds very good right now. Could you bring me a glass of milk, too?"

Ruth smiled. "Be right back." She headed for the kitchen again.

Later that afternoon, as the sun was beginning to sink, she came into the room for a final check. "Ma'am, it's getting late, and I-I think I should be getting on home, unless you think you m-might need me in the night."

The woman turned over and looked at the clock on the nightstand.

"Oh, I didn't realize I'd been in bed so long. Do you have to go, Ruth? I'm still weak. I'm not sure if I could even use my walker. And where is my wheelchair? Is it still down the hill?"

Ruth came closer. "I'll be happy to s-stay here overnight if you w-want me to."

She turned to leave the old woman in peace, but halted. "By the way, I'm feeling really awkward just calling you Ma'am."

"It's Jaeger ... Professor Anna Jaeger," the woman murmured.

Chapter Twenty

A friend loves at all times ...
Proverbs 17:17a

The sun had sunk below the wooded hills, and Ruth switched on lights. She roamed the house. The tree that Professor Jaeger had so carefully decorated had vanished, and a big, brown leather chair had taken its place. In the opposite corner of the living room, a grand piano begged for her to play. She tiptoed over to examine the music sitting on the stand.

Mozart Sonatas. Her fingers ached to press the keys. But not without permission, and certainly not while the professor recuperated from her icy fall. The professor wouldn't object to her thumbing through the music, though. Most of the sonatas seemed familiar. She sat down on the piano bench and placed her hands over the keyboard, fingers moving silently as she tracked the music. The notes on the page formed sounds in her head. *How do I know how to do this?* She pressed her fingers hard against her skull. "Where did I learn to play? God, I want to remember. Please help me, Lord."

Maybe if the professor would let her play, something might come back to her. When she'd played Jesse's guitar, words and pictures had swept through her mind like memories of a world where she had once belonged.

What a lovely, peaceful room. And so many books. Wouldn't it be wonderful to be able to lounge around here just reading books and playing the piano? Was that what Professor Jaeger did with her time? Did she ever go anywhere? Ruth stood up, walked over to the bookshelf and read the titles. The professor must have taught music or music history, judging by the titles of the various volumes.

Tomorrow. Tomorrow, after she and the professor had both had a good sleep, she'd ask the professor questions. She tiptoed back down the hallway and peered into Anna Jaeger's bedroom. The old woman's breathing was slow and regular. Beau raised his head, and his tail thumped the bed again.

Ruth found the guest bedroom and climbed beneath the sheets.

She awoke to the sounds of activity down the hall. Out of bed, she pulled on her boots. The clink of dishes and the gurgling of the coffee pot led her to the kitchen where Professor Jaeger was shuffling about with her walker, in robe and slippers.

"I-I'm sorry, Professor Jaeger, I didn't m-mean to oversleep." Two place settings sat on the breakfast table almost hidden by a stack of unread newspapers and political magazines.

The professor collected them all and dumped them into a basket next to the table. "I'm much better now, and anyway, you'd done so much for me yesterday, I figured you deserve a good sleep, and a good breakfast. And please call me Anna."

Anna poured the coffee and Ruth bowed her head to pray a blessing over the meal. When she raised her eyes, she discovered the professor studying her, mouth tightened into a straight line. Shifting her frail body, obviously ill at ease at the display of faith, she dug into her food.

The room was quiet except for the clinking of silverware. Professor Jaeger reached over to the radio and switched on the classical channel.

"Oh, I love it."

The professor's dark eyes flickered with curiosity. "You know this music?"

"Of course, it-it's one of Bach's Brandenburg Concertos. They're …" Ruth stopped and put her fingers over her mouth. "Now h-how did I know that?" She hummed along with the music. A tingle coursed through her. Was her memory coming back?

"I don't meet too many young people who know any classical music. It seems like they're always listening to pop music. Or they're blasting from their cars with hip-hop or something else equally disgusting. You must have studied music. I mean, the Brandenburg Concertos aren't exactly on the top-40 hits list.

"Well," Ruth answered carefully, "w-when you play the piano, you get familiar with s-some of the great music as a result."

The older woman leaned forward. A small, incredulous smile played on her lips. "You even refer to it as 'great.' Now I'm getting curious. You must have studied music somewhere. In college, perhaps?"

"I … I, well, I'm not sure."

The professor narrowed her eyes at her.

"I, uh, sort of have some memory problems." She pointed at her forehead, and the sad tilt of her eyebrows silenced any more questions.

"Oh, I see. Well, there's always a scholarship for someone who's talented. Maybe I should hear you play sometime."

"I-I'm kind of rusty. I haven't p-played for a while."

"If you really know how to play, maybe you could come here

sometime and practice. That is, if you have something to practice."

Ruth frowned. "When I m-moved here I didn't take any of my music. But I th-think some of my music is still in my fingers. If I could start playing." She fidgeted under the professor's discerning gaze. "Anyway, th-thank you for breakfast." She stood up, trying to tamp down the excitement in case the professor changed her mind. "It-it was delicious. But, if there's nothing more that you need I-I probably should be getting back to my place." She cleared the breakfast dishes and carried them to the sink.

"Oh," Anna said. She looked down at her hands. "Yes, you would have to get back home, I suppose."

Ruth returned the preserves to the refrigerator and the coffee pot back to the stove. She loaded the dishwasher and wiped down the breakfast table, self-conscious because the professor was watching her with a wistful expression.

"You know," Anna remarked casually, "Beau seems to really like you, and I was wondering, if you happen to be in the area, maybe you could play with him for a bit. I can't get around enough to give him any decent exercise. Of course, I'd pay you."

Ruth slid back down into her chair and tried to match the professor's casual demeanor. "How often would you want me to c-come and exercise him?"

"Perhaps every other day for about an hour? He's got a leash and some toys."

Ruth clasped her hands underneath the table. The money would be helpful if she ever got back into a town. But for a chance to play? She'd work all day for nothing. "That w-would be fine. I'll plan on being h-here day after tomorrow."

"Beau will thank you for it."

"I'll get my coat and gloves. Y-you're sure you'll be okay?

Are you feeling well enough to be alone?"

"I can get around just fine as long as I have my little helper." She patted the walker sitting next to her kitchen chair. "But where is my wheelchair?"

"I pulled it up onto the front porch. It was c-covered with snow last night. I thought it would be better to get to it in the morning. I'll pull it inside now."

In another minute, she had removed the snow and wheeled the chair back inside. "Hope you don't n-need to sit in it too soon. That s-seat is cold."

The professor chuckled, and she shuffled into the front hall. "I'll take your advice. Thank you, Ruth, for helping me."

Ruth put her hand on the doorknob and looked back with a smile. Maybe the old lady was as lonely as she was? "Goodbye, Professor Jaeger."

Ruth kept her promise. She took Beau for a long walk around the rural properties nearby. It was exhilarating, yet frightening, to walk by neighboring houses. Did any of those people know Dade?

She had stuffed her long hair up under her hat and borrowed one of Anna's wool jackets, pulling the collar up around her ears. Even Dade wouldn't have recognized her in that outfit. Still, her stomach tightened as she walked. She did not breathe easier until she entered Anna's driveway.

Anna was in the living room, reading a newspaper when she and Beau came through the front door. Beau's claws clicked on the tiled entry while she tried to remove the leash from the excited dog.

Once released, Beau trotted into the living room to be near his mistress.

"How'd it go, Ruth?" Anna called.

Ruth followed Beau into the room. The professor's lap was piled with Sunday editions of *The New York Times*, *The Wall Street Journal*, *The Seattle Times*.

"How do you get through all of those papers?"

"You never know what gem of an article might be hiding in these pages, Ruth. Every educated person should do a daily reading of at least one major newspaper."

Ruth nodded. If you had the time. Most people were probably working way too hard to find the time. She sat down in the leather sofa nearby. "Beau sure loves his walks. He doesn't care about the squirrels or the birds. Just concentrates on m-making sure the other dogs in the area know he's been there." She giggled. "I-I never knew a dog could h-hold that much liquid."

"Well, I feel kind of guilty about Beau," Anna said. "When I first got him, all I was thinking was how a big dog would be protection. I should have arranged for someone to walk him a long time ago."

The dog settled at Anna's feet and panted happily.

Now that her chore was taken care of, she didn't relish the long walk back to her cabin. "Ma'am, as long as I'm here, is there anything I-I can do around here before I go home?"

"Well, there are some boxes of Christmas ornaments that need to go up in the storage loft in the garage. And then after that, you could warm up the piano keys. It's crying for an affectionate touch."

The professor laughed at her delighted reaction. "I thought that would make your eyes sparkle. The boxes are in the closet in the spare bedroom. There's a built-in ladder to the loft. Just pull the cord and it'll come down."

Ruth turned without another word and headed for the bedroom. When she opened the closet door, she found the boxes stacked on one side. At the other end rested three guitar cases. She'd have to ask Anna about them later. She pulled out the boxes and carried two at a time to the garage. In another ten minutes, she'd finished the job, returned the ladder to its place and come back inside, rubbing her chilled hands.

"Now," the professor called from the living room. "If you could just provide me with some reading music, I'd really appreciate it."

Ruth came in and seated herself at the massive piano. She placed her fingers almost reverently on the keyboard and sat with her eyes closed. Scales formed under her fingers. At a slow tempo. Then, faster. She didn't come up for air until she'd played all the major ones. Then the minor ones, all three types. The minor scale jogged her memory and her fingers took her automatically into a Bach Invention.

"S-sorry about the mistakes, Professor. I-I haven't played in a while a-and it's kind of embarrassing, especially c-considering you're a trained musician."

The old woman snorted. "If that's as rusty as you get, I'd like to hear you when you've practiced for a few days."

Ruth beamed. "Any particular style you'd l-like to hear next, Professor?"

"How about something from the nineteenth century?

Ruth nodded and ran her fingers silently over the keyboard. Seconds later a dramatic melody wove itself under her fingers.

"Ah, a Brahms Rhapsody."

"Number 2." Ruth faltered.

"Don't stop, it's beautiful."

"Sorry." Her shoulders slumped. "It's all I can remember. I-I must not have finished l-learning this piece. Wait, I know this," and she segued into a Debussy piece, playing the entire work without flaw.

The professor applauded. "Very nice. You've got a lot of musicality and I can tell that you know how to practice. A few more days of practice and you'll get your fingers back in good shape again."

"Thanks f-for letting me play. Your piano is a really good one, isn't it?"

"I paid a year's salary for it and it wasn't even new when I got it."

"Is-is this what you teach, Anna?"

"No, my primary instrument is the guitar, but I'm a pretty good pianist, although I'm not as good as you. I used to teach music history and theory, and applied guitar, of course."

"Guitar, hmm, like John Mayer?" The name and what the musician looked like had popped into her mind earlier that morning. Another random memory-piece of the puzzle she longed to complete. But now that she remembered his name, she opened her eyes wide and tried not to laugh.

"Good heavens, no, Ruth." The professor's mouth pursed.

Ruth chuckled. She'd successfully baited Anna.

"Oh." Anna's lips quirked upward a little when she caught on. Then she recovered her usual stern face. "You might be surprised to know I've heard of John Mayer. He's an excellent guitarist, if you like that kind of music. But no, I mean classical guitar, like Carulli or Sor or Tarrega. That kind of guitar."

"You know, w-when I was getting the boxes of ornaments out

of the closet I saw your guitar cases. Are-are there actually guitars in them?"

"They're my babies."

Ruth raised her eyebrows. "W-would you consider giving me some guitar lessons in exchange for walking Beau?"

Anna smiled. "When do you want to start?"

Chapter Twenty-One

Dear children, let us not love with words or speech
but with actions and in truth.
1 John 3:18

Afternoons with Anna became the highlight of Ruth's day. The arrangement worked quite well. She could do physical tasks the professor couldn't perform. And, in return, Anna faithfully taught her lessons and let her practice on the piano. Within a couple of weeks Ruth had organized the garage, pruned the shrubs, cleaned the front and back yards, and polished all the silverware.

It had been weeks since Ruth had felt the sting of loneliness. The professor's friendship and the opportunity to make music was a great gift. Had God answered her prayer? And as she worked around the house she smiled to see the old woman sitting nearby, always with a stack of old, as yet unread newspapers.

Occasionally, her chores stretched into the late afternoon and Anna would insist that she stay for the night. "Besides," the professor would remind her, "you haven't spent enough time practicing your guitar music."

They had been working on some difficult guitar technique one evening when Ruth set the instrument on her lap for a brief rest.

"What w-was the college you used to teach at, Anna?"

The professor's eyes darkened as if with some unpleasant memory. "Oh, it was a private college back East. You've probably never heard of it. Smithfield College. Anyway, it's history now." Anna frowned.

"Didn't you like teaching there? I mean, y-you had kind of a sad look when I mentioned it."

"It's very unpleasant to talk about it. Do you mind? It's a dark chapter of my life that I'd prefer to never think about again."

"I'm sorry, Anna. I didn't mean to upset you. I-I guess that, to me, teaching at a college seems so incredible … to have so much knowledge on a particular s-subject that you can stand in front of a w-whole classroom of smart people and lecture. I'd get s-s-so nervous that I-I know I'd start having trouble talking."

The professor's face softened and laughed. "Oh Ruth, you have such a way of looking at things. Yes, you do get nervous at first, but then, after you've done it for a while, you start feeling much more confident. Actually, I could see you teaching someday. You've got such passion for learning and you're very good with people. That's two of the most important qualities for teaching. I guess I lost that."

"But you've been s-such a good teacher for me. Just look at all I've learned in just a few weeks with you."

"No," the old woman answered, "you're different. You actually want to learn. And you don't even seem to mind my—how shall I put it—less than sweet demeanor. No, Ruth," she said when Ruth raised her hand to protest, "I know what I am. Years ago, the kids at the college gave me the nickname, Snaky Jaeky."

Anna reached over and slid the guitar Ruth had been playing onto her own lap. She looked out the window while she played part of something Ruth had never heard.

"That's beautiful. What is it?"

But the professor didn't seem to hear her. "They all thought I was just waiting to sink my fangs into them, so to speak. And, I guess it's true that I did kind of pick on the obnoxious, conceited ones in my classes."

Anna stopped and focused on Ruth again. "Well, after teaching kids like that for thirty years you start to develop a hard shell. And perhaps I wasn't always fair to the ones who were trying to do their best and didn't mean any disrespect. It got to the point that any young person made me suspicious and irritable."

Ruth leaned forward. "So, did y-you get tired of teaching and retire?"

Anna's mood turned into a brick wall. "It's ... it's too. I can't talk about it, yet. You're so young. You couldn't understand about the way people can be." Her voice trembled and she struggled to get up. "It's late, and I'm tired. Goodnight, Ruth."

Before Ruth climbed out of bed the next morning, she'd decided from now on she'd be careful not to upset the professor with too many questions. Maybe it would be better for her to return to the cabin. It seemed awkward, knowing that she'd caused the dignified old woman embarrassment. But when she passed the kitchen door, the professor called to her.

She poked her head around the door. "I was just on my way to my place."

Anna was sitting at the kitchen table with her newspapers and a cup of coffee. "But I've got breakfast in the oven for you, dear. Please stay." Anna indicated the chair opposite her.

Relieved, she pulled off her jacket and gloves and set them on the hall table.

"Pour yourself some coffee." The old woman shuffled slowly to the oven and pulled out a casserole dish of something that smelled wonderful. Setting it on the table, she spooned some of the food onto their plates.

"Wow. That s-smells heavenly. What is it?"

"An old recipe I make from time to time when I'm feeling in the mood. It's a cheese and egg strata."

The professor waited while Ruth said her brief prayer of thanks for the food.

"I want to apologize for last night. I shouldn't have made you feel bad for wanting to know a little more about me. After all, how could you have known about all the miserable things that happened to me in the past couple of years?"

"You don't owe me any—"

"No." The professor put up her hand. "I think I do. You're a kind and lovely young woman and you didn't deserve my rudeness. Please let me explain a little."

Ruth nodded.

"That was arrogant of me to say that you couldn't understand about people. I know, from the little you've shared about yourself, that you've had some unpleasant things happen. Parents? A boyfriend, maybe?"

Anna shifted in her chair. "But what I'm talking about is the kind of relationship problems that break your heart so you want to die. I'm talking about a husband who wanted to destroy me by taking the one love I thought I could never lose: my daughter's. He bought her love with money and special favors and trips to Germany, where he grew up. And all the time he was spending with her, Kurt was telling her how I didn't care, how I could have come on those trips but my job was more important. When she needed to be dealt with firmly, he'd undermine my discipline and tell her she didn't need to listen to me. He spoiled her and made her despise me. And at the same time, I was fighting a battle with my health, and another battle at the college."

Tears welled in Anna's eyes. "I want you to know that I really love my daughter. There's nothing I wouldn't do for her. But you see, I married late, and then I didn't have Greta until I was in my forties. Shortly after she was born I was diagnosed with this exasperating disease. It got progressively worse, and sometimes I had to make decisions about where to spend the little energy I had. Maybe I shouldn't have given so much of myself to my teaching. But you do what you have to do, and I guess, I thought Greta would understand about my work."

Ruth reached over and touched Anna's hand. "I know you l-love your daughter. Just watching your-your face makes me hurt for what you went through."

Anna looked embarrassed. She hurried on with her story. "The day I "quit" at the college was the same day I came home to find the letter from my husband saying that he was leaving—going back to Germany—and Greta had decided to go with him. They say going through a divorce is like experiencing a death. Well, I'd have been grateful if I could have died. I certainly wanted to. I couldn't keep living in the empty house in a college town that no longer wanted me. So, I sold the house and had everything I owned put in storage while I tried to figure out what to do."

"I'm so sorry, Professor. I can't even imagine how that must have hurt."

Anna looked away. "One day I woke up, and it occurred to me that I was a useless piece of old flesh: my husband hated me, my daughter didn't want to see me, and my career was over. I had nothing to live for. I got in my car and started driving west, building up courage to do to myself what they do to old horses and chickens and cows. I drove and drove, past cities and farmlands, and into the wild open spaces of Wyoming. By the time I'd gone down that steep, winding pass heading into Salt Lake City, it suddenly dawned on me that I'd passed up hundreds of miles of opportunity for spectacular self-destruction. I pulled off the highway and sat and cried for a long time. Then I realized that I didn't want to die. Somewhere out there was a new life. Maybe."

The professor paused to dab at her moist eyes. "I know you believe God is good. Maybe that's because you've been granted a measure of good luck. But, if He's even out there, He's pretty selective to whom He grants His favors. My life has been a series of hard knocks and disappointments. My god, if I have one, isn't the kind who cares very much what kind of life I have. He cares just enough to keep me alive and kicking, just for his own amusement."

"Oh Anna," Ruth said softly, "do you think our friendship is an accident? If God doesn't care, then w-why do we find such pleasure in each other's company? You h-have been a tremendous answer to my prayers. I-I thank God every day for you, for everything that you are."

The old woman opened her mouth to speak, but wept, instead.

Ruth held onto Anna's hand, "Your life m-may have been hard but it's certainly not without meaning. Bad th-things happen because this world is messed up. But that d-doesn't mean God doesn't love you. W-why would He love me and not love you? That makes no sense at all."

"You don't understand, Ruth. It's easy for God to love someone as sweet and good as you. If you knew the kind of person

I really am—"

"You say your daughter d-doesn't want t-to see you anymore. That must hurt terribly. B-but you still love her, don't you?"

Anna looked up again through tear-filled eyes. "Of course, I do. Nothing could make me not love her."

"Well, don't you see, Anna? Do y-you think, if your daughter came back to you that you'd throw her out? Of course, not. Th-that's how God is. He'd never throw anyone out who came looking for Him, w-wanting to reconcile."

Anna stopped crying. "No, no. I have to think. That's too simple. Life's much more complicated than that." With an effort, she collected herself, forced a smile, patted Ruth's hand and stood up slowly. "You're a dear to listen to my problems. I didn't mean to tell you so much." Anna's manner turned business-like. "Well, I've got some work to do, Ruth, but thanks for being so sympathetic."

The old woman leaned on her walker and shuffled out of the kitchen, leaving Ruth to her thoughts.

Chapter Twenty-Two

*All those gathered here will know that
it is not by sword or spear that the Lord saves;
for the battle is the Lord's ...*
1 Samuel 17:47a

Ruth spent the rest of the day back in her cabin. But throughout the day, as she cleaned and cooked, she mulled over all that Anna had told her. Alone and neglected by her only child, it would be hard not to grow bitter. And then Anna had made things even worse for herself by choosing to live alone, with no companionship but an animal.

"God, please help the professor."

She pulled out the box of books under the bed and dug around until she found Gregory's journal. Here was another individual who'd shut himself off from almost everyone. He'd probably died alone. Maybe Anna should read his journal entries.

On second thought, the journal was a fairly depressing read. She placed it back in the box.

She would, however, bring Gregory's Bible the next time she went to Anna's house. She hadn't seen one anywhere on the professor's shelves.

Two days later, Beau was outside when she came over the ridge toward Anna's house. The dog practically knocked her over in his excitement.

"Okay, Beau, I k-know, it's time for your walk." Beau danced in circles around her as she walked up the path to the front door. "I'll just get your leash."

She rang the doorbell and waited patiently for Anna to open the door. When the professor did finally answer the door, her face set in a glum mask. "Come on in, Ruth. Where have you been? I thought you'd be here yesterday."

"Oh, I-I'm sorry, Anna. I thought you wanted me to come every other day. I can come every day if you-you want me to."

The old woman shuffled down the hall. Anna returned to her big, overstuffed chair and book and slid down onto the soft cushions. "It doesn't matter. I forgot that you wouldn't be coming until today. I guess my mind's a little muddled." She picked up her book and ignored Ruth.

Ruth waited. Would Anna soften? Probably not. All right, maybe after she took Beau for a walk, Anna would be ready to talk. She turned and headed for the front door.

"I'll be back in an h-hour, Anna." She laid the Bible on the hall table and picked up Beau's leash. As she walked the dog down the county road, she saw many neighbors out cleaning their yards after a wet and snowy winter. More than one watched her curiously as she passed by. The morning was swiftly turning into a bright, beautiful day and her heart delighted in the budding trees, new grass and spring flowers.

When she returned, the house was quiet. She came into the living room and found Anna asleep in her chair. Beau lay down at the woman's feet, and Ruth covered her with a blanket. She tiptoed into the kitchen to prepare lunch.

When it was ready, she returned with a tray, and leaned over to gently nudge Anna's hand. "Time to wake up and have some lunch, Anna."

The woman stirred and opened her eyes. "You're already back?"

Ruth laughed. "I was gone over an hour. It's past noon. After lunch, if-if you're feeling up to it, you should get outside. You wouldn't believe h-how gorgeous it is today." She set the tray on the professor's lap.

"I'm not hungry," the old woman grumbled.

"Well, you should be. Are you feeling all right?" She examined Anna's face. "Y-you don't usually turn your nose up at a roast beef sandwich with all the fixins.'"

"Where's your lunch, Ruth?"

"Oh, I had mine while you were s-sleeping. Now, come on, y-you need to eat or you'll get even skinnier, if that's possible."

Anna reluctantly picked up the sandwich and took a bite.

"Good, isn't it? Take another bite."

When the professor finished her sandwich, Ruth leaned closer. "It seems to me that you're depressed today. N-now don't try to tell me that I don't understand depression because I've h-had my own struggles with the demon. And some things I-I know about it are that, number one, it's better n-not to be alone; two, it's better to-to get involved with other people and; three, y-you'll feel better if you can get outside, feel the s-sunshine and move about a bit."

Anna opened her mouth to protest but Ruth held up her hand. "Come on. Let me h-help you get up. Just look outside and see how beautiful it is."

She helped the professor out the sliding glass door and they looked down at the green tree-filled yard. "Look, Anna, over there. See the two deer down the hill? Even they seem to realize it-it's a beautiful day."

Ruth brought out a pitcher of lemonade and they sat and enjoyed the sunshine.

"You know," Anna said, "when you didn't show up yesterday I started thinking that maybe you were getting tired of me. I couldn't get it out of my mind."

"But Anna, it w-wasn't my day to come over, remember?"

"I know, but I forgot that. And I kept hearing my daughter's voice, 'Mother, I just need some space. Maybe I'll be back in a couple months.' But she never came back."

"Well, I'm here and I have no plans to leave. You're my friend. And even if I do l-leave eventually, I won't ever stop being your friend."

Anna put her glass down. "I've been thinking about our arrangement ... you know, about your walking the dog and our guitar lessons. Don't you think it'd be much easier if you didn't have to keep coming from your place to my house? You could get a lot more practicing done and Beau would have someone to play with every day. There's that spare bedroom and it's getting pretty clear to me that Greta isn't going to be sleeping in it any time soon."

The professor kept her eyes down, and her thin, old hands fidgeted in her lap.

"I'd love that." Ruth smiled so wide her cheeks hurt. "You don't know how lonesome it's been in my little place."

Anna's eyes filled with tears. "You don't know how lonesome it's been in my *big* place."

After more weeks of daily lessons and dog-walking, Ruth

grew close to the older woman. She even shared some of her struggles, like her memory issues. But she kept the terrifying details of her imprisonment with Dade and Mama a secret

But Dade's threat to kill her loved ones weighed on her mind. Maybe she should return to the hidden cabin and not put Anna at risk by spending so much time in her home. The awful dream with Dade and the lovely lady with the dark hair started up again. Ruth jolted awake to the blast of a rifle shot. She sat up in bed and fought to catch her breath. This time the dark-haired woman, lying on the sidewalk in a pool of blood had been replaced by Anna. Ruth got up and paced down the hall and into the living room. The house was silent except for the ticking of the mantel clock. She started when Beau's cold nose contacted her hand.

"It's okay, Beau. Just making sure everything's all right." The dog followed her as she checked all the locks on the doors and windows. Then she padded back down the hallway and peeked into Anna's room.

It took her a long time to go back to sleep. Every time she closed her eyes she saw Dade standing over her, smiling his arrogant, toothy smile. She switched on the light, reached for her Bible and read:

> *Saul and the Israelites assembled and camped*
> *in the Valley of Elah and drew up their battle*
> *line to meet the Philistines....*
> *A champion named Goliath who was from*
> *Gath, came out of the Philistine camp. His*
> *height was six cubits and a span....*
> *And David said to Saul ... "The Lord who*
> *rescued me from the paw of the lion and the*
> *paw of the bear will rescue me from the hand of*
> *this Philistine."*

And the Philistine cursed David
in the name of his gods.
David said, "All those gathered here will know
that it is not by sword or spear that the Lord
saves; for the battle is the Lord's ..."
As the Philistine moved closer to attack him,
David ran quickly toward the battle line to
meet him. Reaching into his bag and taking out
a stone, he slung it and struck the Philistine on
the forehead. The stone sank into his forehead,
and he fell facedown on the ground. So, David
triumphed over the Philistine with a sling and a
stone; without a sword in his hand he struck
down the Philistine and killed him.[6]

Ruth reread David's words: "All those gathered here will know that it is not by sword or spear that the Lord saves; for the battle is the Lord's."[7]

"For the battle is the Lord's." She repeated the sentence over and over until her heart and mind calmed. Then sleep overtook her.

Sitting in her big leather chair one morning, Anna interrupted Ruth's practice by announcing. "You know, you really should be thinking about college eventually."

Ruth stared at the professor. It was the second or third time she'd brought up the college subject. "Anna, I don't know if I could handle college. My speech and—

"Oh, Ruth, it's not nearly as bad as you think it is. And you've already got such a fine musical background, and such talent."

Ruth rubbed her scar and looked down. "I don't know." With

her speech, wouldn't everyone laugh at her?

"Just think about it, Ruth. There are a lot of schools in the state that would love to have you. Believe me, I know. Northmont College is a private college with a great music program. It isn't too far away and it would be a great place for you. And as for money, I'm sure you could get a really good scholarship, and ... well ... I could help with some of the cost, too."

Ruth's eyes widened. "Y-you'd do that for me?" Her eyes filled with tears and she looked down at the piano keys. How could she go to school when she didn't even know her own identity? Wouldn't a college have to have some kind of information about her? She didn't even know her real name or where she'd come from. That wasn't something she could make up.

The only thing she owned from her past was the backpack. Was there anything in it that could help her remember? She hadn't touched it since that horrible day when she threw the dress down the hill. Maybe just holding it or going through it again would bring something back.

She looked up. Anna was watching her with a hopeful tilt of her gray head.

"Do you really think I could handle college?"

Anna snorted. "Of course."

The woman's harsh and bitter demeanor had softened in the past few weeks. Was this all Anna had needed: someone to love who'd respond in kind? That the professor was willing to pay for her education astonished and humbled her.

But before she could take Anna up on her generous offer, she'd have to start remembering more than just bits and pieces of her past. Who were the people in her snapshot memories? The dark-haired woman with the blue eyes? The sweet-faced man with hair as pale as her own? Who were the young people going in and out of those big brick buildings?

Was the answer hidden somewhere in the backpack? The sooner she started remembering, the sooner she and Anna could start looking into college.

Dade retraced the old path where he'd hunted Ruth in the vain hope that he'd find some previously missed clue. Winter storms and seven months' time had washed away most of the clues. When he reached the spot on the hillside where he'd lost her trail in the fall, he stopped. She probably wouldn't have kept climbing this hill. If she'd been around here during that snowstorm she would have had to look for shelter.

He scanned the area. Maybe he should look further west. He hiked back down the hill, crossed several steep ridges and gullies until he reached the lake. He trudged along the northern shore until he encountered a boggy section. The mud forced him to turn uphill. He hiked up the spine of a wooded ridge and stopped when the ground leveled. The area provided an excellent view of the lake and the surrounding land. He found evidence of a camp. He walked about the area and read the signs: a fire pit partially obliterated and a flat patch where rocks, sticks and pinecones had been removed for a tent. Poking through the ashes of the fire pit he found bits of charred fish bones, little else.

He left the camp and headed further west. It was only by luck that he found her trail. He'd stopped to sit on a fallen log so he could remove a pebble from his boot. When he'd swung his legs over the log to stand up he spied the path uphill a few feet. He crouched to examine the many boot prints, traced the outline. There was no variation of pattern or size. All made by the same person. Many of the tracks were fresh and deep, owing to the rains.

He wasn't angry anymore. If she repented, he would take her back. He would have taken her back months ago, but with more force. Now, all he wanted … No, he couldn't think about that now. He needed to put all his mind into tracking.

He straightened and followed the path west until it reached the switchbacks above the lake. He'd explore the area to the west, then he could come back to this spot and follow the tracks the other direction.

The tracks couldn't have been anyone's but Ruth's. Ruth couldn't have made it this far when he was hunting her seven months earlier. The snow would have stopped her just as it had stopped him. She had to have holed up somewhere back east in the woods.

He followed the prints westward and uphill until he glimpsed a house. The tracks lead directly to it. *Careful now.* He approached but stayed hidden behind the trees.

So, all along someone had been hiding Ruth. He recognized the house—it looked different from this viewpoint—and his stomach burned to think that he'd done some carpentry work in another house within view of it only recently. Ruth could have been looking out the window watching him and laughing. He gripped his rifle. He should walk right up to the house and demand that they hand over his wife.

The front door opened and a big black dog bounded out. An old woman, leaning on a walker crept down the front walk while the dog danced around her. Dade crouched behind cover and watched. The woman shuffled down her driveway to the mailbox, then stopped to peruse her mail. He watched impatiently as the woman, followed closely by the dog, inched her way back to the house.

He retreated down the path, staying out of view. The old woman certainly didn't seem like the kind of person who'd be harboring a runaway. But Ruth's tracks led right to the house. What to make of it? What kind of protection would a frail old woman be for Ruth? No, there had to be some other explanation. Maybe Ruth went there to help the woman. After all, Ruth would need money to live on. It could be that the old woman, being a cripple, was paying her to clean and cook or something.

He thought better of his angry impulse to ring the front doorbell. Anyway, the tracks also led east, and if Ruth lived with the cripple, why would she need to keep going back into the forest?

He turned around. Now that he had discovered the path, it was much easier to travel the distance of the lake. The trail made use of level ground, skirting ravines, always providing the best view of the valley. Evidently, the maker of the boot prints valued high and hidden vantage points. The girl showed evidence of real thinking and planning. Of course, she would have known that he'd be searching for her. He had told her that he wouldn't ever give up hunting her if she were to try to run away.

It hadn't occurred to him that Ruth might possess intelligence. After all, not only was she a woman—and young at that—but she was brain-damaged. If she couldn't talk, she must also be incapable of rational thought. Or so he'd thought.

Shortly after he passed the lake's eastern border he met the little stream as it tumbled down the hillside, glistening in the sunlight. Recent snowmelt had created cascades of shimmering, iridescent bridal veils, spraying the surrounding rocks and earth. The footing was treacherous. He searched until he found a safe place to cross, and leaped the distance. He took a step and halted. Something caught his eye, something that didn't fit in the wild landscape, something shiny. He bent over the object to get a better look. He plucked a brass button from the dirt. Along with the button came the garment it was attached to. He held it up and examined it. Dirty and ripped. But he had no difficulty identifying the dress that had once covered Ruth's form. He closed his eyes and breathed deeply. Ruth's sweet face filled his mind. His gut, lungs, heart, muscles stirred for action. He looked at the sky and raised his hands. *God, you have rewarded me for my faithfulness to my marriage vows.*

He shook the dirt and debris from the dress. Stuffing it into his jacket, he started back up the hill to find the trail again.

He dodged rocks, undergrowth and trees. The tracks led between two bushy-covered mounds of earth and then … a cabin. His breath caught. He backed up quickly and crouched behind the smaller mound. He stared at the door and window. Ruth might suddenly appear. Minutes passed. Nothing. He grew impatient. He crept around the mound, and approached the cabin from the side. He peeked through the window. The room was dark. No movement. He turned the door handle and stepped in. The cabin seemed in order, nothing lying about that would have identified the cabin's occupant. Maybe he'd made a mistake. Then he saw the backpack. He lifted it, opened the flap, and rummaged through its contents. He pulled out the handmade soap and recognized his fishing lures and hooks. At the bottom, carefully wrapped in cloth, he uncovered a piece of wood that had been skillfully carved into the shape of a woman's head and neck. Delicate face, large eyes. Long wooden tresses. Just below the jaw, the artist had carved his name. Dade's lip curled. Jesse. The bust snapped in two in his grip. He wrapped up the pieces and thrust them into the pack, then threw it back into the cabin corner next to the door.

He stationed himself by the window to wait for Ruth. Shadows darkened the area in front of the cabin. Still, no Ruth. She would come. She had to. He'd wait all night. And the next day, and the next day, if needed. He dropped Ruth's dress on the floor by the bed, and hung his jacket on a hook.

He woke just as the first glimmer of dawn filtered through the small window above the bed. He had lit no lamp the night before nor used the wood-burning stove. Nothing to alert the girl to his presence.

He waited most of the morning, pacing about the cabin floor, often checking the front window. Where was she? More than once he stepped out and walked down the path, hoping to see her coming home. The more impatient he grew, the more his anger flared. The girl deserved a good fright when she finally did return. Something to scare her into submission.

The dress. Why had she dumped it on the hill? Why was it all cut up? "Oh, Ruth." He chuckled. "You must have hated this ugly dress. Well, I've got more dresses waiting for you back home."

He went back inside, lifted the mangled dress from the floor, and shook it to straighten out the wrinkles. "This'll make a nice calling card for you, Ruth."

Chapter Twenty-Three

*"The Lord is my light and my salvation—
whom shall I fear?
The Lord is the stronghold of my life—
of whom shall I be afraid?
When the wicked advance against me to devour me,
it is my enemies and my foes
who will stumble and fall."
Psalm 27:1-2*

Ruth came into the living room, carrying her jacket. "Anna, w-would you mind if I went back to my place? I need to get some of my belongings. I-I won't be gone for more than two or three hours."

The professor looked up from her stack of newspapers. "You go right ahead. I've got a couple weeks' worth of newspapers to catch up on. Do you want to take Beau?"

"Oh, no thanks. I'll be fine. Just a quick there-and-back trip."

"All right, Ruth, take your time."

Dade was too restless to stay in the cabin any longer. He positioned himself uphill from it and settled himself. He listened and watched for an hour. Maybe it would be better to go back inside her little hideout. Then he heard the snap of a twig and, in another moment, a soft footfall. Ruth. His heart pounded. It had been seven long months since he'd laid eyes on the girl. She approached the cabin, an expression of joy lighting her beautiful face. She hummed a tune as she stepped onto the porch. The cabin door opened, then closed with a click. Noiselessly, he scrambled down the hill and into the clearing. He positioned himself a few yards from the front porch and held his rifle at belt-line.

Anna planned to begin with the oldest issue of the *Monroe Times*—dated two weeks earlier—and move forward from there. She loved the local news almost as much as the big national newspapers. She plowed through the two-week old Sunday *Monroe Times*, then took a break from reading long enough to hobble into the kitchen to fix herself a hot mug of tea. She returned to her comfortable leather chair in the living room, seated herself and bent over to retrieve the next old newspaper. She put on her reading glasses, then stared at the front-page article: "New Lead in Disappearance of Oregon Woman." She squinted at the photo, not wanting to believe what her eyes told her. Anna read the article. Her eyes riveted to one paragraph. "A local handyman, John "Buzz"

Fisher, is considered a person of interest in Ellingsen's disappearance. The man stated that he had picked up a hitchhiker on or around July 6th who matched Haven Ellingsen's description, but that he had let her out of his truck fifteen miles west of Lily along Highway 2."

Anna reread the article, then looked again at the pretty, blonde woman in the photo.

"Oh Ruth, Ruth, why does it have to be you?" she moaned. For a second, and only a second, she wondered what would happen if she just kept silent about Ruth. Then she reached for the telephone.

Ruth entered the cabin with a buoyant step. She shut the door, lifted the backpack from its dark corner behind the door and turned to set it on the kitchen table. She opened the pack, but a faint, disturbing odor stopped her. Antiseptic. Familiar, somehow. Almost like—

She tried to swallow. But her throat constricted as if by an invisible noose, tightened by cruel hands.

Look. But she didn't want to.

You have to look. The spasm in her neck made it hard to turn her head. But she needed to focus. She turned slowly and squinted through a beam of light that bisected the interior of the cabin. *What is that?* On her bed. A blue thing.

It couldn't be. But a closer look confirmed it. The horrible denim dress, filthy and mutilated, lay draped over her pillow. Like a punch to the gut, her vision funneled and her knees started to buckle. She tried to breathe.

Oh, God, no! He's found me. Please help me. Get away, get away now. She dashed to the door and flung it open. *Run, oh, run for your life!*

She made it as far as the porch before she saw him.

An expression of smug triumph played across Dade's lean, bearded face. "Time to come back home where you belong, Ruth," he drawled.

She gripped the door jamb for support. "I-I don't belong with you. I never will."

Dade's eyebrows arched. "So, the dummy can talk." His expression darkened and his voice took on that hard quality that had so effectively terrified her back in the dark cabin. "You belong anywhere I say you belong, girl."

Dade watched her. "So, what's it going to be, Ruth?" His lips curved into that familiar and horrible toothy smile.

For a slim second, Dade and his gun disappeared and another image filled her mind.

"What happened that night after your piano concert?" Jennie asked, her face filled with compassion.

I closed my eyes and saw it all again. "After the concert, my mom and I went out to celebrate with friends. I parked less than a block from the restaurant. We got out of the car. A tall man holding a rifle came out of nowhere. For a second that's all I saw. It didn't seem real. I know it's strange, but I thought, this is weird. On TV, they always mug you with a handgun. Then he pointed the rifle right at us."

"I can still see him, holding that rifle, looking so wild and mean. That night, I felt helpless. I just stood there, behind my mom. I should have done something."

Jennie spoke gently. "What could you have done? The man was holding a rifle."

"I don't know. But later I promised myself I'd never feel so small and helpless again."

Dade's sneering smile seemed frozen on his lips. Oh, how she wanted to claw that toothy grin off his face.

"I'm waiting." His tone grew ominous. "What's it going to be? You can make this easy or hard. Either way, I win."

Dade took a step toward her.

"The man with the rifle said, 'Hand over your purse, lady.'

My mom hesitated.

Then he said, 'You can make this easy or hard.' He raised the rifle to his shoulder.

Mom stood tall. She tried to block the man from seeing me. But the man with the rifle was way taller. He saw right over her shoulder.

'Well, well, what do we have here? Not one pretty lady, but two pretty ladies.'

Mom threw her arm out. 'Leave my daughter alone!' She lunged toward him.

The man jerked back and pulled the trigger.

Mom crumpled to the pavement.

'Mom!' I threw myself on top of her. 'No!' I screamed and screamed and screamed. 'No! No!'"

Ruth slid her hand behind the doorframe. *Lord, help me.*

She touched and recognized the basket containing her hunting rocks. She reached in, fingered one of the rocks and gripped it. *The battle is the Lord's.*

"I don't know why you've come for me." Her voice sounded like steel in her own ears. "I'm not ever going to go back with you."

"I'd be a pretty poor husband if I just let my wife walk away without a fight. Remember what I told you? Anyone tries to help you get away from me ... your father, that old lady. If you care about them ..." Dade's eyes narrowed. He took another step toward her.

"Stop," she shouted. "Don't come any closer."

Dade paused and his strange eyes fixed on her like a cougar preparing to pounce.

"I don't want to hurt you." She raised the rock, but kept it hidden behind the wall.

He snorted, incredulous, then advanced, rifle raised to his shoulder.

"No!" Her first rock struck his trigger hand. Dade's rifle jerked sideward and a roar of pain burst from his lips.

"No!" The second rock struck him in the shoulder with enough force to make him stagger back a step. The rifle clattered to the ground. Dade clutched his shoulder and bared his teeth like a rabid animal. He moved to retrieve his rifle.

"No!" The third stone, rocketing with deadly aim, hit him in the knee with bone-crunching force. The big man tottered, then crumpled in agony. Ruth jumped off the porch and approached.

Arm raised, she aimed the fourth rock at his head.

Dade lay helpless. He threw his arms up to shield his face.

Her arm, poised with its weapon, trembled. *Would God judge me if I killed Dade?* No court would. Self-defense. One well-aimed rock and she could be free of the man forever.

The battle is the Lord's.

The rock spun expertly from her hand. It struck the ground an inch from Dade's forehead.

"No," she said with deadly calm. Then she marched around Dade and picked up his rifle.

"You devil," he cursed through clenched teeth. He half raised his body. "Come here," he roared. In spite of his agony, he threw himself backward and lunged for her legs.

Ruth yelled and jumped clear. "Leave me alone." The authority in her voice surprised her. "Stop following me. I don't ever want to see you again. Y-you're evil."

She carried the rifle to the edge of the clearing. Gripping it, she swung it with all her strength against a tree trunk. *Crack.* The sound echoed throughout the valley like an ax through dead wood. Snatching the mangled weapon, she threw it down the hill. As she turned to run she caught one last glimpse of Dade lying on the ground, his face contorted in pain and malice and his one good arm outstretched toward her.

"It'll never be over, Ruth," he snarled through gritted teeth.

Then she was gone, running, running till her muscles burned and her lungs ached. But this run was like no other she'd done in her beautiful forest. No joy in her heart, no exulting in the crisp fragrant air and warm sunlight. Heedless of the chatter of the squirrel overhead or the call of the jay, she ran down the path she'd created over the past seven months. She did not stop to look back, but her ears were tuned for any sound of pursuit. None came.

Chapter Twenty-Four

The LORD will watch over your coming and going
both now and forevermore.
Psalm 121:8

Ruth passed the lake, not even aware of it. Scrambling up the steep switchbacks above the western shore of the lake, her breath came in ragged gasps. At last she reached level ground. Her chest heaved from the exertion of traversing three steep and rugged miles. A light from Anna's house pierced the murk of moss-covered cedars and dense ferns. After covering another hundred yards she saw a black vehicle parked in the driveway.

"Anna, Anna!" She made herself run again.

Had Dade found Anna and hurt her? "Please be okay, Anna. I need you to be okay. Not just for your sake, but for me, too."

"Oh Lord, he knows where I am. Will he ever stop coming after me?"

She trotted around the corner of the house, past the squad car. No one was sitting in it. The front door opened. Anna and a police officer stood framed in the doorway. The man supported Anna's arm, but when she caught sight of Ruth, she held her arms out.

"Anna, are-are you okay? I saw the p-police car and I—"

"Don't worry about me. You're … you're that—oh, my poor girl!" Anna wailed as she clung to her. "Why didn't you tell me? Why didn't you let me help you?" Anna choked up.

"Ma'am," the police officer said, "let's bring her into the house." He took Anna's arm, and Ruth followed them into the living room. After Anna was seated, Ruth noticed a woman sitting in a chair with a black briefcase resting on her lap.

"This is Detective Romerez," the police officer said. "She's been in charge of your case since last summer. Don't be afraid. She just wants to ask you some questions."

Ruth trembled. "My case? Did I do something wrong?"

"No, honey," Anna said, her voice still shaking with emotion. "The police are here to help you."

Detective Romerez said, "Here, please sit down." She indicated toward a chair next to hers.

Romerez pulled a file out of her briefcase and opened it. She flipped through some pages before lifting a photograph from the file. She looked at the photo and then at Ruth. Nodding, she handed the photo to the police officer.

"Ruth" the detective said, "Mrs. Jaeger tells me that you've been having some problems with your memory. Please take a look at this photograph."

The police officer handed the photo to her.

"This was taken a couple of years ago," Romerez said. "It's your college ID photo. Your real name is Haven Ellingsen and up until last summer you were living with your father just outside Beaverton, Oregon."

She stared hard at her photograph. "My name is Haven?" She looked up at Anna, who started to cry again.

The detective touched her shoulder. "We've been looking for

you for a long time. Can you tell me where you've been?"

Haven pictured Dade, lying on the ground and shuddered.

Romerez held up another photo. "Do you know this man? His name is John Fischer. Most people call him Buzz. He says you were hitchhiking last July and he gave you a ride."

"No, I-I don't recognize him."

"He doesn't look familiar?"

Haven shook her head. "I may have accepted a ride from him—my memory isn't clear—but what does this Buzz guy have to do with me?"

Detective Romerez exchanged glances with the police officer. "I guess this man isn't part of our investigation." She stuffed the man's photo back into her case. "Haven, please think about the last nine months. Can you tell me where you've been?"

"I-I've been ... out there." She waved her arm in a wide arc.

"Where, Haven? Can you be more specific?"

"I've been l-l-living in a cabin east of that lake out th-there. Is that w-what this is about? I didn't mean trespass, I mean, t-to trespass. But I was lost and ... and I found it and there w-was nobody l-l-living there."

The detective turned to the professor. "Ma'am, we'll be making some phone calls in a minute."

She turned back to Haven. "Just one more question. We know from your conversations with the Life Ventures people in Lily and our own investigations that you were trying to get to see your father when he was in the hospital in Monroe last July. Do you remember that? And do you remember where you were before that time?"

Haven jerked forward and gripped her photo. "My father?" She looked at the professor again, then the detective. "Do you know where I was? Are you here to tell me about myself?"

The detective put her hand on Haven's and focused on the scar at her temple. "We're sure going to do all we can."

"We'd like to put you in touch with your father." Detective Romerez took out her cell phone.

"But w-what do I say? What do I call him? I-I don't even remember what he looks like."

"You just say hello and let him hear your voice. I'm sure he'll take it from there." The detective dialed the phone number, then listened to it ring. Someone must have answered, because she said, "This is Detective Romerez from the Monroe Police Department in Washington State. May I speak to Mr. Guy Ellingsen?"

Whoever answered must have gone away from the phone. Romerez turned to Haven and smiled reassuringly. "Just call him Dad."

A man's voice answered.

"Hello, Mr. Ellingsen, Detective Romerez from the Monroe Police. We have great news for you. We've found your daughter and she's sitting right here. But before I let you speak to her I should let you know that she seems to have suffered some memory loss. So just say hello to her and hold off with any questions until you actually see her."

The detective offered the phone to Haven.

"Dad?" She said in a small, trembling voice.

"Baby?" The man's voice sounded nearly strangled with emotion. "Is that you? Are you all right?" He started to weep. "I knew you were okay. I knew God would take care of you. I'm coming up right now. Don't you go anywhere till I get up there, okay?"

"Okay, Dad." The voice of her father had not aroused any

memories. She handed the phone back to the detective, then sat down next to Anna while the woman finished her conversation with her father.

"Anna? Do you th-think that really was my father on the phone? I mean, how would I know?"

"Oh Ruth, I mean, Haven. Of course, it's your father. The police have all sorts of information on you and your family."

"But I'm scared. What if he-he sees me and doesn't l-like me? What if I went missing because we had a fight?"

"Haven, even if you weren't on the best terms with your father a while back, now's your chance to square things with him. And also, if he's had the police searching for you all this time, he must really love you and want you back."

Haven pressed her shoulder against Anna's. "C-can I stay with you while we wait? I-I really don't want to go to the police station. Would you-you mind if I met my father right h-here with you beside me?"

The professor put her arms around her. "I'm not going to leave you. You don't have to go anywhere you don't want to go."

When Guy walked into Anna Jaeger's living room, Haven stared at him with a confused and blank stare. Something like a vise wrapped around his heart and squeezed hard. She did not recognize him. But he could not resist gathering her into his arms tenderly, weeping with relief and joy. He pulled back for a moment to take her in; Haven was back, alive and well. He stifled a surprised gasp at the sight of the scar. Then, smoothing back her hair, he gently kissed the ragged scar and hugged her tightly again.

By the time the police left it was late in the evening. Haven made up a bed for her father in the office. But she did not sleep well. When she woke in the middle of the night, she was startled to see a large lump on the floor just outside her open bedroom door. When she got up to investigate she found her father lying there, wrapped in a blanket.

The next morning, she groaned in dismay to see that Anna's driveway had been taken over by news vans and reporters, waiting eagerly for the story that would make national headlines: "Woman, missing since July, found alive and well, living in wilderness."

The professor put her frail hands on her shoulders. "They're not going to get in here if I have anything to say about it," she whispered fiercely. She pulled all the blinds shut and refused to answer the doorbell.

Her father came into the kitchen, rubbing his tired eyes. "What's all the noise?'

"Oh, the newshounds are out there waiting to get a good story. They've got your car hemmed in and I've a feeling you're not going to get out of here easily."

Dad huffed. "Oh, is that so? Well, I can fix that." He pulled his cell phone out of his pocket and dialed the police.

The professor prepared breakfast. Haven went back into her bedroom and dressed hurriedly, then rejoined Anna and her father in the kitchen. She lifted one shutter and peeked out the window. The reporters weren't budging.

Her father grimaced. "Don't worry, Haven. I'm not going to let them get near you."

"But w-we're going to have to walk through them to get to the car. I-I wouldn't know what to say to them."

"Then don't say anything. Just let me talk." He stared at the front door. "But I'm going to have to give them some information. We don't want them making up a story. Don't worry. I won't tell them much, just that you've lost your memory due to an injury. We won't go outside until the police arrive."

Anna stood up and leaned on her walker. "Here, let's go pack your things."

In the guestroom, Haven sat down on the bed, shaking her head at the wonder of the past twenty-four hours. "I'm going to miss you so much, Anna. It-it doesn't even seem real that I'm about to go home with a father I can't even remember. Y-you're all I know." She jumped up and threw her arms around the professor.

"Now, now," Anna soothed. "Don't go getting all emotional on me. You know you're going where you belong. And your father loves you very much. Besides, we'll be seeing each other a lot. Remember we talked about Northmont College? I've already spoken to some associates there. And it's not even very far away. Why, you could come and visit me on the weekends."

Haven released Anna. "I don't have too m-much to pack, just a few bits of clothes."

"Hmm." The professor's eyes held a mischievous glint. "I think there's something in the closet that you may have forgotten. Open up the left side."

Haven went over to the closet and slid the door open. "Your guitar. Oh, Anna, I c-can't take it. It's yours."

"Please, I want you to take it. You'll need it when you get to college. Besides, I have my other two guitars and they suit me just fine."

"All right, I'll take it. But only on one condition, th-that when I do go to Northmont, you'll come hear me when I play. Deal?"

"Deal."

Guy did not let the reporters near Haven. As he addressed the media on the steps just outside the professor's house, he was brief and to the point: his daughter had suffered memory difficulties due to an injury and had survived in the wilderness for nine months living in an abandoned cabin. No, he did not know how she had survived for so long all by herself. That information would come later. Yes, he and his daughter were looking forward to returning to a normal life and he was confident of Haven's eventual full recovery. No, he would not care to address any rumors or speculations about how his daughter was injured. No, he would not allow any questions for Haven at this time.

The picture in the local newspaper the next morning showed a young woman with her face hidden in her father's chest being firmly escorted through a sea of reporters.

Dade ripped out the page containing the newspaper article, folded it and stuffed it into his wallet. "Difficulties with memory."

Well, she wouldn't have any trouble remembering him, or the events in his home. But she hadn't told the police anything about him yet. Maybe that would come later. Ruth had seen enough of his tracking and shooting skills to know he could easily snuff out her father or the old lady any time he wanted.

He had hobbled back to his truck parked along the county road, and treated his injured knee and broken thumb as best he could. He'd spent two uncomfortable nights, camped out in the cab of his truck, wondering what to do. But now, standing outside Hayfork's only diner, a few miles from Monroe, he wondered if he should chance going back to his place. They could already be looking for him, depending on what Ruth told the police. Of course, it was her word against his. He could always say that the girl wanted to come with him. But if she ever starting remembering how she got that scar, he might be in trouble. But then, he wasn't the one who had injured her. It was that stupid, old barren sow of his.

And what would he say about marrying the girl? Well, he and Brenda weren't really married, not the way most people would think of as legally married. They just kind of shacked up together for such a long time—and with those two raven-haired children she'd adopted—that anyone would have just assumed they were married. And, anyway, there were lots of places in the country where a man had more than one wife and the local government just winked at the practice. And Ruth had never objected to the marriage. She could have said no. She went along with it. Yes, she had. He had witnesses to that. Besides, he hadn't touched her.

If the police questioned his family, they wouldn't talk. Even Jesse wouldn't talk. He'd make sure of that.

He'd have to keep reading the papers. She wouldn't be home with her father for long. The news article mentioned the girl's plan to continue her music studies at college. And college students roamed all over campus alone and unwatched. Late nights at the library. Lonely parking lots. There'd be lots of opportunities in the future to reclaim his wayward Ruth.

Epilogue

One morning in the middle of summer, three months after her rescue, Haven woke and, with her eyes still closed, remembered. It did not all come back, but when she opened her eyes, her bedroom held a sense of history. Once her room had been done all in little-girl pink, but she and her mother had redone the room in a more mature pale blue. Her mother had been beautiful, with dark hair. And she remembered that the color of her mother's eyes was a deep, deep blue.

The aroma of coffee wafted into her room. Haven smiled as she slipped on her robe and slippers and hurried down to the kitchen.

"Morning." Her father finished pouring water into the coffee maker, and turned to face her. "Pancakes or waffles?"

Haven chuckled. The waffle maker sat on the kitchen counter, already plugged in. "Definitely waffles." She opened the pantry door and pulled out a canister of flour, along with the baking powder, and salt.

Dad brought out the eggs, milk, and butter.

"You know, this isn't the healthiest meal. I hope you haven't been fixing waffles every morning while I've been away."

"Only on weekends, sweetheart. Believe it or not, your old dad is taking care of his health."

And she needed to look out for his health, too. Not by nagging him about eating too many waffles, but by keeping her mouth shut about Dade.

She would do anything to protect her dad, and Aunt Joy and Anna. A man with a rifle had murdered her mother, and she aimed to make sure Dad didn't suffer the same fate.

Her dad hummed an upbeat tune as he set two mugs on the counter. *He's so happy to have me back. How can I say, "Dad, I have a dark secret, but if I tell you, Dade will kill you? And me. But don't worry. The police probably wouldn't believe me, anyway. Because I'm still recovering from Post-Traumatic Stress Disorder. I watched my mom get shot to death and now they'll say I'm suffering flashbacks, and falsely accusing Dade. And, oh yeah, I got this big bump on my head so I can't talk well, and my memory is spotty, at best. And any accusation I make can be knocked down by Dade and Mama. And their kids won't talk, either."*

That same morning, Haven and her father drove up to Anna's for a guitar lesson. He had insisted that any time she traveled to the professor's house he would accompany her. She did not argue. It wasn't too hard to imagine how he might worry about her going off by herself, especially to the very area where she'd disappeared a year earlier.

But this morning, she wouldn't think about the events of the past year. The carefully wrapped package that she'd placed in her music bag added a better kind of excitement to her impending visit. Anna would have something to put on her walls that would be a tangible reminder of Haven's love.

After the lesson, she drew the gift out and presented it to the professor.

"It's something she's been working on for a couple of weeks," Dad said as he sat down next to Haven.

Anna took the package and her eyes seemed to express both delight and unworthiness. She removed the paper and gasped in wonder. The oil painting depicted a young woman being instructed on the guitar by an older woman.

As Anna examined the art, tears filled her eyes. "You know, last Christmas I bought a Christmas tree, and I spent days decorating it with all my old ornaments. Some of them had been made by Greta, and I put them on the tree wishing, somehow, that she'd come and see me for Christmas. Of course, she never did. By Christmas night, I was feeling so lonely and depressed that I actually prayed.

"Yes, I know, you're surprised. But I said, 'God, if you're really out there, would you send my daughter so I can feel loved again.'"

Anna paused to trace her fingers around the wood frame. "Then, one morning I was on my way down the driveway to get my newspaper, and I wound up falling down the hill. I lay there shivering and helpless, thinking how God must hate me. I felt someone touch me and when I looked up, I thought an angel was bending over me. You pulled me up that steep hill and somehow got me inside the house and into my bed. And I remembered how I'd been so mean to you and yet you were doing everything you could think of to help me. I felt so ashamed. I thought, isn't that how I always am? I've driven everybody who ever cared for me away. Maybe, if I'm careful, I won't make the same mistake with this lovely young woman who looks so much like my own Greta."

"It took me a while, but I finally realized, after you'd gotten back with your father, how God had answered my prayer last Christmas. He'd sent me a daughter. And this time I wouldn't be too busy to show her how much I love her."

"Oh, Anna," Haven whispered, overcome with tenderness. She leaned over to embrace the professor.

"See you next month. I l-love you, Anna." Haven waved from the passenger side as her father reversed the car out of the long driveway.

The professor leaned with one hand on her walker and waved with the other. "Give me a call when you get home."

"I will. Take care."

They finished backing onto the road, then turned and headed for the main highway.

"Hey, I'm hungry." Dad said.

"Me, too. We stayed so long at Anna's we c-completely forgot to have lunch."

"How about we stop off in Monroe and have an early dinner?"

"That's fine with me, Dad." She settled back into her seat and watched the tall pines whiz by.

In less than half an hour they exited the highway that ran through Monroe and drove into the business center. Dad pulled into a parking lot. "I had breakfast here with Joy last summer when we had that car accident. It's a pretty good café."

It had begun to rain heavily and neither Haven nor her father was dressed for it. They ran inside and settled into a booth, laughing and shaking the rain from their heads. The waitress poured coffee, and they ordered sandwiches.

Haven studied her place-setting. All the things she wanted to tell her father crowded into the front of her mind, each thought begging to be first. But she wouldn't, no, she couldn't tell him about Dade. Better to leave all that horrible stuff in the past. It wasn't only Dad's physical protection she needed to think about. If people knew his daughter had lived with a crazy man in a cabin for three months, they'd wonder what took place behind those four walls. She couldn't live with that speculation and suspicion. And pressing charges against Dade would drag her entire family through the humiliating stages of a court case with the media publishing every awful detail.

But she'd beaten Dade. With God's help, she'd defeated her giant with stones, just like David had defeated Goliath. Dade now knew that she was no longer a weak, frightened, speechless victim. And he'd have to wonder if she'd told her father or the authorities about him. Hopefully, that doubt would keep him from pursuing her any more.

After all her father had gone through this past year, she couldn't load any more burdens on him.

She sat up straight, took a deep breath, and exhaled as if she could hurl thoughts of Dade and Mama like a javelin. Hurl it into space and on into oblivion. She forced a smile. "Dad, you probably know that one of the reasons I'm excited about Northmont College has to do with Anna."

"How so?"

"Well, she's kind of—I hope you don't take this wrong—but she's become s-sort of a mother for me." Haven studied her father's face for any trace of jealousy. "I mean, of course, I'm an adult, but even a grown woman still cherishes that mother-daughter kind of relationship."

Dad waved his hand to stop her. "You don't have to explain. Do you think it would disturb me that you love Anna, and enjoy her companionship?"

"Well, no, b-but I was afraid that you'd think that I'd replaced Mom. But now that I remember Mom, th-there's no way that anyone could ever c-compete with her memory."

"I know that. You must have been very lonely out there. And Anna is such a good match for you. It's obvious that God put you two together and I'm proud of you for remaining loyal to her even after returning home."

The waitress set their plates on the table and refilled their coffee cups

"It's over now. You're safe." He set his lips in a flat line as if his statement were more of a pronouncement than a conclusion.

She would be safe. Dade was sick, and obsessive, but not crazy enough to imagine he could show up at her father's home and try to snatch her. In a year, maybe two, she'd finish her music degree and become a fine concert pianist. And this whole awful chapter of her life would remain logged in faded ink in dusty old pages, shelved in an ancient, forgotten library.

Her father reached over and gently ran a finger across the red scar on her forehead. Then he pushed his empty plate away and picked up the tab. "Let's go home."

Notes

[1]   Psalm 91:1, 4, 11
[2]   Ramsey, Tea Table Miscellany (1724) "Waly, Waly, Gin Love Be Bonny"
[3]   Psalm 91:1-2, 4-5
[4]   Psalm 118:5-7
[5]   Psalm 139:7-10
[6]   1 Samuel 17:2, 4, 34a, 37, 43, 47-50
[7]   1 Samuel 17:47

**If you enjoyed HAVEN'S FLIGHT,
please consider returning to its
Amazon page and leaving a positive review
with hopefully 5 stars,
for the author!**

From the Author

Dear Reader:

Thank you for reading my story. The idea for **Haven's Flight** was birthed years ago, when an image popped into my mind of a young woman standing in a snowy field, surrounded by dark forest. She was looking nervously over her shoulder as if someone were pursuing her. The image was so emotionally compelling that it stayed in my mind for several days. Eventually, I sketched the girl in the snow on a sheet of artist paper and stuffed it into my desk drawer. But every time I opened my drawer, I saw her. What was her name? Why was she alone, and why was she so frightened?

I wanted to tell her story, but knew I wouldn't be able to do it justice. I wasn't a writer then, just a teenaged girl who loved to read and who stayed awake late at night, lying in my bed, spinning stories to entertain myself.

I had lots of other stories developing in my mind, too. But I was busy studying to be a professional musician, and musicians have very little time to learn how to write novels.

Three decades later, after retiring from teaching and performing, and after my three children grew up and moved out, I felt God's nudging: "Now, write."

Haven's Flight was my first attempt at writing a novel. I laugh when I tell people, "This story has been my writing workbook." I've lost count, but I think the story of **Haven's**

Flight (and its two sequels) went through at least nine or ten versions and as many titles.

What I've learned from writing ***Haven's Flight*** is this: be patient, give yourself time to learn your craft, don't let disappointment stop you, listen to criticism and be teachable. And finally, listen to God. He will guide you if you let Him.

Discussion Questions

1. In the Prologue, Thomas shocks the reader by killing the only person he loves. How did this make you feel about Thomas and why?

2. We meet Haven in the middle of her first day of wilderness exercises as a counselee in the Life Ventures Therapy Program. List several ways a wilderness therapy program might help people who are struggling with traumatic life events?

3. At the Life Ventures camp, Haven suspects someone is stalking her. If you were in her shoes, what would you do? In whom would you confide and what would you share with him or her?

4. Haven's reaction to the news of her father's car accident led her to make an unwise decision to slip out of the hotel during the stormy night. In what ways can you adequately prepare yourself to make wise decisions in the midst of devastating news?

5. Mama is very submissive to Dade. Define *submission* based on Mama's practice. How does that definition of submission in line or not in line with God's definition of submission?

6. If you were a prisoner of Dade and Mama, how would you cope with your situation and their abuse?

7. Mr. Colton twists scripture to control his wife and children. In what environment does scripture-twisting thrive? How do you ensure that you are not twisting scripture to control others or get your own way?

8. Considering that Dade has such control over all the family, explain why it would be difficult for you to trust Jesse to help you escape?

9. Haven's father, Guy, convinced her to register for Life Ventures and may have blamed himself for her disappearance. What advice/counsel would you give him regarding his feelings of guilt?

10. Haven lived alone in Gregory's cabin for several months. What's the longest you have ever lived in complete isolation from another human? What emotions did you experience during your isolation?

11. Selfish and bitter, Professor Anna Jaeger also lives alone. If you became her friend, how might you help her overcome her self-pitying? When your life gets difficult, how can you guard against becoming selfish and bitter?

12. When Haven encounters Colton again, she remembers how small and helpless she felt the night her mother was shot and killed. In what ways does Haven respond that indicates she is no longer the helpless, traumatized victim she was when first met her?

About the Author

Dena Netherton was born and raised in the San Francisco Bay Area. Living in a musical family, she was blessed to study with great piano and voice teachers and given many opportunities to perform both in church settings and professional secular venues.

Although Dena wrestled with whether to study music or to study writing, her relatives counseled her to "live life first, then write about it." Looking back, she's glad she studied, taught, and performed music first until all her three children were grown and out of the house. There's nothing that compares with a life of loving a husband and children, pouring one's life into helping little hands and voices sing praises to their Heavenly Father, linking arms and "doing life together," as her husband likes to say.

Now a retired teacher, she enjoys sitting in her office and imagining her literary characters—usually the musical ones—

jumping up and down, using pillow fights, while squealing, "Me! Write about me next!"

Recently, a new adventure has called Dena and her husband, Bruce, from the Colorado Rockies to the wet and misty forests along the San Juan Islands in Washington State. So, don't be surprised if the towns in her novels bear some resemblance to actual towns around Seattle.

Dena's biggest prayer as a writer is that God speaks a word of comfort or encouragement to you through her words. And her goal is to write stories that are compelling enough to keep you up all night. Find Dena on her website: denanetherton.me.

Recent Suspense Releases
by Write Integrity Press

Her dad's gone, her business
is failing, and her car's
in the lake.
What more does she have to lose
... except her life?

How can a small-town girl
survive
when ultimate power
wants her dead?

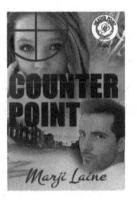

The walls have ears ...
and voices.
Voices that threaten ...

Abra Carmichael's husband,
Beau, has been murdered. She
begins to realize that the man
she loved was never who he
seemed. Beau's secrets endanger
Abra, their twin sons, and
everyone who loved him.
When Abra's life and the lives of their boys are
threatened, she flees to Amazing Grace,
North Carolina, and to Beau's family--people she
never knew existed until the day of Beau's funeral.

Thank you for choosing
Write Integrity Press.

Find more of our books
at our website:

WriteIntegrity.com.